TALES OF ADVENTURE #2

MICHAEL KINGSWOOD

ISBN 13: 978-0692564318

ISBN 10: 0692564314

ABOUT THIS BOOK

A sword-for-hire quests to defeat an evil Necromancer.

A young girl discovers that music has a magic of its own.

An FBI interrogator discovers a chilling conspiracy.

A shipwreck unleashes a supernatural monster onto the inhabitants of a tropical island.

A washed-up electrician battles a monster from beyond our universe.

Tales of Adventure #2 is a collection of five science fiction and fantasy novelettes and novellas: The Necromancer's Lair, A Note Of Magic, Facilitated Interrogation, The Beast And The God-Woman, and What Lurks Between.

———

Enjoy the book! After you're done, please come to Michael's website and sign up for his mailing list at www.michaelkingswood.com/newsletter-signup/. Guaranteed to be spam free, he uses it to announce new releases and special promotions for his fans.

Michael Kingswood

THE NECROMANCER'S LAIR

Valor vs Magic...and the Undead

THE NECROMANCER'S LAIR

Gareth's chest heaved as he sucked in gulps of air. His heart pounded in his ears, and he tingled all over with a mixture of exhilaration and fear. He leapt backwards, leaving grimy claws to scratch harmlessly along the front of his steel breastplate before he got out of reach.

This thing was relentless! Gareth had hit it a dozen times before, each blow of his axe tearing out large bits of flesh and muscle, but it kept on coming. Even losing an arm did not stop it.

The creature shambled forward, the putrid scent of rotting flesh leading the way. Its mouth lolled open in a brainless snarl and its eyes shown with a ghostly light that did not come close to resembling life. And yet it moved. Ragged cloths, the last remains of its funeral raiment, Gareth was sure, still clung to its body in places, but were at best an afterthought. If such a thing as this had any thoughts at all.

Gareth drew a deep breath and adjusted his grip on the handle of his axe. He wondered for a heartbeat how much longer he could keep hacking at the thing before it simply wore him down from fatigue.

Then it was on him. The nails—claws—of its sole remaining arm thrust toward Gareth's throat. It was an awkward attack, as clumsy as the thing's stride, and Gareth easily sidestepped it. He gritted his teeth and, with a grunt that was nearly a shout, brought his axe down.

The thing's arm went flying, cut off at the elbow.

No blood flowed; there was none remaining in its body. Neither did the thing seem to feel pain, or slow. It stumbled forward, turning to face him, before launching itself straight at him, its rotting teeth its last weapon.

Except for the stink. It became overpowering as the thing's mouth drew near. Gareth nearly gagged, only years of training stopping him from losing his composure.

Would the thing never die?

He recoiled and struck again with his axe.

The half-moon of steel struck the beast in the forehead, cleaving its head nearly in two before lodging in place.

The light in the creature's eyes flickered and it shambled forward another half-step. Then the light went out completely and it fell forward. It hit the ground with a sickening, squishy thud, and lay still.

"Ye Gods," Gareth muttered as he wiped his brow with the back of his hand. He took a deep breath and had to stop himself from shuddering.

"Well fought, my lord," said Hatherle from behind him, "but if I may make a suggestion?"

Gareth scowled and looked over his shoulder.

The slender man behind him and to his left was less armored than he was: just a leather breastplate, mostly hidden by the dark grey tunic he wore over top. His pants were light brown, tight-fitting, and tucked into calf-high turned-down boots. He wore a pack on his back, and a grey scull cap covered most of his head, leaving just a few strands of his blond hair falling out. His hands rested upon the pommel of his longsword, which he held point-down into the dirt before him.

"What?"

Hatherle cleared his throat. "I would avoid flesh wounds for such as these," he nodded toward the still corpse at his feet, its head was severed from its body, "and go for the head instead."

Gareth stared at him for long moment, then rolled his eyes, bent over, and grabbed the haft of his axe. "No kidding." The axe was stuck fast. This was going to take a bit of work. He stepped over the rotting corpse and took hold with both hands. "You could have helped, you know, if you figured it out so fast."

Gareth practically heard Hatherle's shrug. "You seemed to have things well in hand, my lord."

Gareth heaved upward, his breath leaving his lungs in a long grunt as he strained against the axe handle. For a long several seconds, nothing happened. Then, without warning, the axe came free. Gareth stumbled backwards, almost tripping over the creature's severed forearm. Decaying corpse-matter of some variety or other—Gareth did not want to think about what it was exactly—sprayed out of the thing's head where his axe used to be.

He shuddered, trying not to inhale the newly-increased stench.

Instead, he turned away and stalked further into the cave, pausing only to remove a rag from behind his belt. He wiped the blade of his axe clean of slime, bone, and the rest, as he walked.

Hatherle followed.

"I asked you to stop calling me that. I'm no lord," Gareth growled over his shoulder.

Again with the semi-audible shrug. "Lord Hadley offered a title to whomever rids the county of the Necromancer, so I expect you will be soon. Besides, I am sworn to your service, my lord. What else should I call you?"

Gareth ground his teeth. They had argued this point several times before, and he had never been able to get Hatherle to budge. Best to just let it lie.

"What do you make of those things?"

"Necromancers *are* masters of all things dead, my Lord. Considering our quest—"

"Yes, I know. I just meant, what do you think about them?"

There was a long pause. "My lord?"

5

Nevermind.

The reanimated corpses were clearly watchdogs. That meant Gareth's notion was right: there was a passage from the cave into the Necromancer's tower. Hatherle either really did not see it or was just playing dumb because that was what he thought a man servant was supposed to do with his Lord. It would be less annoying if he was consistent about it, if the later.

The light was beginning to fade. Gareth took a moment to look back.

The cave mouth was about twenty-five feet behind them. The jagged rocks around its entrance really did make it look like a mouth, come to think of it. The floor of the cave was relatively flat, littered here and there with rocks and boulders…and two hacked-up corpses. But as far as caves went, it was easy to navigate.

Looking back to the passage ahead, the cave bent around to the left. Very soon the light from the entrance would be gone.

"Break out the torches," he said.

Hatherle nodded acquiescence and took off his pack. He spent a moment digging around before coming up with two of the torches they had made back in town.

Gareth set his axe down and took out flint and steel. Hatherle held the torches out toward him, and he began to work. In a few moments, both torches were alight, and the two men set off once more.

"Keep a close eye out," Gareth said softly, receiving only a short grunt in return.

Glancing aside, Gareth noted an expression of annoyance on Hatherle's face that disappeared as soon as the other man felt his eyes on him. He had to suppress a grin; it was not often that Hatherle let his facade crack.

The cave continued to twist to the left and ascended. It gradually became more narrow, and the ceiling lowered as well. The small pools of light cast by their torches only heightened the sense that the world was slowly closing in on them. Gareth felt the hair on his arms stand on end and he began to get a queasy feeling in his stomach. He had to force himself to breath normally, but nonetheless he felt a deepening pressure on his chest. He had never cared for tight spaces.

Finally, the passage leveled, though it became noticeably more rough, with more rounded boulders strew hither and yon, along with the occasional stalactite and stalagmite. Then there was a whisper of moving air. Gareth would not have noticed it except for the stillness of the rest of the cave. The slight breeze carried with it the odor of dampness, with a hint of corruption beneath.

Gareth rolled his shoulders, settling the shield he kept slung on his back a bit more comfortably. Then, flexing his fingers on the haft of his axe, he stepped around a particularly large boulder.

And found himself flailing his arms to keep from falling as his foot came down on only empty air. Only Hatherle's quick reaction, grabbing his shoulder and hauling him back, prevented disaster.

Shivering from a surge of adrenaline, Gareth exhaled deeply and nodded thanks. Hatherle returned the nod, but said nothing. His eyes said enough: Gareth needed to be more careful. It would not do for Hatherle to lose his Lord this quickly into his tenure as Gareth's sworn man. Gareth managed not to scowl at the man before he turned back to the fall that had almost taken him.

His heart sank.

The floor dropped away on the other side of the boulder, becoming a sheer crevasse that descended farther than the torch's light could reach. The crack ran in both directions as far as he could see and was about fifteen feet wide, too far to jump. Except for a narrow ledge leading off to the left on his side of the crevasse, there was no way forward.

"That is discouraging," Hatherle said as he eyed the crack.

"That's one way to say it. I didn't see any branching passages or anything that looked like a door. Did you?"

Hatherle shook his head.

Gareth sighed and stepped to the left left-hand wall, where the ledge lay. It was about two feet wide and proceeded on for quite some distance, well past the illumination from the torches. It was not a very inviting route.

"I'm not sure I like the notion of sliding along that ledge, but I don't see any other way to go," Gareth said. He glanced back at Hatherle. "What do you think?"

The slender man shrugged. "I go where you go, my Lord."

Great help, that one.

Gareth sighed. "All right. Let's go."

With a deep breath, he inched his foot out onto the ledge.

It was too narrow to walk properly, not without great risk of overbalancing and falling, so he pressed his back against the cave wall and slid along sideways. It was slow going, and awkward. Very quickly in the process, he switched his axe to his left hand—the one that was leading the way—and the torch into his right. At least he would have a chance of defending himself that way, and he was not staring directly into the torch's flame.

At one point, Gareth's foot came down on the very lip of the ledge, and part of it broke away. He pressed himself back more tightly against the wall, expecting the rest of the ledge to fall away beneath him at any moment. The various prayers that he had not spoken since he was a boy flew through his mind as he awaited the end, and he felt a cold sweat beading on his brow.

But the rest of the ledge held. After a long moment, Hatherle cleared his throat, rousing Gareth from his near-panicked state. He shook himself and blinked, then managed a rueful grin and continued on.

Finally, after what felt like forever, but was probably only a few hundred feet, the wall expanded back into an oblong alcove that almost appeared carved out of the rock face, it was so smooth. About twenty feet deep and half again as many wide, the walls were rounded, rising to meet in a sort of dome in the center of the alcove area. Aside from that, however, the alcove was unremarkable.

And empty.

The walls were bare rock, with no protuberances, the floor

smooth and level. Even the ledge did not continue beyond the alcove.

This was it. End of the road.

"Dammit," Gareth muttered. "I thought sure there was a way."

"The presence of our previous adversaries certainly suggested as much, my Lord," Hatherle replied. "Though I hesitate to imagine beings like those successfully navigating that ledge."

Gareth was forced to nod in agreement. He had been wondering that himself as they crept down the ledge; those walking corpses were not particularly nimble. How had they managed to not fall off the ledge? Of course, there was nothing to stop the Necromancer from simply bringing them in through the cave mouth.

By why go to all the effort to do so if the only thing in the cave was...*this*?

"There's got to be more here than meets the eye," Gareth said. "Take left, Hatherle. I'll start on the right. We'll meet in the middle."

He did not wait for the man servant to respond, but strode over to the far end of the alcove. Moving slowly, he tapped the flat of his axe against the cave wall. A metallic "tink" rang out, almost eclipsing the softer ring of the stone as the metal touched it. Not particularly melodious, but true. The wall was solid there.

Gareth continued in that manner, ranging up and down the wall at random as he eased his way around the alcove, until he met Hatherle halfway around, as planned.

"Anything?"

The man servant just shrugged. "Sounds solid to me, my lord."

"Hmmph."

Gareth frowned at the stone wall for a long moment, his thoughts whirling. He had been so sure! The wasted time and effort rankled, but more than that the thought that another may have already breached the Tower's walls ahead of him drove a spike of irritation that bordered on rage into him.

"If I may suggest—"

"Stow it, Hatherle!" Gareth could not keep himself from shouting.

Hatherle blanched and drew back on himself, his already slight frame seeming to shrivel as he recoiled from his Lord's anger.

His Lord. Gareth had no claim to that title. Nor did he want one. Why would the little fellow not listen when he explained that? It was almost enough to bring the rage full-on for a moment. Then Gareth got ahold of himself, forced himself back to calm. Or at least just more-than-mild irritation. He knew exactly why Hatherle had sworn to him, why he called Gareth his Lord.

And Gareth did not have the heart to force that devotion from him.

He drew a deep breath and forced the last of his anger away. "I'm sorry, Hatherle," he said, making his tone as kind as he could.

Hatherle blinked. He actually looked confused. "No need to apologize, my Lord. I serve at your pleasure."

How to explain? The issue almost made Gareth angry again, but he was back in control. "Nevermind. Let's go. We'll take the short, direct way. Straight through the front door." He barked out a laugh that he hoped sounded confident. "That ol' Necromancer will never expect something like that."

Gareth turned and walked back toward the ledge, his earlier trepidation about taking it forgotten, at least for the moment. The sound of Hatherle clearing his throat brought him to a halt.

Gareth looked back at Hatherle over his shoulder. "What?"

Hatherle gave the slightest of shrugs. "I go where you go, my Lord, but…"

"Out with it, man."

Hatherle frowned. "Not to contradict you, but I suspect the Necromancer expects that very thing. He counts on it, and has his defenses arrayed against it. The odds of success, or even survival, in a frontal assault are…"

"Never tell me the odds."

Hatherle's teeth clacked together and he managed a rueful smile. "Pardon, my Lord. I forgot."

Gareth looked at the slender man servant for half a minute, then rolled his eyes and threw up his hands. "Well what do you suggest?"

"My Lord, I would not presume—"

Gareth's stare carried daggers. Hatherle's speech slowed and came to a halt beneath its weight. Finally, he made a vague gesture toward the top of the ceiling, where the dome reached its zenith.

Gareth frowned and walked over to the center of the alcove. As he stepped beneath the ceiling's zenith, it was like a key turning in a lock. He suddenly saw what Hatherle was referring to. Standing exactly there, the patterns of the rock came together and formed a sigil of a wolf biting the neck of a fallen deer, the sigil of the Necromancer Gareth presumed. The wolf's eyes were open. They stared behind Gareth and to his right…toward the stone floor.

Gareth turned around and looked down toward where the wolf was gazing. There, he saw a circle surrounding a five-pointed star inlaid into the ground.

He felt his eyes going wide as his jaw dropped. "Hatherle," he began. Then he caught himself as a realization hit him. He rounded on the slender man, his earlier anger rekindled. "You knew?"

Hatherle shook his head. "I saw the sigil in the ceiling, yes."

"Why the hell didn't you say anything?" Gareth felt his heart rate beginning to climb.

"I was sure you would find it, my Lord." He smiled, his face becoming pure admiration and devotion. "It was not my place to interrupt."

Gareth bit back a curse, instead grinding his teeth to keep a vicious tongue-lashing from spewing forth. He glared at Hatherle for a minute—the man did not have the grace to look embarrassed —then sighed and looked back at the star and circle on the ground.

"Well…what do you make of this?"

Hatherle walked up next to Gareth, his expression curious. When he stopped beneath the sigil on the ceiling and followed Gareth's pointing finger with his gaze, his eyes widened.

"I did not see that, my Lord," he began. His lips pursed together. "Interesting. As you well know, that symbol is used by magicians and wizards everywhere, as the center of a summoning circle."

Gareth knew no such thing, but he did know better than to interrupt when Hatherle went on a tear. He nodded, putting on an encouraging grin, or at least one he hoped was encouraging. But Hatherle seemed not to notice as he kept right on talking.

"The symbol's power constrains the beings the wizard summons, allows him a certain amount of control during the meeting." Hatherle's tongue clicked behind his front teeth. "I suspect a Necromancer would be especially comfortable with this symbol. The dead are…quite unhappy…when disturbed." He cleared his throat. "Or so I hear."

Gareth supposed Hatherle's last comment made sense. Sort of.

"So now we know the Necromancer was here at some point." Gareth left the area beneath the ceiling's zenith and stepped toward the symbol on the floor.

He half expected the symbol to fade from his vision when he left the zenith, but it did not. It was as though once unlocked, the symbols were easily seen. On a hunch, he looked back at the zenith. The wolf sigil was still there. Yep, whatever it was that had prevented him from seeing it before was gone.

Gareth wished that did not make him feel so frightened.

He crouched down and examined the symbol. From up close, it almost appeared to be etched into the floor. But that did not make any sense; if it had been, he would have seen it before.

Setting his axe down, he ran his fingers along the symbol. Sure enough, the lines of the star and circle were recessed into the stone of the floor.

"I'll be damned," Gareth murmured.

"I should hope not, my Lord."

Hatherle's ears were entirely too keen sometimes. Rather than respond, Gareth just grunted and went back to examining the symbol. The edges of the lines were abrupt, hardly weathered at all. Which was not surprising considering how little traffic came through this cave. All the same, that meant they had been made relatively recently.

Gareth traced out the lines of the symbol again, more slowly. There was something…

"Well how about that?" Gareth looked up at Hatherle. "The engraving is a bit deeper at each point of the star, see?"

Hatherle frowned slightly and crouched down next to Gareth. After a moment, he nodded.

"Indeed, my Lord. And it looks like there is something embedded within, as well."

Gareth blinked and lowered his head to examine the points of the star more closely. As he did so, he moved the torch, now back in his left hand, and he saw a glint of reflected light from one of the points.

"Is that metal?"

Hatherle shrugged. "It does appear so, my Lord."

Gareth bit his lip in thought for a moment. This was becoming more and more interesting. Clearly the necromancer had left this symbol here, and gone to no small amount of effort to do so. Maybe…

"Maybe it's like a doorknob," he said, voicing his thoughts aloud.

Hatherle shrugged again, but did not reply.

Gareth glanced at him and sighed. Sometimes the man's penchant for speaking his thoughts became annoying, but he was knowledgable about many things; scholars and sages were useful that way. But he seemed to pick the strangest times to go silent, and that was almost *more* annoying.

"Back up, Hatherle. I'm going to try something, and I have no idea what it's going to do."

"As you wish, my Lord." The slender man stood and moved over to the wall. Gareth noted he was right near the ledge, no doubt ready to make a quick escape if things went badly wrong.

Smart man.

"Here goes nothing."

Gareth kept a dagger sheathed on his belt, opposite the iron ring that he slung the haft of his axe through when he did not want to carry it. He withdrew the dagger, hardly noticing the familiar sound of steel drawing across hardened leather, and paused.

Where to begin? There were no markings to make any one point of the star more important than another. No indication of where to start and where to end. If Gareth had put this little contraption together, he would make sure to have something horrible happen to a person who did not execute it correctly. It only made sense the Necromancer would have done the same.

But there was no way to know that without trying, was there?

"I am a sodding fool," he muttered, then he pressed the tip of his dagger into the lower right point on the star.

Scarlet light, somehow beautiful despite its unearthly hue, began shining from the point as soon as the steel of the dagger made contact. The glow continued after Gareth removed the dagger, but nothing untoward occurred. He must be on the right track; he was not dead.

Yet.

Moving with careful slowness, he pressed the tip of the dagger into the remaining four points of the star. Each time, the points began glowing just as the first one did. As he removed the dagger from the final point, Gareth felt a certain satisfaction, and he grinned. Turns out this little riddle was not so difficult, after all.

He rocked back on his heels and his grin faded. The points of light were dimmer…or was that his imagination?

No, they *were* dimmer. What—?

The lights went out.

"Dammit! What the hell just happened?"

Hatherle was next to him again; Gareth had not noticed his approach, so caught up in the moment he had been. He had to resist the urge to slap himself. That was the sort of carelessness that could get them both killed.

"I suspect," Hatherle began, rubbing at his chin with the fingers of his left hand, "that you are correct about this device's purpose, my Lord. It may well open a portal of some sort. But it will need to work as a whole, not as a collection of individual parts."

Gareth blinked. "Come again?"

Hatherle gave him a look that said he was missing the forest for the trees. "The star is a series of lines, not a set of five points."

The realization hit Gareth in a flash. Idiot! He should not have needed Hatherle to come to that conclusion.

Grumbling, Gareth thrust the tip of his dagger into the lower right point on the star. This time, he did not remove the dagger but instead traced the star out, line by line and point by point, until he had completed the entire thing. As he did, the glow began from the first point, then continued down the line to the second, getting brighter as it went. By the time he was tracing out the line between the fourth and fifth points, the glow was bright enough that he had to squint to avoid being dazzled.

Done! Gareth pulled his dagger from the engraving, and the circle began glowing on its own, a blue glow this time that complimented the star's crimson but also added to the glare so much that he had to look away.

He saw Hatherle shielding his eyes with a raised hand, a look of surprised awe on his face.

Then the light flicked out, leaving them both in blackness.

At first, Gareth thought he was blind. The light, as bright as it was, had overcome him completely; he had turned away too slowly, and he was doomed to live out the rest of his life in darkness, begging passersby for whatever coins or scraps they deigned to share with him.

It was almost enough to make him open a vein with the dagger in his hand.

After a minute or so, however, he realized he could see. Ever so slightly. There was a light, extremely faint, streaming in from somewhere, off to his right, he thought. It was difficult to tell, because the light was so dim he almost thought he was imagining it, at first.

Once, when Gareth was young, he had locked himself inside a padded chest while playing hide and seek. He had almost died of suffocation before his parents finally found him, but while he waited, he experienced near total silence. The padding of the chest blocked the outside noise so well he could not hear anything. After a short while, he began imagining he heard things: dogs barking, laughter, whispers...the sort of faint whispers that would drive a man mad if he listened to them for too long.

The light he experienced now reminded him of that day, and he felt a cold shiver of fear run down his spine. Swallowing to repress the bile he knew would try to come up if he let it, he pushed himself to his feet.

"Hatherle," Gareth said, trying hard to not let his sudden fear show in his tone. "Are you still there?"

There was silence for a long moment, then a discontented snort announced the man servant's presence. "Here, my Lord. That was...most instructive." Hatherle normally was extremely pleased to learn something, remnants of his old profession, no doubt. Not this time. He sounded positively chagrined.

Not that Gareth felt much better. Sheathing his dagger, he peered around, trying to get his bearings, and failed.

Then, all at once, he realized he still felt grainy wood in his left hand—the torch. He had not extinguished it; why was it not shining?

Gingerly, Gareth raised his right hand to the end of the torch, where the flame should have been. He felt no heat, even when he closed his hand around it. The top of the torch crumbled, ash falling away where the fuel and underlying wood had burned, but aside from that he would never have been able to tell the thing had ever been lit, as cool as it was.

"What the—?"

"It would seem," Hatherle said, "that our quarry is a bit more clever than you gave him credit for." There was a brief pause before he added, "My Lord." Clearly he was re-thinking his pledge of service. Or he was just annoyed because he did not see this turn of events coming. Gareth would not give odds either way.

"Wonderful." Gareth tossed the torch, useless now, to the ground, then crouched back down and felt around until he found his axe.

Feeling a bit better with the weapon's solid weight in his right hand, he stood back up and shrugged his shield off his back, then slipped it onto his left forearm.

What was making that light? Gareth turned his head left and right, but no matter which way he looked, it was all the same. Just darkness illuminated by the faintest hint of light, just enough to remind him he was not blind. He could find no source, see no details.

But there had to be something there.

He rolled his shoulders and straightened; he found himself hunching over without realizing it, an instinctual response to the oppressing gloom no doubt. "Hatherle, grab the back of my belt."

He did not wait for the other man to respond. He just stepped forward, trusting in Hatherle's seemingly instinctive need to obey. Gareth felt a reassuring tug on his belt as he moved forward; Hatherle had grabbed on before it was too late.

One direction was as good as another, so he continued forward in as straight a line as he could manage. It would be very easy to get turned around with no visual reference, but there was nothing else to it. And he had always been good at walking along logs, even with his eyes closed. Sooner or later, if he kept straight enough, he had to run into something.

Sure enough, he did exactly that. One moment he was walking slowly forward. The next, he found himself falling, his outstretched foot having come down on nothing but thin air. The cry of chagrin behind him, and the desperate tugging at the back of his belt, told him that Hatherle, too, had fallen, but he had only enough time to throw his axe aside—it would not do to land on it and impale himself—before he struck ground. Hard.

A heartbeat later, Hatherle landed atop him.

Gareth's breath left his lungs in a rush, and the momentary lack of breath clouded his other pains for a time. Finally, when he was able to inhale again, he took stock.

He hurt all over; he had landed flat on his belly, spreading the impact all over his body. A small mercy, that. Had he landed any other way, he would likely be nursing one or more broken bones. But after a short consideration, Gareth decided he would have bruises pretty much everywhere. But he was functional. If that was the right word for it.

"Get off me," he said, his voice harsher than he intended it between his aches and difficulty breathing.

It was only after Hatherle rolled off and Gareth forced himself up onto his hands and knees that he realized he could see again. Or rather, that the light was bright enough that he could make out his surroundings without difficulty.

He almost wished he could not.

He and Hatherle sat in a small room, maybe ten feet on a side. Although room was probably a misnomer. All around him were steel bars, beyond which he could make out little of the chamber beyond. The floor was rock, as was the ceiling. And how did that work exactly? He could see no hint of the hole he fell through, though it must have been there.

"Bugger me," he breathed.

He looked around again. Whether it was because the light grew more bright or because his eyes were becoming more accustomed to it, he found he could see the chamber housing his cell a bit better. It was made of stone, chiseled blocks that fit together tightly enough that he wondered whether the builders had bothered with mortar, and was empty save for their cell.

And his axe, lying about five feet beyond the bars of the cell, off to the right.

"Bugger me," he said again, more emphatically.

"Not even if you paid me, my Lord," said Hatherle as he pushed himself to his feet. He took a moment to brush himself off, smoothing his clothing at the same time, as he looked around. "Well," he said, "this is rather…discouraging."

He had a way with words, Hatherle did.

It was difficult to tell how much time passed with no external reference. But regardless, they remained stuck in that small cell for far too long.

At first, Gareth plotted ways to escape. They could team up to bend a bar out of shape and then Hatherle, the thinner of the two, could slip out and figure out how to free Gareth. Hatherle could stand on Gareth's shoulders and work the stone where it encased the bars with Gareth's dagger. Given enough time and effort, he would surely be able to remove enough stone that Gareth could knock a couple bars out.

In truth, Gareth was surprised Hatherle went along with those ideas, oaths or no. Regardless, it did not work. Nothing worked.

And so they sat idly, letting time pass by as they steadily grew more thirsty and hungry, and as fatigue began to set in. Those sensations, and the urgings of nature, were the only way to measure time's passage. It must surely have been a day, maybe more, before their captor revealed himself.

All at once, the seemingly unbroken wall of the chamber housing their cell became...broken. A portion of the wall swung open, like a door. Except before it swung open there was no indication of hinges or any break in the stone at all. In fact, the "door" bisected several of the stones that made up the walls of the chamber.

A rush of air accompanied the door's opening, bringing with it a sickly-sweet odor that Gareth could not quite place. It was familiar, but...off, somehow. His contemplation of the odor was short-lived though, his attention being taken by the man who stepped delicately into the chamber.

Delicate summed the man up perfectly. Hatherle was slender. This fellow made him look like a hulking slab of muscle. Gareth was not entirely certain how he managed to support his own weight, let alone the weight of the black robes he wore. They were cowled, the robes, though he wore the hood thrown back, and were cinched around his waist by a length of red-brown cloth of some sort. The man's features were sharp, almost skeletal, which was fitting in a way, but far from weak. His dark eyes peered at Gareth and Hatherle intensely from beneath narrow black brows that matched the short-cut black hair atop his head.

The Necromancer, Gareth presumed. Of course, the shambling figures of two reanimated dead men that accompanied him on either side as he strode into the room would have given that away even if he did not look the part.

"Welcome, friends," said the Necromancer. His voice was surprising: deep and strong, belonging to a much more substantial man. And cultured. Gareth had encountered Lords who spoke with less precision and elegance than this man. No simple power-hungry lunatic, this one.

"Glad to be here," Gareth replied, trying to keep his tone steady despite the shiver crawling up his spine.

The Necromancer smirked slightly. "I've no doubt." He

stopped his approach about ten feet from the cell. The walking corpses halted as well as he crossed his arms over his chest. "You are the first to stumble upon my back door," he said. "The others all tried a more...direct route." He made a vague gesture toward the corpse on the left. Gareth followed the gesture with his gaze and found his bowels turning to liquid.

He knew that man.

Man. Hard to call him that now. But Ranulf had been powerful, jolly, and loyal once. To see him standing there, barely recognizable from the decay of his flesh even as the Necromancer's ghastly art kept him from his rest, nearly unmanned Gareth. He had not known that Ranulf had sought to challenge the Necromancer; he had simply stopped coming to the pub one day. Gareth assumed he had just moved on, or found a different watering hole.

Though why he would not have at least said goodbye to those he had become friendly with stung a bit.

Apparently Gareth had been wrong, and that error filled him with fear.

If such a mighty man as Ranulf could not defeat the Necromancer, what chance did *he* have? Especially considering the circumstances.

He kept his mouth shut. Better to let the Necromancer speak. Perhaps he would give something away.

"What did you hope to accomplish?" The Necromancer's tone was conversational, though tainted with a hint of derision.

Gareth shrugged and spread his hands. "Do you really need to ask?"

Amusement flashed through the Necromancer's eyes, and he shook his head. "No, I suppose not. I am, after all, *the great menace*. The *threat to all humanity*." He took on an ironic, almost mocking tone as he emphasized those last words. There was a moment of silence as the Necromancer just looked at Gareth. Then he sighed and shook his head. "Does it never occur to any of you that I might have a good reason for my studies?"

He did not wait for Gareth's response. He just turned away and strode back through the doorway. "A pity," he said, and made a circular gesture with his right hand. Then he was gone, but the animated corpses remained.

Gareth blinked. "Um…ok…"

A sharp crack from overhead drew Gareth's gaze to the ceiling, and he leapt backwards, pushing himself off the ground with a powerful spring of his legs. He did not go far before slamming into the bars behind him with a loud CLANG of steel striking steel. Had he not been wearing his breastplate, the impact would have hurt. A lot.

But the ceiling stone coming dislodged and falling down right where he was standing would have hurt a lot more.

Hatherle, too, dove to the side. He hit the ground and rolled to his feet to Gareth's left, his eyes wide.

"My lord," he began.

"Yes, I know. We're in trouble. I'm working on it."

Hatherle shook his head vigorously, his eyes locked on the ceiling, where the block used to be. "No, my lord…look!"

Gareth looked back up, and his heart sank. Hands were reaching through the hole left by the block that had just fallen. Rotting, dead hands, with the flesh hanging in strips from them like so many torn rags. They scrabbled around, blindly for all Gareth could tell, until they reaching the next block over.

They began tugging at it.

The block, slightly larger than the one that had just fallen, had to have weighed a quarter of a ton. There was no way those dead limbs could move such a piece of stone.

Yet they did.

Slowly at first, then more quickly with each passing second, the stone began to rock. Dirt and dust fell from around its edges: a trickle at first, then a steady stream as the block came, inexorably, free.

Gareth shuffled to the side to avoid being crushed as the second block came down, Hatherle following suit.

This was not good. Not good at all. If the falling blocks did not do them in, Gareth did not want to think about how easily such strong arms could tear he and Hatherle limb from limb if the creatures opted to come down and join them. And his axe lay out of reach, at Ranulf's corpse's feet!

Gareth took a second to wonder why Ranulf and the other corpse had stayed behind, if the intention was to crush or bludgeon he and Hatherle to death. Then he had to leap forward to avoid yet another block.

By then the ceiling was more a dark, gaping hole than anything else. Dark as it was, though, he could see the walking corpses shambling around toward their next project. Hear their unnatural silence—the lack of breath and speech—beneath the sounds of their movement. Smell the stink of their advanced state of decay, a stink so strong he could almost taste it.

Adrenaline prevented bile from rising in his throat despite the surge of revulsion he felt. Time enough for that sort of thing later. Now was for figuring out how to survive.

The hands appeared again, tugging at yet another block. But this one was next to the first block that fell.

Gareth dropped his shield to the ground, hopped up onto the fallen block, and reached up. With the added height from his perch, a pair of rotting wrists were easy to reach. He grabbed and pulled, twisting his torso to add more force to the movement. For a heartbeat, there was resistance, then the moving corpse came free and fell, and he spun completely around, to hurl it across the cell. Toward Hatherle.

"Hatherle," he roared as he threw.

The corpse landed at the serving man's feet and moved quickly to right itself. But not quickly enough. Hatherle's sword took its head off in one smooth cut. The corpse collapsed in a heap.

Hatherle glanced at Gareth, his expression, for once, openly impressed. "Well played, my Lord," he said simply.

Gareth grinned in reply, then reached up for the next set of hands.

The five corpses in the ceiling managed to drop two more blocks before Gareth and Hatherle killed them all. Again. They never even tried to change their tactic, but simply kept on tugging and digging as Gareth pulled them down one by one. Hatherle proved efficient at dispatching them, though the last two required Gareth's intervention as well, as much due to the limited room to maneuver with all the fallen stone as anything else.

But finally, the last of the corpses lay at Gareth and Hatherle's feet. Gareth drew in a deep breath and wiped sweat from his brow, then stepped over to Hatherle and clapped him on the shoulder.

"Well done, Hatherle. We may just make it out of this yet."

No sooner had the words left his mouth when a metallic clang followed by the groan of metal being stressed beyond its capacity caused Gareth to turn around.

Ranulf and the other re-animated corpse the Necromancer left behind, a man who in life had been even larger and stronger than Ranulf from the look of him, stood right up next to the bars of the cell. Between them, they held an exceptionally stout iron rod, which they had thrust between two of the bars making up the cell's walls.

The two corpses pulled on the rod. Hard. The bars of the cell groaned in protest again and slowly bent outward.

"Oh no," Gareth breathed.

The Necromancer's reason for leaving them was plain: they were his backup plan in case the ceiling corpses failed. He felt his eyes growing wide as his grin of triumph, which he wore so briefly, faded. His mouth suddenly dry, he glanced away from the two powerful corpses toward where his axe lay, so close but yet so far. If only he could get to it, they might have a chance.

"My lord," Hatherle began as though he intended to say more, but when Gareth looked at him, the serving man was pale, his eyes wide as well. He stared at the massive corpses as they worked at the cell bars and it was plain that, for once, he was not referring to Gareth when he said Lord, but instead to his personal deity.

Gareth could not blame him for that. A few choice prayers came to mind, the ones he had recalled back on the ledge and more. He quickly shoved them away. If they were to get through this, he needed his wits, not meaningless words spoken to a being that might not even exist.

The bars were bending more quickly now, their groans of protest becoming more pronounced. Dust puffed down from the ceiling where the bars were driven in. Very soon either the bars themselves or the mortar holding them in place, if any, would give way, leaving a space that the corpses could squeeze into.

Or a space that Gareth could exit.

It was a long shot, but there was no choice. He bent over and picked up his shield, then strapped it back onto his left forearm. "Get ready," he said, glancing at Hatherle over his shoulder. "When those bars go, we charge."

Hatherle looked at him as though he were daft. He might have a point there.

"Are you with me, Hatherle?"

The slender man hesitated then, licking his lips nervously, nodded.

It only took another minute or so, then with a final scream first one bar then the other reached the end its endurance and snapped. The top half of each clattered to the ground, falling free from their ceiling holes. The lower halves remained fixed in the holes in the floor, but bent over as they were it would be only a small challenge to vault past them.

The corpses released their great pry bar and it too clattered to the floor. Ranulf stepped forward, his hands lifting, revealing fingers that had decayed enough that the tips were better called bony claws than anything else. The unearthly glow in his eyes dimmed as his eyelids, somehow still intact despite the decay of the rest of his body, narrowed. Gareth had seen that expression on the powerful man before, in life.

He was readying himself for a fight.

A new chill of terror swept over Gareth. How much of a man's personality, his experience, his…self remained when he became undead? Did Ranulf know what had happened to him? If he did…the man Gareth had known would have viewed this sort of existence with revulsion, horror. Did he reside, even now, within his own skull, screaming for release yet powerless to bring it about or resist the commands of the Necromancer?

"Not me," Gareth said between barred teeth. "I'll not go like that."

Ranulf stepped forward, into the gap between the broken bars.

Gareth drew a deep breath and forced his fear down with the fiercest battle roar he could muster, then he raised his shield in front of himself and charged.

Behind him, he thought he heard Hatherle take up his own roar as he followed. Then there was only the stink of Ranulf's corpse as Gareth lowered his head and raised his shield a bit further. He struck Ranulf in the midriff. The impact was more than he expected and he almost lost his feet. For a moment he got a sinking feeling in his belly as he thought sure the large corpse would resist the attack.

Then, abruptly, Ranulf fell backwards and Gareth found himself following. It would not do to get into a wrestling match, so Gareth tucked his shoulder as he struck the floor next to the fallen corpse. He rolled with the momentum of his fall, trying to put distance between himself and his foe.

He almost succeeded.

Gareth rolled to his feet and turned, looking for his axe. It should be right here…

Then something grabbed his ankle and pulled. Hard. He lost his balance and fell to the ground before he could even begin to resist the pull. Unprepared as he was, he struck the ground hard, and once again found himself struggling to draw breath as the air left his lungs.

The noise of his armor striking the stone rang in his ears, stunning him almost as much as the loss of his breath. For a moment, he lost track of himself, disoriented. Then a stabbing pain shot up his leg and only the fact that he had lost his breath prevented him from screaming out. Then he was moving backwards, the grip on his ankle drawing him inexorably away.

He looked back and saw that Ranulf's corpse had ahold of his right ankle with its right hand and had dug the claws of its left hand into the meat of the same calf. The corpse wore an expression of insatiable hunger, but beneath that...satisfaction? Glee? Then it pulled with both hands, and any ability to analyze fled Gareth's mind before a second, deeper agony as the claws dug deep furrows in his leg.

Somehow he was screaming. When had he regained his breath? It did not matter. He was caught. He was going to die, and become...

No!

Gareth kicked with his left foot, hard as he could. The sole of his boot impacted the side of Ranulf's head with the snap of breaking bone combined with a sickening squish. The corpse's head canted to the side, knocked off true by the force of Gareth's kick. The tugging on his leg ceased and the pain diminished slightly as the claws' burrowing stopped.

Gareth pushed himself away from the corpse, and his wounded leg slid out of its grasp. Madly, hope surged within him. Had he actually won?

Then the corpse twitched. Again. It moved its hands to its head and, with a quick jerk, set it back aright. Then its gaze leveled on Gareth and its eyes narrowed. He could have sworn he saw fury in that expression.

It pushed itself up onto its hands and knees, then to its feet.

"Bugger me," Gareth said aloud. No, actually he shouted it, he realized as soon as the words left his mouth.

There was no way he could walk, not with his leg wounded as it was. Desperately, he pushed himself away from Ranulf's corpse, scrabbling against the floor tiles with his hands and his left foot. Hatherle! Where was Hatherle!

Grunting and…a curse?…drew Gareth's gaze to the left, and his heart sank. Hatherle was firmly set upon by the other burly corpse. The nimble man servant ducked beneath a raking claw attack, but he bled from cut to his left shoulder and right thigh.

He countered then, his longsword whipping toward the corpse's throat, but the thing dodged backwards with nearly the agility of a living man. It took a cut to the front of its neck, but seemed to not even notice as it renewed its attack.

They were in trouble.

And then Gareth ran out of time to think. Ranulf's corpse bounded forward and swept its clawed hand down toward him. In desperation, he rolled to the right, bringing his shield up above his body. The corpse's hand struck the shield hard. Harder than any living man could have struck it. Gareth's shoulder flared with pain and he found himself driven into the ground, stunned.

Above him, he heard Ranulf draw back for another attack. Gareth gritted his teeth and pushed himself off the floor with his right hand.

He rolled onto his back in time to see the claws sweeping down at him. Somehow, despite the pain in his shoulder, Gareth forced his shield arm up. Again the claws slammed into his shield, and again his arm buckled.

Ranulf pulled his arm back again. Gareth could not take another hit like that; he could barely move his shield arm at all now.

He pushed away, his left heel digging into the crack between two floor stones, but he did not go far enough. He reached out with his right hand, to grab onto to something, anything to pull himself away faster.

His hand came down on a rounded, grainy piece of wood. He blinked and moved his hand up the wood. It was wrapped in leather an inch or so from its end. He knew the feel of that leather like his own flesh.

His axe.

Ranulf's corpse swung at him again. Gareth grabbed the axe and swung it upward with a roar.

Axe met rotting hand in midair, and the axe won. The shock of impact was less than Gareth would have expected; maybe the decay was even more pronounced than it appeared. As a result, his follow-through went farther than he had intended.

Had Ranulf pressed the attack, he could have taken Gareth with ease. Instead, the corpse recoiled, an expression that looked almost like pain—or fear? Gareth should be so lucky—flashing across its face.

Ranulf's hand, severed from its arm, landed a few feet away with a dry thud. And began crawling towards Gareth, dragging itself toward him inch by slow inch.

Gareth swallowed hard and kicked himself away from hand and walking corpse alike, fear and revulsion lending his muscles extra strength. He only made it a couple feet before his back hit the wall of the room.

And then he was out of time. The respite ended as Ranulf's corpse charged back in, reaching for Gareth with its good hand and opening its mouth in a snarl, soundless except for the creaking and popping of joints that had long since lost their natural lubrication.

Seated, with his back to the wall, was not a good fighting position, but that was what Gareth had. He was sure not going to end up this thing's lunch, or worse the Necromancer's new pet. He shouted something unintelligible—or at least, *he* had no idea what it was—and shoved himself forward and to the left.

He came down hard on his already injured shoulder and a new surge of pain lanced out. His vision blurred and he saw spots.

It was so tempting to just let go and collapse.

For half a heartbeat, he almost gave in. Then he felt the breeze of Ranulf's claws passing through the air where his head was a moment before, and he forced himself to his senses.

Gareth looked up to see Ranulf's corpse bent forward next to him, the follow-through from its miss causing it to overbalance slightly, placing all of its weight onto its right knee—the one that just happened to lie within the swinging radius of his axe.

The impact was more substantial when his axe bit into the side of the corpse's knee, but the satisfaction Gareth felt as his blow struck home was even greater. A gravelly crunch advertised the breaking of bones that had been made brittle through desiccation, and the knee gave way, sending Ranulf's corpse sprawling head-long into the wall.

Gareth nearly lost his grip on his axe as the walking corpse fell. The blade caught on something, a piece of bone he thought, for a moment. Panic over being disarmed in such a situation over-whelmed his satisfaction in an eternal instant. Then the bone gave way and the axe pulled free in a small shower of bone fragments and scraps of flesh.

Ranulf's corpse still had its leg, but the knee was ruined, cleaved at least halfway through the bones and connecting tissue, with a large chunk missing where the axe pulled free. It would never again bear Ranulf's weight.

The animated corpse thrashed around when it struck the wall. It tried to lift itself off the floor, but fell again when the stump of its right arm did not perform the way a hand would have. It hesi-tated, and Gareth imagined he saw something resembling thought in its glowing eyes. Then it placed its good hand on the floor and pulled its legs beneath its body.

The walking corpse pushed itself up onto its feet.

Gareth's jaw dropped open and he felt his eyes growing wide as his bowels turned to water with fear. No! It could not do that!

But it had. It righted itself and turned its head to regard Gareth coldly, without feeling or thought. Except, perhaps...was that grudging respect in its unearthly gaze?

Gareth scrambled backwards, but the blood from his wounded leg made the stones of the floor slick and he got no traction.

His terror increased. He was going to die! Die, and become a slave in undeath.

The corpse opened its jaw in a macabre imitation of a smile, and it stepped toward Gareth.

The knee gave way completely.

Gareth reacted out of pure instinct. He rolled onto his right side, putting his shield between himself and Ranulf's corpse as it fell atop him. The weight of the impact was substantial, but less than he would have expected had Ranulf been alive. Still, he found himself driven onto his back, his shield arm splayed out uselessly to his side.

Ranulf clawed at him. Gareth grit his teeth in anticipation of further agony, and was surprised when it did not come. Instead, the corpse's claws simply scraped harmlessly down the front of his breastplate with a sickening high-pitched squeak.

The thing must truly have been without thought. How else could it have made such a mistake? Beside himself with a mixture of relief and incredulity, Gareth remained still while the claws completed their transit of his armor. The horrid blue lights in Ranulf's eyes flared with chagrin, or confusion, or...

Gareth did not stop to consider what exactly what was or was not going through the thing's head. Silently blessing the fates that led it to blunder at that exact moment, he raised his axe even as the corpse drew back its own hand for another attack, then plunged it down toward Ranulf's head.

The sound Gareth's axe made as it clove through the side of his old drinking companion's head was solid, final. Sickening. In spite of himself, he felt a tinge of regret, guilt almost, as the gruesome light in the corpse's eyes flickered and went out.

Hatherle tied off the final stitch in Gareth's calf with a particularly rough jerk. It hurt. Not as much as what Hatherle did with his shoulder, but it hurt. Gareth grimaced and had to suppress a snide comment; it would not do to upset Hatherle after he had gone to all the trouble of playing doctor.

Besides, the manservant had emerged from the battle with the animated corpses quite a lot better off than Gareth had. That was worth quite a bit.

"Thanks, Hatherle," Gareth said after he regained his breath.

"Of course, my lord," Hatherle replied. He took a moment to coil the remaining thread then he tucked it and the needle he was using into a case, which he placed inside his pack. Then he stood and offered Gareth a hand.

It took some doing, since he outweighed Hatherle by a fair amount, even without the heavy steel of his breastplate, bracers, and greaves. But after a bit of huffing and puffing Gareth got to his feet. The pain in his right calf immediately flared, growing worse from the weight suddenly placed upon it.

"Son of a whore," Gareth muttered, earning a quirked eyebrow from Hatherle.

"It will be some weeks before you regain full use of the leg, my lord," he said in a clinical tone that Gareth had come to recognize well. "For that matter, your shoulder will be some time in recovery as well. Just because I was able to force it back into its joint does not mean—"

"Got it, Hatherle. Anything else?"

The serving man shook his head, and Gareth felt a small surge of relief. He was right, of course.

Hatherle was always right. That was why he did such great business as a scholar-for-hire—Hatherle preferred the term Sage, but what was the difference?—before the incident with the bandits that led him to swearing fealty to Gareth. It would have been nice if he were wrong this time, though. Since Hatherle had worked his magic, Gareth's shoulder almost felt good again. Sore, but at least he could move it. He would not want to test that under combat conditions, though.

Or his leg, for what it was worth.

And here they were, within the Necromancer's domain. Small chance he would just let them go so they could come back when Gareth was fully healed and ready. He nodded, resigned.

"I just hope the stitches hold. There will be more action ahead."

Hatherle's other eyebrow joined its twin, high on his forehead. "My Lord?" He cleared his throat, taking a moment to glance back at the shattered cell and the now unmoving corpses littering the room. "Perhaps it would be more prudent to go."

Gareth had to suppress an amused smile. For once, he had made the leap of logic before his manservant? Wonders never ceased, it seemed.

"If I thought we had a chance of making it out without conflict, we would be on our way now," he said, truthfully. "That Necromancer will not let us escape, though. And besides," he gestured toward the ceiling they had apparently fallen through, somewhat more believable with the new hole in it, he had to admit, "we cannot go the way we came. Do you have any idea where the exit is from here?"

Hatherle shook his head and his lips lowered into a frown. Was that uncertainty Gareth saw in his eyes?

"Don't worry, Hatherle. We'll be fine. You'll see." Gareth heard the undertones in his voice as he spoke, and was surprised to not hear the mountain of uncertainty he felt come through. Maybe he was getting better at this 'being a leader' bit. Hatherle was not the first who seemed to expect it of him, though he was the first to flat out swear himself to Gareth's service. Crazy fellow.

Hatherle just looked at him in silence. Gareth began to grow somewhat uncomfortable under his gaze.

Finally, Hatherle grunted and said, "Very well, my lord." He stepped back toward the cell and bent over. When he returned, he held a length of metal out toward Gareth: the upper half from one of the broken bars. "Makeshift, but this should work as a crutch."

Gareth blinked. A crutch? What did he... He moved slightly, settling more weight upon his injured leg, and almost collapsed from the immediate protest his wounds made.

Indeed. A crutch was quite the thing.

He made a shallow nod of thanks then took the length of metal. It was bent and, where it had been sheared off under the force of the animated corpse's pry bar, jagged. But it was about the right length. So he placed the jagged end on the ground, the more gently rounded end under his arm, and tried to take a step.

It hurt.

But it worked. He was at least slightly mobile again. That was the best he could hope for.

There was not much to the level of the tower—assuming they really were within the Necromancer's tower and not somewhere else—that held the room with their cell. The doorway opened into a featureless hallway that encircled the room completely. And did not appear to have any other exits. It was well-lit, but there was no obvious source of the light. The light was just...there. It was more than a bit unsettling.

They made two complete circuits of the hallway before Gareth finally stopped. This was getting nowhere, and besides his leg hurt like hell. He needed a rest.

"Now what?"

"It defies probability that there is no way to get to and from this level," Hatherle said, his voice contemplative.

Gareth snorted. "He's a bloody spellcaster. For all we know he could just...you know..." he waved his left hand in the air "... poof himself to and fro."

Hatherle shook his head. "I've heard that sort of spell is very difficult and requires great skill. But more importantly, it is very expensive."

Gareth looked askance at him. "Come again?"

"The components required for a spell like that are very rare, or so the writings say."

"You would know, oh sage of sages." Gareth sighed and straightened his back. It had felt good to slouch, to put more weight on the makeshift crutch. Alas, there was work to be done still if he wanted to see his own bed again.

Hatherle inclined his head in response to Gareth's words, a flash of a smile appearing on his face for a moment. He had apparently decided to take the remark as a compliment. Good thing, too, because Gareth had not meant it as an insult. A friendly jibe, a bit of teasing maybe, but certainly not an insult.

"Alright. Let's makes another pass." He forced the little voice, now grown quite a bit larger after the first two laps, in his head that begged him to quit and sit down into the back of his head. This was no time for ninnies. "Check the floor and walls carefully as we go."

As we go more slowly, he meant. There was no need for him to even considering voicing the thought, however. Hatherle lagged considerably during the lap, forcing Gareth to slow his pace to avoid leaving him behind.

The man was an absolute saint sometimes.

They had almost completed a third circuit before Hatherle found it.

It should have been Gareth. It was on his side of the corridor. But the ever increasing protests from his injured calf had begun intruding ever more steadily onto his consciousness until it was all he could do to put one foot in front of the next without breaking down. And to blazes with the makeshift crutch. It had helped at first. Hell, it still helped. But the blunt end was beginning to dig into his armpit something fierce, becoming almost as much a source of discomfort as assistance.

All that was lost when Hatherle spoke up, though. Well, most of it.

Gareth bit back a curse as he turned to look at the spot in the wall where Hatherle was pointing, and had to admit the revelation hardly suppressed any of his discomfort at all. But at least it provided a distraction.

At first he could not see it. Hatherle was crouched next to the wall, pointing eagerly at a place just an inch above the floor. But there was nothing to see to Gareth's eyes. He was just about to tell Hatherle to stop being a bloody fool when he recalled the carvings in the alcove.

He moved backwards, away from Hatherle and whatever he was looking at. Still nothing. Gareth moved again, and struck the opposite wall. Nothing. That left just one more thing. He gritted his teeth in anticipation of pain to come and bent his legs, lowering himself into a deep a crouch as he could manage without either passing out from pain or falling over.

And then he saw it.

It was the same symbol as was on the ceiling of the alcove in the cave, carved into the stove as though by a fine chisel. But it did not come into view until he had lowered his line of sight. Which meant it was not a simple carving at all, but some sort of magical sigil. Just like in the alcove.

Gareth grinned. "Well done, Hatherle," he said. He straightened his legs and very nearly fell down; if he had not had the piece of metal there was no way he would not have. All the same, he had to take a deep breath and forced the protests from his injured leg away before he could speak again. "What now?"

Hatherle's triumphant smile faded slightly and he shrugged. "I doubt it functions the same as the sigil in the cave, my lord. Could be this is just a lure to draw us in."

"A lure leading nowhere?"

Hatherle inclined his head, conceding the point. "In which case it likely marks the location of something important."

Thanks for stating the obvious, Gareth did not say. "Well, play with it. See if you can get it do do something."

Hatherle nodded and turned to the sigil. He began probing it with his fingers, and Gareth winced. That was probably not a good idea. *He* really should be the one to do this... Stupid leg.

Gareth watched his manservant working on the sigil, impatience born from frustration and embarrassment at his own ineffectiveness growing all the while. Finally he could not contain it any more.

"Anything?"

A slight shrug accompanied Hatherle's response. "There appears to be a small protrusion here, near the wolf's snout. Maybe if I press it..."

Hatherle's hand moved and there was a loud CLICK that echoed down the hallway.

This was either going to be very good or very bad. Gareth would not give odds either way.

Gareth found himself counting the seconds in his head as nothing else happened. At ten, though, he began to hear a low rumbling from beneath the floor. It grew louder over the next several seconds and the floor began to shake slightly. Then, at thirty, the paving stones in the floor before he and Hatherle began to rise up. At the same time, the stone ceiling began to pull back, creating an opening above. Finally, the stones' movement stopped and there was a stone staircase leading upward where before there was only the circling hallway.

The two men stepped back. Hatherle looked stunned; Gareth had no doubt he looked similarly.

"Well." Gareth cleared his throat. "That did the trick."

"Indeed, my Lord."

"I guess this confirms that we *are* in the Necromancer's tower. Seems we have to up to get down."

Gareth looked up the stairs, then down at his injured leg. This was not going to be easy. But there was no point dilly-dallying. He took a deep breath and hauled himself up the first step.

"Let's go."

The stairs climbed for what seemed forever, circling in the same manner as the hallway below. After ten steps, Gareth's injured leg was screaming in protest and he had to sit down to rest before continuing.

Hatherle kept a watch, his longsword at the ready, as Gareth worked out the kinks as best he could. But it took far too long to get moving again. The Necromancer had to know of their movements—this was his tower, after all—and he was doubtless preparing the next surprise for them. Gareth half expected to hear footsteps descending toward them at any moment. But that did not happen, and after a few minutes he felt ready to continue upwards.

Ten more stairs and Gareth was sorely tempted to sit again. But he instead gritted his teeth and pushed on. No need to give the Necromancer any more time than necessary.

Finally, the staircase ended at a small landing that backed up to a stout wooden door that was reinforced with strips of iron. It was ordained only with an iron ring where a doorknob would be and a dark iron square in the center of the door, about at eye level, which was engraved with Necromancer's wolf and deer sigil.

Gareth paused on the landing and looked the door over. Nothing seemed unusual about it, but he had a feeling there was more there than met the eye. Not that anything so far had met with expectations, so why should this door?

"I wonder what sort of trap the Necromancer may have placed here?" Hatherle said, echoing Gareth's thoughts.

"Not sure. Why don't you try it, and we'll see?"

Gareth glanced aside at Hatherle, a teasing smile forming on his lips, in time to see the serving man flinch then square his shoulders and take a deep breath. He stepped forward toward the door.

"No!" Gareth said, forcefully. "Goodness, man, I was joking."

Hatherle blinked, then frowned back at Gareth, his expression one of reproach.

Gareth rolled his eyes. One of these days he was going to figure out the fellow's sense of humor. Some day.

"Hit it with a piece of wood or something first. Do you have any more torches?"

Hatherle nodded and pulled his pack off. He rummaged through it for a moment then put it back on, unlit torch in hand. "Brace yourself, my lord," he said, then he reached out and tapped the door with the torch.

Nothing happened.

The two men exchanged glances, Hatherle's questioning. Gareth shrugged and waved him onward.

Hatherle tapped the door again, this time on one of the iron strips. Again nothing. The same with the iron ring and square. He shrugged again and set the torch down, then reached out and took hold of the ring with his bare hand.

Hatherle stiffened and let out a low groan. His body began shaking.

"Hatherle!" Gareth surged forward, ignoring a stab of pain from his leg, and pulled the man servant back. His grip loosened from the door easily and very quickly he was back out of danger.

"Are you alright?" Concerned, Gareth looked him over. Only to find him wearing...an impish grin.

"Pardon, my lord," Hatherle said. "Just joking."

Dumbfounded, Gareth stared at him in shock for a long moment. Sudden anger conflicted with relief and then finally gave way to wry amusement, and he found himself laughing, his earlier thought about Hatherle's sense of humor returning to mind, ironically.

"Bloody hell, man, don't do that again," he said. He could not force his tone to sternness, however much he wanted to.

Hatherle's smile slipped a bit, and he nodded. "At any rate," he said after clearing his throat softly, "the ring does not appear to have any function, my lord. It did not rotate, and would not budge when I pulled on it."

Gareth frowned and looked back at the door. His eyes alighted on the iron square, and the Necromancer's sigil. "That must be the key," he murmured, and stepped forward to examine it more closely.

The sigil was the same as it had been the last two times, the square of iron plain, unadorned. The sigil was engraved in the iron, but not deeply; Gareth ran his hand over the square and could barely feel the lines of the engraving. He could not see or feel any part of it that stood out in any way.

Yet it must be there. The previous sigils had pointed the way; this one must as well.

Unless this was all a sick joke of some kind, designed to keep them running around pointlessly until the Necromancer was ready to take them out. Or until they died of thirst or hunger.

That thought made Gareth's stomach growl; they had eaten through what small morsels they brought with them during their stay in the cage, and the water flasks were running low as well. The Necromancer, if he had been keeping tabs on them—and Gareth was certain that was the case—had to know or suspect their state of affairs. Why go to the trouble of killing them when he could just let nature take care of it for him?

The was a depressing thought.

"Is it just me, my lord," Hatherle said, from behind Gareth's shoulder, "or are the wolf's and deer's eyes a bit larger on this sigil?"

Gareth did a double-take and peered at the sigil more closely. "I'm not sure. I suppose maybe. What if I..." He reached out and touched his fingertips to the eyes of both beasts.

There was another resonating CLICK, this time from within the door itself.

Gareth retreated, as much a retreat as he could manage with his leg anyway. After several seconds, nothing more happened and he let out the breath he was holding. If they were lucky, the click was the door's locking mechanism acting in response to his touching the sigil that way. He did not want to think about what it could be if they were unlucky.

Gareth took a few moments to shift his axe into his left hand. It would be of no use trying to wield it in his right, not with the crutch he needed to use. Then he had Hatherle strap the shield onto his right upper arm. It was an awkward fit, but at least it would offer some small amount of protection.

Hatherle prepared himself, drawing steel and getting a good grip on his sword. Then, at a nod from Gareth, he grabbed the ring on the door and pulled.

The door swung open immediately, revealing...a plush office.

Plush was probably not the right word to use to describe the room beyond the door, but it was the only one that sprung to Gareth's mind. The room was circular, about the same size as the cell room on the level below. And probably located directly above it. It was well lit by a number of gilded stand lamps, though the lamps were not burning any sort of visible fuel, leaving the question of what was producing the light unanswered. The floor was stone, but covered in thick red rugs that were lined in thread-of-gold tassels. A trio of full bookshelves were spaced equidistantly around the perimeter, and there was another wood and iron door directly across from the entrance. In the center, facing the open door, was a long desk that was constructed out of dark reddish wood and polished until it gleamed. A quill and ink lay to one side, opposite a stack of papers, but aside from that the desk was clear. A pair of chairs, simple but of obviously high quality, and padded, were arranged before the desk, to receive visitors no doubt.

The Necromancer sat at the desk. He was garbed as before and appeared completely at ease as he regarded Gareth and Hatherle over steepled fingers.

Gareth stood rooted to the spot for a moment in surprise. Of all the ways he thought to meet the Necromancer again, *this* was not one of them.

The moment stretched, then the Necromancer broke the silence by slowly clapping his hands together.

"Well done, gentlemen. I am impressed." He gestured toward the empty chairs. "Will you sit? I'm certain your leg must be paining you by now."

Gareth, taken aback, remained silent as he hobbled into the room. After all that had happened, *this* was all the Necromancer had to say? Amazing. And even more amazing, he looked as though he was genuinely concerned about Gareth's comfort. Gareth made a mental note to use this man as a comparison for any actors he ever watched perform in the future. He was good.

"I prefer to stand," he said in reply.

The Necromancer shrugged. "As you wish. May I offer you and your man some wine, to take the edge off?"

"Thank you, no." Gareth spoke quickly, seeing Hatherle licking his lips with poorly-suppressed eagerness. He had seen the former sage in a wine bottle enough to recognize that weakness and nip it in the bud quickly.

Again the Necromancer shrugged. He took a moment to pull open one of the drawers in his desk and remove a wine bottle and a simple but obviously well-made goblet. He poured the wine, and the faintest hint of its aroma wafted across to Gareth's nose.

Oh my. To smell that good from that far away, it must have been a heavenly vintage. His thirst, growing all the more intense by the second especially now that he could see drinkable fluid so close by, screamed at him to just have a drink.

What could it hurt? It took a force of will to not renege on his refusal, but he managed. Somehow.

The Necromancer smelled the wine with closed eyes and a serene smile on his lips, then lifted the goblet to his lips and sipped. Enjoyment seemed to flow through him. When he opened his eyes, they twinkled with an inner light they did not have before.

"I fear we've gotten off on the wrong foot," the Necromancer said.

Gareth snorted. "Says the man who locked us in a cage and then ordered my friend's corpse to kill us. Can't see how that could have gone right."

The Necromancer raised one eyebrow as he fixed Gareth with a contemptuous gaze. "You broke into my house with the intent to kill me. How would *you* respond to that, hmm?"

His words sunk in and Gareth had to admit he had a valid point. Still…it's not like the Necromancer was some peace-loving fellow who just sat around minding his own business all day. He was, well, a Necromancer. Those sorts of people were just a menace.

He was clearly waiting for Gareth to respond. Gareth obliged him with a noncommittal shrug, but said nothing. There was not much to say, and besides, his leg was beginning to ache…bad. Gareth was half afraid if he spoke too much, his discomfort would show through. And though the Necromancer knew he was probably in some measure of discomfort, it would not do for Gareth to give him a more accurate estimation of his condition.

After a short moment of silence, the Necromancer, too, shrugged. "No matter, I suppose." He took another sip from his goblet. "What do you hope to accomplish here?"

Gareth was taken aback. This was not going *at all* the way he had envisioned. Attacking monsters, parrying blows, taking down foes: those things he could deal with, and expected on a job like this. Reasoned discourse? That was another matter altogether.

"Just looking to collect a bounty," he said, in as straightforward a tone as he could manage.

The Necromancer smirked. "It's all about the money, isn't it." Sipping his wine again, he looked amused more than anything else. "So you have no interest in rooting out my *evil*," his voice dripped sarcasm as he said that, "or of righting whatever wrongs I have committed?"

"Well, there *is* that, too, now that you get to it."

The Necromancer was silent for a moment, then burst out laughing. It sounded genuine and was disturbingly human, not at all the maniacal laugh one would expect from the depraved and evil. "Ah, my friend," he said after his laughter subsided, "you are droll. Which is something I can very much appreciate, I assure you."

Gareth did not respond. Beside him, Hatherle shifted on his feet, his expression one of distaste.

The Necromancer noted this, and the amusement faded from his features. "Your man does not approve of me. But then, he is clearly not as...practical...as you."

Gareth could almost hear Hatherle's teeth grinding, and for a moment he thought he would have to restrain the former sage from doing something rash. But in the end, Hatherle restrained himself, even schooling his expression to one of stoic readiness. Though knowing him as he did, Gareth could tell he was more than a little peeved.

"What would you say if I were to tell you I understand your friend's disapproval. And your lord's as well."

"I bow to no lord."

The Necromancer snorted. "Tell yourself that if you wish, but we both know the truth." He set the goblet down on his desk and leaned forward. He clasped his hands together and regarded Gareth with an earnest expression. "If I were in their shoes, or yours for that matter, I expect I would disapprove of me as well." His eyes narrowed, his stare becoming severe, piercing. "But they do not know the facts. If they did, they would sing my praises, not set trifling bounties on my head."

Gareth snorted again. Five hundred crowns was far from trifling. With that much money, he could buy himself some property, settle down, give up the life of a wandering sellsword. Sell-axe. Whatever.

Not that he would. He knew himself well enough to admit he enjoyed the work. Most times. But still, it would be possible.

"You don't believe me?"

Gareth blinked in confusion. It took a second to realize the Necromancer misunderstood his snort. Although truth be told, now that he considered it, he truly did not believe the various priests and lords, let alone the rest of the people out there, would change their views on Necromancy any time soon. "Can't say I do," he said, honestly.

"What if I told you that all this," the Necromancer waved his hand, including the entire room, the entire tower, in his statement, "existed for one purpose only." His eyes flashed with something. Passion? Reverence? Insanity? "I believe I am close to discovering a way to defeat death."

"Beg pardon?"

"Death is the price all men pay, my friend. But does it have to be? What if there were a way to eliminate death completely?" The Necromancer's pace of speech increased, his tone becoming more impassioned, excited. "How much suffering, how many crimes, have their root in a fear of death? How much better could humanity be if that weight were lifted from its shoulders?" He grinned. It was an unnatural-looking smile, the upward curving of his lips revealing his gleaming white teeth and making him look almost like a carnival freak. "I am almost there. I only need a short time more and I will have it, the answer to every man's desire."

Gareth had to work to suppress a shudder. The man *was* insane. He had to be. Right off the top of his head, Gareth could think of half a dozen terrible consequences of a discovery like that, if it was even possible. Which he seriously doubted.

"So what, you want me to go back and tell Lord Hadley to just leave you alone? I don't think he will buy that."

The Necromancer's smile faded, becoming instead a frown of annoyance. "I have no faith in his ability to reason. Though you *could* assist me in another way."

Here it was. Gareth flexed his fingers on the grip of his axe, willing his muscles to relax into readiness. "And how is that, exactly?"

"You are clearly very capable. None have made it as far into my realm as you, or defeated as many of my servants. I could use a man like you at my side, watching my back, managing my forces."

He was joking, right? Gareth opened his mouth to retort, but the Necromancer beat him to it.

"Unfortunately," said the Necromancer with a malicious grin that was, if possible, even worse than his earlier one, "you are no use to me alive."

He made a little flick of his left hand, and Gareth heard a sharp CLICK from behind him. He turned to see that the doorway he had entered through had changed. Before it opened onto a landing; now it led into a large room that was empty except for a number of columns running down its length.

And a horde of animated corpses.

Gareth should not have been surprised. What else could he expect from a man such as the Necromancer? All the same, he could not deny that the man's genteel demeanor had lulled him into lowering his guard. So when the first pair of corpses stormed through the door and reached toward him and Hatherle, Gareth stood rooted to the spot in shock.

"Goodbye, my friends," the Necormancer said from behind. "If it comforts you at all, I am very confident your passing will help me make great progress toward my goal." Did he really expect Gareth to find that notion appealing? "Who knows, you may end up being the key to the entire experiment."

Another click from behind. Gareth looked back quickly, in time to see the latch on the door on the other side of the room lowering into place. The Necromancer was gone.

Then the corpse was on him. Dead fingers clawed through the air toward his face. Reflexes honed through years of training saved him on the first pass as he turned his body away, placing his right shoulder—and the shield strapped to his arm—closest to his attacker. The claws struck the shield and scraped harmlessly down it, though the sound they caused as they did so made his hair stand on end.

There was no time for subtlety. He lunged forward, ignoring the screams of protest from his injured calf, and brought his axe straight down atop the corpse's head. It split open like a melon and the corpse instantly stopped, falling to the floor at Gareth's feet in a heap and spilling grey matter—it was surprisingly fluid, and rank; the poor fellow must not have died the first time all that long ago—all over the floor.

Beside him, Hatherle was hard pressed. His wounds were not as bad as Gareth's had been, but he did not have the advantage of Gareth's years of training. What he knew of the sword, and combat, was what Gareth and his various acquaintances had taught him. This corpse was more nimble than the last couple Hatherle had faced, easily dodging a riposte from the slender man and responding with a bull-rush attack that knocked him to the floor.

Hatherle's expression when Gareth's axe took the corpse's head from its shoulders was a classic blend of relief and revulsion. And small wonder; Gareth would not have enjoyed being splattered with corpse-fluids either.

Gareth helped Hatherle to his feet as best he could, but was drawn up short by the renewed pain in his leg. He glanced down and saw that his pants bore fresh bloodstains. He could feel fluid seeping into his boot; one or more of his stitches must have pulled. Dammit.

"Thankee, my lord," Hatherle began, but then there was no more time for talk as another pair of corpses entered the room.

Those were more easily dispatched. The men were not

surprised this time, and both corpses were older, more brittle and less quick.

Still, it was obvious, from the multitude still approaching the door, that they would be overwhelmed sooner or later.

Another pair of corpses shouldered their way through the door and Gareth lurched forward to intercept them.

"Hatherle, the door!"

Hatherle nodded and ducked to the side. The corpse nearest him turned to follow, but Gareth leapt to place himself ahead of the monster.

Or rather, he tried to. His right leg, already pressed beyond what would have been prudent, picked that moment to fail him completely. Gareth fell hard, taking a painful bump on his cheek as his face struck the floor. Above the pain, he felt a surge of despair. He missed his chance, and the animated corpse was going to get to Hatherle before he could get the door shut.

They were going to be overwhelmed, overrun.

Then something struck him in the side and an instant later he felt a weight land on his back. Whatever it was thrashed around, and it stank of decay. The corpse! It must have tripped over him and fallen.

Hardly believing his luck, Gareth squirmed and pushed with all his might, trying to get out from beneath the undead thing before it realized what it had fallen upon and choked the life out of him. Fortunately, being reanimated did not seem to convey intellect very well—at least with this corpse; Gareth tried not to think about how quick Ranulf had seemed—and Gareth managed to get some distance from the thing with just a very little struggle.

He pushed himself to his knees to find the corpse also rising. His axe ended that, severing the thing's desiccated left leg at the knee. It flopped onto the floor. Gareth would have sworn it was surprised by that turn of events, if he was not sure it had no mind to be surprised with. Its surprise, if it existed, was momentary, though, before Gareth's axe split its head in two.

Gareth was just beginning to feel good about himself and their chances when something grabbed him by the back of his breast-plate, lifted him off his knees, and threw him into one of the book-shelves.

The impact was incredible. He struck it with his already-injured shoulder, sending a surge of pain through him that was so intense he could only see red for what felt like eternity. He did not feel himself strike the floor, or anything at all for that matter, except for the pain.

Somewhere in his mind a voice screamed at him to get up, to move, to do something, because if he did not, he was dead. But that voice was faint, easily ignored beneath the screaming agony that washed over him. Had the end come right then, he would have welcomed it without hesitation.

But somehow, it did not.

Some time later, he had no idea how long, his vision cleared and the pain faded so that he could process other things. At first, all he could see was a blur, but after blinking a few times, he was able to make out a face staring down at him.

Hatherle's face.

The manservant looked like hell. He had a deep cut running across his forehead and down the right side of his face toward his ear. It had bled intensely, coating his face with a sheen of red that at first made Gareth think he was a devil of some sort. But devils never wore expressions of concern that melted away into joyous smiles when the object of their attention woke. Or whatever the right term was for what Gareth did when he came back to his senses.

"Are you well, my lord?"

Gareth barked out a bitter laugh. Or at least he hoped it was a laugh; it was hard to tell. "Do I look well?"

Hatherle shook his head and helped Gareth to his feet. As he stood up—he very nearly collapsed again when his wounded leg felt even a small amount of weight—he looked around.

The door to the room full of animated corpses was shut, but it shuddered periodically as something—no, several somethings—

pounded on it from the other side. The corpse Gareth had done for lay where he expected it. The other, the one that had thrown him across the room, was slumped against the desk. The blade of Hatherle's sword was stuck into its eye and protruded through the back of its skull. Only the blade.

Gareth blinked. Hatherle was not strong enough to make that strong a thrust. "What happened?"

Hatherle shrugged. "I got the door shut as it," he nodded toward the impaled corpse, "threw you. I tried to distract it, but it was so strong." The slender man paused, swallowing. "It leapt on me, and impaled itself on my sword somehow. But it did not stop immediately. I tried to pull the sword out, but..." He gestured toward the ground near the desk, where the pommel of his sword lay. The blade was sheared off near the crosspiece.

Cold anger burned inside Gareth as he considered everything that had happened to them over the last hours. Or was it days? "Let's go, Hatherle. I'm going to kill that bastard."

Hatherle nodded agreement. "Let me check your leg first, my lord."

Gareth hated to take the time, but the shuddering door seemed solid enough, at least for the moment. And Hatherle was right. He had burst at least one stitch, and he would not be able to fight well if he was losing blood.

A few minutes later, Gareth shouldered his way through the door the Necromancer had disappeared through, ready to deal out some punishment.

***

Gareth did not truly expect to find the Necromancer on the other side of the door. More likely it would lead to another corridor with confusing twists and turns and more riddles to solve. Or even better, to some sort of magical trap that would burn he and Hatherle alive while the Necromancer watched and laughed.

So when he forced his way through the portal and found

himself in a well-appointed bed chamber, and the Necromancer bent over a small chest of drawers next to the four-poster bed that dominated the room, he found himself stopping in complete surprise.

Which meant he was at best half as surprised as the Necromancer, from the look on the skinny man's face.

"What?" said the Necromancer. "How?" His eyes flickered from Gareth to the door to Hatherle and back to the door.

"Were you expecting someone else?" asked Gareth as he stalked, limped really, and calling it limping was being charitable, toward him. He swung his axe slowly back and forth at his side, and he knew he had a murderous expression on his face, an expression he had practiced long and hard, one that had struck fear into strong men on many occasions before this.

The Necromancer was not a strong man, at least not physically. But, credit where credit's due, if he felt fear he never let it surface. "Actually yes."

"Sorry to disappoint." Gareth reached the corner of the bed and rounded it, grabbing the corner post with his right hand to steady himself as he did so. The Necromancer was almost within reach. Gareth should have known better.

The Necromancer smirked slightly, then inclined his head toward Gareth. "I did not think you would be able to fight my servants off, given their numbers. Not in your condition."

"And they say wizards are smart." Gareth did not even try to keep the scorn, the derision, from his tone. No point in showing respect to a man whose brains you were about to splatter all over his fine rug.

"Oh, we are."

The Necromancer snapped his fingers, and everything went black.

He was not dead.

That was a surprise, actually. Gareth had heard wizards could kill easily with their magic. Presumably, Necromancers, as attuned to death as they were, would be particularly adept at it. But when several seconds passed and he found he could hear his heart pounding in his ears, smell the faint odor of the freshly re-killed corpses in the adjoining room, feel the sweat beading his brow, Gareth was certain he still lived.

But for how long?

He realized he had dropped into a combat crouch, his reflexes responding to the changing condition even as his mind struggled to make sense of it. His injured leg screamed at him; the crouch was pulling on his stitches again. He could feel them, about to give way. But he pushed away the impulse to straighten, instead forcing himself to move forward, toward where he last saw the Necromancer.

Something passed over his head, causing a slight breeze that ruffled his hair.

Behind him, he heard a surprised-sounding grunt, then a long slow sigh followed by a limp thump. That could only have been Hatherle hitting the floor. Gareth clenched his teeth in anger and turned toward the sound, raising his axe in preparation for a swing. He may not be able to see the Necromancer, but he could damn well hear him. He was not going to get away without tasting the bite of Gareth's axe!

Or at least that was the plan.

Suddenly something snatched the axe out of his hand. One moment he was holding it in readiness: not in a death grip, but hardly loosely by any means. The next, the axe was gone, plucked from his hand before he could even think to resist, and with a strength that would have been irresistible regardless.

Gareth had only a heartbeat to wonder what had happen before he felt a vice take hold of his throat and lift him off his feet.

Shock, pain, and sudden loss of breath all worked in unison to confuse him; it took longer than it should have to realize that the vice was in fact a hand. Thin, skeletal fingers wrapped around his throat with a strength Gareth never imagined possible.

Panicked horror surged through him. It was another of those walking corpses!

Then a voice spoke in the darkness, its source mere inches in front of his face from the stirring of the air. "You fool," it said in a tone that dripped contempt. "You actually thought you could defeat me." A half-laugh, half-snort punctuated the words. "Now it is you who are defeated, and I gain a new pair of servants."

The Necromancer. It was the Necromancer speaking, and who had hold of Gareth's throat. Why had it taken so long to recognize his voice?

Gareth's heart pounded all the louder. He began seeing flashes of light in the darkness and his lungs cried out as though ready to burst. He had to get out of the Necromancer's grip. Had to breathe.

But flailing with his hand was like beating on a tree trunk, for all the result it had in getting the man to remove his hand from around Gareth's throat. Amazing that so scrawny a fellow could harbor such strength!

The Necromancer laughed again, in amusement. Gareth imagined he could see, somewhere behind the flashes of light, the other man's lips turned upward into a mocking sneer. It was not an image he wanted as his last.

He tried to struggle more, to strike the Necromancer with the edge of his shield, but his right arm would not move; it was too heavy. Hell, his *free* arm felt like it was made of lead.

He could definitely see the Necromancer now. Whatever he had done to get rid of the light had faded. Or then again, maybe not. The edges of Gareth's vision contained only darkness, which was slowly spreading toward the center. After a moment, he realized when the darkness spread fully, it would be all over, and felt another surge of fear.

That fear turned to terror when the thought passed ever so slowly through his head that it might not be all over. Would he be aware of himself, of his status, once the Necromancer turned him into one of his undead servants?

He had to escape. He raised his arm, leaden as it was, to punch the Necromancer in the face. But the blow fell well short of its mark and his hand dropped, limply, down until his hand fell onto something on Gareth's belt.

The Necromancer's sneer grew more gleeful. "Soon, my friend," he said in a tone that was nearly a purr.

The growing darkness had eclipsed the room, its furniture, Hatherle lying face-down on the floor, everything except for the Necromancer's face.

It could not end like this. Gareth tried to clench his fist for one last attack, but for some reason his fist would not close. Something prevented his fingers from reaching his palm. Something round, hard. Something cold.

The pommel of his dagger, where it was sheathed on his belt.

Final desperation gave strength to his fingers as Gareth clutched at the dagger's grip and withdrew it from its sheath.

The Necromancer's eyes flickered downward as he noticed Gareth's movement. They went wide, the sneer leaving his face to be replaced by an expression of shocked disbelief as Gareth plunged the blade into his chest.

He was definitely dead this time. He had to be; all he saw was darkness, all he felt was cold.

But then, once again, the light slowly returned, revealing the bed chamber's ceiling, Gareth had to consider that maybe his assumption had been wrong on that point. He blinked, focusing in on a hand that was reaching down toward him, then followed the hand up to its owner.

Hatherle was crouched by his side. He still had that nasty bloody gash across his forehead, but now the other half of his face was bruising up as well. Somehow the un-bruised half of his face was ashen beneath all the blood, as though he was deathly afraid. Small wonder, that. Despite all that, however, he somehow managed to look ready for action.

A lot better than Gareth felt.

Gareth took Hatherle's hand, and the manservant pulled him to his feet. There he had to stand still for a long moment, leaning against the former sage for support to avoid falling again as the world spun around him. Finally it settled down and he examined his surroundings.

The bed chamber looked the same as it had, but the Necromancer was nowhere to be seen. Blood stained the stone floor where he had been—or where Gareth thought he had been—but that was all.

"What happened?" he asked.

Hatherle shrugged. "When I came to, you were unconscious, my Lord, and our foe had vanished." He held up his free hand; he was carrying Gareth's blood-stained dagger. "This was lying on the floor."

Gareth nodded and took back the dagger, cleaning it on his pants leg before re-sheathing it. "He hit you on the head."

It was not a question, but Hatherle nodded anyway. "In the darkness, my Lord. I heard him coming, but he was too fast, and…" He left off talking, sounding embarrassed.

Gareth snorted. "He got the better of both of us, Hatherle. Don't beat yourself up." He took a hesitant step toward the pool of blood. When he did not immediately fall over, he took another, then crouched down next to it, again ignoring the protest from his leg. "I can't imagine he could have not killed us with magic. Why didn't he? Why fisticuffs?" he said aloud, glancing over his shoulder toward Hatherle.

Hatherle shook his head. "I concur, my lord." He swallowed. Hard. The color was slowly beginning to return to the unbruised portion of his face. "Of course, killing magic takes some preparation. Likely he had not planned on using those sort of spells when he set out his plan for the day. Or he just figured his minions would do the job well enough."

"Or he really *does* like me."

Hatherle looked at him askance. "I suppose that is…possible."

So where did he go? There was only one other exit besides the one leading to the office, an iron-reinforced door that swung open easily at Gareth's touch. Beyond the door were stairs leading straight downward until it reached a landing some thirty feet below. Unlike the previous corridors, however, this stairwell was illuminated by natural sunlight that streamed in through periodic windows on the left wall and through a stained glass design inlaid above the door down on the landing.

"That can't be the exit…can it?" It was too easy.

Hatherle made no reply, but the hopeful expression on his face said it all.

Gareth sighed. The Necromancer was gone and, frankly, Gareth had no desire to figure out where he had gone to. For whatever reason, it looked as though there would be no payoff on this one. Lord Hadley had been quite clear on that point: no body, no bounty.

A great thump, much louder than any of the previous, reverberated into the bed chamber from the office. Hatherle looked back, and blanched.

"The door is almost off its hinges. I'm not sure what hit it, but…" He left the rest unsaid.

"Let's get out of here." Gareth hated to leave with nothing to show for this expedition, but that was how it was. He turned back toward the stairway out, but stopped halfway there. "Well I'll be."

Resting atop the chest of drawers the Necromancer had been rifling through was a good-sized strong box. Gareth stepped over to it, and found himself grinning. Maybe his luck was about to turn around. He forced the lock and flung the box open, and his grin grew even wider.

Gold always made him smile.

"Grab that, will you Hatherle?" He would not be able to carry it, wounded as he was. And besides, what was the point of having a manservant if not to have him lug things?

Hatherle sighed. As he picked up the strong box, he spoke in a tone of resignation, with perhaps a tiny bit of irritation beneath. "I am sworn to carry your burdens," he said.

Gareth shook his head in amusement.

He took a minute to pull flint and stone out of his belt pouch, then struck alight a few pieces of paper he found in the chest of drawers. He set the burning pages beneath the bed, and soon the bed was beginning to burn as well. With luck, maybe the entire place would go up. At the very least it would slow down their pursuers.

"Looks like we live to fight another day," he said.

Then he turned and hobbled down the stairs.

Hatherle followed.

A Note Of
Magic

Michael
Kingswood

Author of the Climmer Vale Chronicles

A NOTE OF MAGIC

Lilly wet her lips quickly, then rested them on the mouthpiece of her clarinet and waited. The reed pressed against her tongue, its rough texture and wooden taste familiar and comforting as she readied herself.

All around, the other members of the McClain High School Performance Band—more an orchestra than a band, really—had their gazes locked on a slender woman in a white and yellow sun dress that set off her greying hair, who stood at the center of the semicircle of musicians.

Mrs. Quigley smiled and raised the baton that she carried loosely in her right hand. Then, with a negligible flick of the baton, the band commenced.

It usually did not take very long for Lilly to become caught up in the pleasure of performance, all else forgotten but the notes on the sheet music before her, the imagined ticking of a metronome in her head, and the movement of her fingers along the clarinet's valves as she played her part, and today was no different.

She played, and lost herself in the ecstasy of the moment, not noticing the heat of the bodies all around her—so many that the air conditioning, weak as it was in this part of the school, could not keep up—or the sweat that dripped down her back, making her ruffled blue shirt stick to her skin.

The music was all.

She played, and it seemed as though a force other than herself sent her fingers over the valves, controlled the quick inhalations and slow exhalations that created the notes she played.

Henry, the spindly Freshman who sat next to her, as second Clarinet, reached over to flip the sheet music over, but she paid him no heed.

Onward, the music carried her, and she began to feel truly a part of it. It seemed she would float away, carried on her clarinet's tones to a state of pure bliss, pure light. For a second, she almost thought she could see that light, a beautiful pink-white radiance that bathed over her.

And then that second passed, and with it, the oneness that she had felt so clearly.

Abruptly, she realized she was no longer in her seat. She stood, alone amongst all the others in the band except for the bassists. Hers was the only music being played, and all eyes were on her.

Her last note turned into a squeak and then ended abruptly. She lowered her clarinet, her face growing hot in embarrassment.

"What was that, Lilly?" Mrs. Quigley said, one eyebrow raised in what normally passed for her stern expression. But her tone did not convey anger, only curiosity and…admiration?

Lilly swallowed and tried to grin, but it felt fake. She glanced around at the other musicians and forced out a little laugh. "I'm sorry," she said. "I just got…caught up."

"Please do so again. That was wonderful."

Lilly gaped at Mrs. Quigley's words.

"But," the teacher added, "save the improvisation for after Mozart, hmm?"

Lilly nodded and hastily sat down, still flushing. She made a point of re-arranging the sheet music on her and Henry's music stand, determinedly not looking anyone else in the eye. How much time was left in this period? She was not sure she could stand to remain there much longer, mortified as she was.

Just then, as if cued by her thoughts, the bell rang.

Half the band stood up and began putting their instruments away. Mrs. Quigley had to rap her own music stand twice with her baton before they gave her their attention.

"We have one more rehearsal on Wednesday, and then the recital on Friday night." Mrs. Quigley beamed a brief smile. "Be ready."

There was a quiet murmur from the gathered students, then, en masse, they packed up and bolted for the door. Such was the danger of scheduling rehearsal for the final period of the day. Most of the upperclassmen had missed free periods—an early departure form school, really—to be there, but that did not mean they wanted to remain even a minute longer than necessary.

Lilly did not hurry, though. Even had she felt up to dealing with their stares, she would not have left with them. She actually liked playing her clarinet. Loved it, really. Oh, she had no doubt the others enjoyed band as well, to some extent or other, but it did not compare with the joy she took from it. That much was obvious. And so she always remained after for a while, practicing on her own.

She raised the clarinet to her lips and inhaled, but Mrs. Quigley's voice broke her concentration. "Did you come up with that solo part during these little extra sessions of yours?"

Lilly looked back at the teacher and found her staring back at her curiously, her hands resting on her hips. She shrugged. "Not sure. I lost track of what I was playing, just then."

Mrs. Quigley watched her in silence for several seconds, and Lilly felt the hair on the back of her neck stand on end. There was something odd about the way the teacher was looking at her. Something almost... She could not put words to it, but all of a sudden she felt extremely wary of Mrs. Quigley.

Then the moment passed and Mrs. Quigley flashed that smile again. "See you Wednesday," she said, then she, too, turned to leave the room. She paused at the door and looked over her shoulder at Lilly. "Practice hard."

The door shut behind her with a barely audible click, leaving Lilly alone with her clarinet, and with the notes.

Twenty minutes later, Lilly stepped out of the front entrance to the school into the bright warmth of the late spring afternoon and looked around. The student parking lot off to the right was mostly empty. Few of the extracurriculars held meetings on Mondays, so there was no reason for most of the upperclassmen to remain after the final bell.

All the same, a few of her fellow Seniors gaggled there, chitchatting and laughing together. Football jocks mostly, from the look of the boys, and cheerleaders. Lilly watched the empty-headed hussies for a minute as they threw themselves at the muscled guys, marveling at how they could be so transparently brazen without catching any hell for it. If she ever thought of behaving that way…

And of course, there was Katrina, the first violin, all long legs and graceful curves, her perfect blonde hair tossing as she laughed at one of the jocks' words, her violin case tucked under her arm. It was simply not fair. She was everything Lilly wished she could be: beautiful, popular, smart, and a brilliant musician.

Their eyes met, and Katrina's smile turned slyly vicious. She gestured Lilly's way, and the group of jocks and hussies looked over in her direction. One of the cheerleaders said something, and the group of them laughed, still staring straight at her.

Lilly made a point of turning left, away from the parking lot and the other students. She lived close enough to walk home; even if she had a car, she would not have had a need to go to the parking lot.

She was not fleeing from their mocking stares. She was *not*.

Or at least that was what she told herself.

She turned the corner of the building, leaving the floozies to their victims, and headed down the edge of the athletic fields toward her street, at the far end of the complex. Off to her left, the baseball team had suited up for practice and was in full swing. Idly, she noted that the cheerleaders did not bother to practice in view of these particular jocks. All the better for them.

She passed the baseball backstop and continued on, her thoughts already leaving the boys and their diversions. A tune passed through her head. She recognized it from earlier, when she had gone off during rehearsal. It had seemed so clear then, but now it echoed through her memory like a dream half-remembered. She knew that tune, somehow. But it vanished as soon as she tried to take hold of it. She should be able to hum it, but somehow it eluded her, the notes flitting out of her mind as soon as they came.

What was...

Something slammed into her and she fell forward onto the turf, letting out a high-pitched yelp that sounded horrid in her own ears. She threw out her hands to catch herself, her book bag flying wide from the effort, but only managed to land jarringly on her left wrist.

Damn, that was all she needed was to hurt herself before the recital.

Something heavy lay atop her, and she had to squirm to get out from beneath it. She rolled over onto her back, working her wrist gingerly and biting her lip, both from the pain and from the effort of holding back a salty curse one of her mother's boyfriends had let loose one time.

A boy rolled the other way—it must have been he who landed atop her—and she scowled. "What do you think you're - "

The words cut off in her mouth as the guy pushed himself up onto his hands and knees and looked at her, concern on his face. She recognized him immediately: Josh Harrington. Her stomach did a little flip in her belly as his bright green eyes met hers and he flushed with embarrassment.

"Sorry, Lilly," he said, getting to his feet in a hurry and offering her a hand up. "Didn't see you there."

She should have snapped back some witty retort, but right then all thought left her as she looked up at him. A few strands of his dirty blond hair hung out dashingly below the brim of his ball cap, and his practice uniform was grass-stained where he had landed on the turf. On *her*. She forced down a little shiver as her mind tried to take that thought another six steps farther than it should have.

"S'ok," she managed to say, and started to her feet. She took his hand, not wanting to refuse the effort at politeness, and a second later almost wished she had not.

A little jolt excitement, almost electricity, seemed to run down her hand and into the rest of her body at his touch, and her legs stopped working for a second. She half-collapsed back to the ground before she caught herself and got back to her feet.

She turned away, so he would not see the flush she felt running through her cheeks, and looked around for her book bag. There it was, off to the left. And, next to it, a baseball.

"Guess I made you miss your catch," she said. He was an outfielder. It was not good for him to miss catches. She hoped he would not get in trouble for that. "Sorry."

Josh laughed softly, bounding past her to scoop up her book bag and his ball, both. He turned back to her, an easy grin on his face as he held her bag out for her. "Not the first time." How many girls had he run into out here? "Are you alright?"

She was about to nod, but right then the alarm on her watch went off. She glanced down, surprised. She did not remember setting the alarm. Then she saw the time.

3:45.

Something…shifted…within her. A force seemed to shove her aside within her own head, and everything went black.

She needed to hurry; she was almost late.

She snatched the bag away from the boy, murmuring something—she had no idea what—and spinning away from him toward the street. She caught a brief flash of confusion, becoming irritation, on his face before he left her field of view, and then she was off.

She covered the remaining distance to the street, and then down the three blocks to the girl's house, at a run.

She burst through the front door and hardly spared a second to glance around the foyer with its gleaming hardwood and sparse, tasteful furnishing before dashing upstairs. She did not announce herself; the mother would not be home from work for some time. She got to the girl's room and kicked the door shut behind herself, dropping her book bag in a heap on the floor. A quick scan showed everything still in place: the double-bed, neatly made with white-lace blankets off in the corner to her left, the writing desk beneath the window at the foot of the bed, the dresser against the wall to her right, and there, against the wall directly ahead, the music stand.

A rush of relief flowed through her; nothing had been disturbed.

More slowly now, she lifted the foot of the mattress up and pulled out a small bundle of paper from its place of concealment. She flipped through it and, spying the familiar lines and notes of the music, smiled in satisfaction. The pages were still intact.

That thought struck her as silly; nothing on this earth could destroy these pages, or render their notes unreadable. But this was not a game that allowed for mistakes; the consequences of an error would be disastrous beyond the understanding of the simple people around her.

She set the sheet music on her music stand, feeling the weight of her burden distinctly, as she always did when she prepared herself. As she assembled the girl's clarinet, she spared a glance at her watch.

3:55. This would not do.

But there was no help for it. She finished her preparations and set the reed to her lips, her eyes focusing on the first note as she gathered her will. She inhaled slowed, through her nose, then set to it.

The notes came easily, carrying through the room on a wave of energy that made the hairs on her arms stand on and. Her skin tingled in a thousand places as the music took her, pulling her onward almost against her will, her fingers flying across the clarinet's valves and her breathing strong and steady as she played. This was the spell that had touched the girl in band rehearsal multiplied a hundredfold, and she reveled in it.

And yet…what had happened in rehearsal gave her pause. That should not have happened; the girl should not have been able to tap into this, not without guidance. How had…?

She brought herself back to the present with a flash of chagrin. Focus. Focus was required now, lest it all go wrong.

The music began building in a crescendo that filled the room until it seemed the walls would burst apart. And then, all at once, another series of notes joined hers, a lilting harmony that matched and lifted her part to a level greater than she could have managed on her own.

And with the expanse of the song, the light from outside—bright and pure on this nearly cloud-free day—faded, dimmed. In the center of the room, and new radiance began to grow. Pink-white, it pulsed in time with the music, beckoning. Weakly at first but quickly growing more intense in time with the growing harmony until it seemed she must go blind from looking at it. And then brighter still it became until it eclipsed all perception, replacing the world she had been in, leaving nothing behind. Nothing but the music.

Her fingers were a blur; she could not remember when she had last taken a breath. But she felt no fatigue, no shortage of breath. The music carried her, nurtured her, lifted her up into the vortex of light. She billowed upward and her heart gave a little jump at the sudden feeling of weightlessness; familiar and expected though it was, the transition always had that effect. Strange, that. She should have been used to it by now.

She reached the end of her part of the music and let the clarinet lower from her lips, but somehow the melody and harmony continued on without her. The strands of the song reinforced themselves, each preventing the other from fading lest the connection be broken.

Drifting in the pristine glow, she pushed aside the body's reaction and allowed herself to bask in the sense of warmth, of belonging. Of power. She closed her eyes for a moment and just...felt.

When she opened them again, she was no longer alone.

A figure floated in the light before her. Its was blurry, obscured as though being seen through a warped piece of glass, but it was humanoid, with strong features framed by long pale hair. Flowing iridescent robes, their color difficult to determine in the surrounding brilliance, hung from its shoulders, giving the figure air of formality.

She inclined her head respectfully in greeting.

The figure did not speak. Rather, words appeared in her mind. "You are overdue."

"I know," she said, voicing her thoughts aloud. "The girl became distracted. I was forced to intervene."

The figure's features twisted in disapproval. "Is she going to be a problem?"

She paused for a moment, considering, then shook her head.

"Very well. Report."

"I am certain I have located the target. I'll only need a short time to complete preparations."

The figure again looked disapproving. "Time grows short. You know the consequences of error."

"I do."

"See that you keep them in mind." The figure paused. When it "spoke" next, it was with greater warmth. "You have been apart from us for a long time. Your presence is missed."

She felt a flush at the change in tone, and could only incline her head again, more deeply.

"Have you anything else?"

She considered mentioning the incident during the girl's music rehearsal this day, but decided against it. It was nothing she could not handle, nothing to worry over. She shook her head.

"Very well. Report again in two days, and be prepared to complete your task quickly." The figure was back to formality and command. "Much depends on your success."

She inclined her head again, in farewell this time.

Then, with a flash of brilliant white, then connection broke and the figure was gone.

"What's going on in here?"

Lilly gave a little start and almost fell off her bed. She blinked her eyes, bringing them into focus, and sat up, confused.

Her bed. What was she doing on her bed? The last thing she could recall was picking herself off the grass where Josh had run into her, the way the sunlight glinted in his eyes... She shook her head, suppressing the thought, and looked over toward her bedroom door, where her mother stood with her hands on her hips, staring at her with a mixture of concern and irritation.

Mother was everything Lilly was not: tall and willowy while Lilly was short and—how did grandmother say?—big boned. Mother's hair was dark, just a shade less than black, and she wore it up, giving her an elegant but businesslike look when matched with the dark pants suit that seemed to both show off her curves and conceal them at the same time. She spent plenty of time at the gym to keep herself looking that way, Lilly knew. But—and Mother would be mortified if she realized Lilly knew this—she also had made use of professional help to do so. That's what Lilly heard one of the girls at school call getting plastic surgery once.

"Are you alright?" Mother asked, concern growing on her face as she took in Lilly's appearance.

"Yeah." But was she? She glanced at the clock hanging on the wall above her desk, and stopped short. 5:45. She had lost two hours this time.

Lilly shivered. Several times over the last weeks, she had found herself sitting someplace, or lying on her bed, unable for account for some amount of time. Sometimes just a minute or two, sometimes more: a half hour or forty-five minutes. It had made her nervous, but she had never lost *this much* time before.

That was downright frightening.

"The front door was standing wide open. I thought someone had..." Mother stopped, shaking her head. "Are you sure you're alright?"

Lilly nodded quickly, not trusting herself to speak just then. Mother already thought her strange. If she knew about the lost time Lilly had experienced lately... Lilly had no desire to be poked and prodded by a bunch of doctors, or worse get taken to a head-shrink. She had just been very tired, and had fallen asleep is all. Nothing more.

Easy to say.

"I'm going to get started on dinner. Come down and help?"

Lilly nodded again, quickly. "Be right there."

Mother smiled then, reassuringly, and turned to walk back downstairs, leaving Lilly to sit on her bed and try to get her thoughts in order. She was not very successful.

Lilly walked into the band's rehearsal room, feeling strangely anxious. It had been building up within her all day, the feeling that something momentous was about to happen. She tried to shrug it off as nerves over the impending recital, now only two days away, but could not. She had played in many recitals, both solo and in an orchestra, over the years, and before audiences far larger than they expected in the school's auditorium.

No, there was something more that had her worried. She just could not figure out what.

Mrs. Quigley turned from where she stood near her conductor's music stand, baton in hand, and smiled in greeting. As usual, she was dressed conservatively. Also as usual, her smile seemed just a tad wider for Lilly than for the boy carrying a violin case who brushed past her.

"Ready to go?" the teacher said.

Lilly just shrugged and moved to her seat.

Henry was already there, his clarinet fully assembled and the music sitting on their stand. His blond hair was frizzled as usual, his blue t-shirt wrinkled, and he was sucking on his instrument's reed like it was a lollipop.

Gross.

She sat down next to him, smoothing her loose, flowery skirts absently before setting her clarinet case down and opening it up.

Henry pulled the reed out of his mouth and grinned at her. "Excited?"

Lilly pulled the pieces of her clarinet out and began fitting them together, pausing only to shrug slightly in answer.

He was not to be dissuaded. "I can't wait. Friday is going to be awesome!" He tested the reed with his thumb then nodded and slid it into place on the mouthpiece of his clarinet. "My grandpa's coming to town just for this."

Lilly tried to give him an encouraging smile, but her heart wasn't into it. For whatever reason, his talking about the coming recital set her heart to racing all of a sudden and she felt a flash of something that was not quite fear.

But that didn't make any sense.

She finished assembling her instrument and wetted the reed, then set it into place. She looked around the room quickly.

The rest of her band-mates were all seated. From all around the room came the sounds of various instruments being tuned or run through arpeggios, a chaotic mass of sound that somehow managed to be pleasing, despite its lack of structure.

It was a familiar pattern, oft repeated, and she found herself calmed by it. There was nothing to worry about, nothing at all.

A couple minutes passed, then Mrs. Quigley tapped her baton onto the top of her music stand. It did not make a loud noise, but the rhythm of it cut through the various musicians' preparations easily, and the noise around the room died out.

Mrs. Quigley's eyes moved over the group, assessing. And was Lilly imagining things or did they pause on her longer than on anyone else? Again she felt a shiver of almost fear, but then the feeling passed as the teacher's gaze swept past her.

"Two days to the recital," Mrs. Quigley said. "This is our last rehearsal, so let's make it a good one." She raised her hands, and, in unison with her motion, the band raised their instruments to positions of readiness.

They began.

Almost immediately, the tension that had been filling Lilly seemed to wash away. The notes flowing out of her lungs and through the valves in her clarinet seemed to lift her; she almost felt she was going to float away. Her head swam, and the musical symbols on the pages Henry had placed on the music stand wavered and blurred. Still, she played on. She knew the part by heart, and anyway she could not have stopped herself if she tried.

The song progressed, and she lost herself more and more as the seconds passed. Nothing existed except the next note she was going to play, nothing mattered except the pace of her breathing and the rhythm of her fingers on the valves. Her vision narrowed, the faces of her bandmates fading into a blur all around her.

And then, a light. A glorious white-pink light that warmed her to core of her being.

Unbidden, a different piece of music came into her mind, familiar despite her certainty that she had never played it before. Without thinking about it, she changed the rhythm of her breathing, and her fingers moved to key the new melody.

It came so naturally. It was so...right.

No!

A voice that was not her own seemed to shout in her head, knocking her off her rhythm.

Not now, not yet!

She faltered, shaken to the core, but the call of the music was so strong, the light so welcoming. She could not stop herself...

She felt a...wrenching. Heard an inaudible curse inside her head.

And then everything went black.

Lilly floated in nothingness, for how long she did not know.

Slowly, she came to realize that she existed, that she was, in fact, able to think. But she could not see, could not hear. Could not move. It was like she was a thought without a body, unable to do anything.

A shiver of fear ran through her. What had happened to her? Where was she?

All around, there was only blackness, only silence. She tried to speak, but no sound came out of her mouth.

The fear grew, nearing panic. Her hair felt as though it were standing on end, and her body was damp with cold sweat.

That was something at least. She could feel.

And then she could hear. Slightly. A distant murmuring, like voices speaking softly from across a room. She could not quite understand...

She strained toward the sound, struggling to move.

Finally, after what seemed a year, her head turned, just the slightest bit. And that small motion unlocked the floodgates. First her fingers and toes, then her wrists and ankles began to respond to her commands, and through the blackness, a light began to grow.

Dimly at first, just the faintest of red in the black. But gradually increasing in intensity. And with it, the sounds grew louder as well.

"...don't know how she did it," a voice, sibilant and gentle-sounding, said with more than a hint of confusion.

She turned her head again, and the sounds fell to a murmur once more, before a second voice, deeper and more commanding than the first, became understandable.

"This could ruin everything." The second voice sounded upset.

The redness of the light struck a memory in Lilly's mind: closing her eyes against her mother suddenly flicking on a light switch, to keep the sudden brightness from overwhelming her. The light was just like that, like a lamp shining against her closed eyelids.

She strained, and her eyes opened a crack.

Immediately she knew where she was: her bedroom. She recognized the pattern on the ceiling, where she had once tried to paint a scene when she was little. She was lying on her bed.

But the light that shown around her was not from any lamp. It was white-pink, and warm. Just like the light she had glimpsed in rehearsal earlier. What was going -

She raised her head, and her breath caught in her throat. A nimbus of pink-white floated in the air at the foot of her bed, and within it was a being of some sort. More a silhouette than anything else, but it was a creature, she was sure of it. And sitting next to her, on the bed, was another creature, seemingly made of pure light. She could not make out many details of either being except that they were human-shaped, with long pale hair and clad in translucent clothing, and lovely beyond anything she had ever seen.

The stern voice continued, coming from the being in the air. "You must - "

Lilly's squeak as she finally found her voice cut the being off, and both creatures spun to face her. The intensity of their gazes froze her muscles; she would have shrunk back, sunk through the bed if she could to avoid those eyes. Eyes that glimmered pink-red and seemed to see through to her soul.

"She's awake!" the stern being said. A second later, it turned its gaze away from Lilly and toward the being next to her on the bed. "How is she awake?"

The being on the bed was visibly shaken, recoiling from the question and from Lilly both as it sprang to its feet. "I don't - "

"Who are you?" Lilly managed to say, through trembling lips. She did not like how squeaky her voice came out. "*What* are you?"

The being who had been with her on the bed gathered itself quickly and moved closer, reaching out an arm toward her. "Lilly, don't be afraid. We - "

Lilly pushed herself away from the being's touch.

"This is unacceptable. Put her back to sleep immediately." That was the being in the air again.

"I think it's a bit late for that, Allona," said the being that had been sitting next to Lilly. It looked back at Allona, floating in the glowing nimbus in obvious displeasure, for a moment. Then, after Allona gave a little nod, it turned back toward Lilly.

"I know this is hard," the being said. It slid back onto the bed and approached her.

Lilly pushed herself backwards so hard that her head hit the wall at the head of her bed. She could not bite back a yelp as pain flared from the contact.

The being edged closer, again reaching out to her. "My name is Selene, Lilly." A pause. "*Selene.*"

Selene.

The name froze Lilly in place.

No. No, it couldn't be.

Memories flooded into her, of a time when she was little. Playing with her best friend Katrina in the back yard, their games alternating between duets on violin and clarinet and make-believe adventures with their magical friends. They danced through the flowerbeds, careful not to disturb Mother's gardenias, laughing as they saved the princes from the evil witches that had taken them prisoner. And all the while, they imagined their friends laughing with them. Lilly could not remember the name of Katrina's imaginary friend, but hers was named...

"Selene." Lilly said the name softly, her voice wavering as fear, uncertainty, and wonder all fought within her.

The being—Selene—nodded.

Lilly shook her head. "This isn't real. I hit my head or something, and - "

Selene's hand touched her arm, and a feeling of warmth and certainty, of well-being, spread up from her touch and filled Lilly's entire body. The throbbing in the top of her head, where it had struck the wall, faded away between one breath and the next.

Lilly blinked in confusion, and Selene smiled gently. "Lilly," she said. "We've been together for years. You know better than that."

She shook her head. "It was make-believe."

Behind Selene, Allona made a sound that could have been a snort if it wasn't so dainty. "That's your grown-up mind explaining what the child's mind simply accepted. You two have never been apart."

"I don't understand. I've never seen you before. Where have you - ?"

Selene lifted her finger to her brow, then extended it to Lilly's temple.

The warmth from Selene's touch faded and a shiver went up Lilly's spine and her stomach did a little flip. "In my head?" Saying made the reality strike her, and her blood turned to ice. "You've been *inside* me??" He pulled away and bounded off the bed. She had to get away, and the door to the hallway was so close. Surely she could make it before they could catch her.

"Haven't you wondered why music comes to you as easily as it does?" Allona said, some of the sternness leaving her voice. "Why it makes your very soul sing?"

Lilly froze with her hand hovering halfway to the doorknob. "Everyone likes music."

"But not everyone feels it, or can channel it, as you do." Allona paused meaningfully. "People like you are exceedingly rare. Special. It is our purpose to protect them, guide them. That is why Selene has been with you all this time."

"What do you mean?" She looked back at the two glowing beings, some of the revulsion that caused her to flee fading beneath a growing curiosity.

The pair exchanged a look and Selene slid off the bed onto her feet. "There is a power to music, a magic," she said, approaching Lilly slowly. "You've known this your whole life."

Selene's words resonated within Lilly, touching on a feeling that she had experienced seemingly forever, but could not put into words. She nodded slowly.

"Some people are able to tap that power, to shape it, and with it, the world. These people rise above mere competence into virtuosity. If they were left unguided, the effects on both your world and ours would be potentially severe."

Lilly frowned. "So you just jump into people's heads without asking?"

Selene stopped her approach, now a bit more than an arm's reach from Lilly. A slight smile appeared on her face and she shook her head. "No, never. You agreed, don't you remember? You said you wanted me to be with you forever."

"No. When did I - ?" She started to object, but another memory arose. Practicing in the backyard after Katrina had gone home. Giggling as she imagined Selene telling her a joke. Saying she never wanted Selene to leave her.

And Selene replying that they would always be together, no matter what.

Lilly shook her head in denial. "I was *seven*."

"A child sees and accepts truths an adult often will not," Allona said, her tone growing stern once more.

"Katrina had an imaginary friend too. Does she - ?"

Selene shook her head before Lilly finished the question. "The offer was made, but she refused."

"Ok... So you've been, what, riding around in there, watching everything?"

Selene nodded slowly. "And giving a little nudge here and there, to help you learn to best control your ability."

"I see." Somehow, that didn't seem so bad. Although... Lilly froze as an icy lump formed in her stomach. "And...my lost time."

Selene's gentle smile slipped, and that lump became a chill that swept through Lilly's entire body.

"That was you." Selene didn't respond after a second, and Lilly knew she was right. The chill gave way to growing anger. She lifted her chin and scowled mightily. "That was more than just a little nudge. What did you do?"

Selene glanced back at Allona again. "I was...teaching you."

"Teaching me. *Teaching* me?" The anger was real now, a burning fire within her, and he felt her fists clench unconsciously. "Teaching me what?"

The two beings locked eyes for a long several seconds, and then Allona seemed to slump, as though defeated. She gave a little nod and Selene turned back to Lilly.

"You have to understand, Lilly. Not all of our people act for the good. There are some of us - "

"Fugitives," Allona interjected.

Selene nodded agreement and continued. "Some fugitives who reject our people's teachings and seek their own gain through your magic. Most times, we are able to prevent them from causing mischief before they reach your world, but occasionally..." She seemed to take a deep breath. It was the first time Lilly had seen her or Allona make any movement that resembled breathing at all. "Occasionally, they manage to bridge the gap, and we are forced to act more directly."

Lilly raised her eyebrows at them. What this had to do with her, she could not figure, and it didn't explain them mucking about with her memory.

As though reading her thoughts, Allona said, "These fugitives act as any of us would, with humans. They convince a promising musical talent to accept their help, and then take up residence." Lilly flinched at that turn of phrase, but if Allona noticed—or cared—she gave no sign. "But while we nudge and guide, they wrest control almost completely, and the human becomes little more than a puppet in their grasp."

Lilly shuddered. What Selene and Allona had done to her was bad enough, but that was awful. "So…they become possessed."

Selene nodded briskly. "Yes, that is the term your people have used for it. A possessed person can be forced to do great harm if he is not countered. So when we learn a possession has happened, a nearby talent is trained to counter the fugitive's actions and free the possessed." She smiled again at Lilly.

"You mean me."

Allona nodded at Lilly's words. "We believe a possession has occurred at your school. A former acquaintance of ours has crossed over. Since Selene knows the fugitive's methods, she has been teaching you means to counter her magics and force her back to our world, where she can be taken into custody. It had to be done without your knowledge, and quickly, because we only just located her and her plan is nearing fruition." She frowned. "Normally, the instruction could have been spread out over a longer period of time so you wouldn't notice it, and you would have countered her efforts and been none the wiser. But," an accusing look in Selene's direction accented her words, "we were sloppy."

This wasn't helping Lilly be less angry. "You could have just asked. You're no better than your fugitives if you just take over."

Both creatures lowered their eyes.

Selene said, softly, "I'm sorry."

"There was a good reason to not tell you," Allona said, not sounding nearly as contrite as Selene had.

Another lengthy pause. Lilly pressed her fists to her hips and tapped her foot no the floor. "I'm waiting."

Allona gave a little shrug. "In the past, we actively enlisted the aid of talents. They knew of our presence, and we formed powerful partnerships. You've heard tales of seers, prophets, divinely inspired bards, have you not?"

Who hadn't? Lilly nodded.

"Have you ever wondered at their lack in recent centuries?"

"Not really. They were just stories."

Selene chuckled softly. "I think you know better than that, now."

True enough. "Ok. Why haven't there been any prophets lately?"

Allona replied, "Because of Mozart."

That caught Lilly off guard. She blinked in surprise and her mouth dropped open of its own accord. "Mozart. What do you mean?"

"You've heard of the rivalry between him and Salieri?"

"Yeah. It was made up, a story that guy invented to make his play more interesting. And then they made the play into a movie and everyone thinks Salieri was this bad person, when he wasn't at all." And oh, had that made Lilly angry when she learned the truth of it.

"That is mostly true. Salieri had no reason to feel threatened by Mozart at all. He was far more successful than the young upstart from Salzberg, *the* name when it came to opera in Vienna. But," Allona leaned forward, "there is a hint of truth to the tale, all the same. Can you guess what it was?"

Lilly frowned, pondering. Where was Allona going with this? If there was no real rivalry between them, what... Her eyes widened. "Mozart was possessed?"

Allona shook her head. "The opposite, actually. When his guide told him of Salieri's affliction, he worked himself to the bone to learn how to counter the fugitive's designs. But even after he succeeded in helping us capture the fugitive, he began to see signs of possession in others, despite his guide's assurances that it was not so. He pushed himself harder and harder, working to counter a threat that was not really there. And so he died young." She made a loud sigh. "Far too young, and both of our worlds lost out on the music and the magic that he would have created, had he lived."

Allona lowered her eyes again, going silent.

After a couple seconds, Selene said, "That was not the first time a talent was lost early, but his loss was the most poignant. After that, we decided it would be best for the talents to not know of us after they reached a certain age. For their own protection, and ours as well."

The anger had faded, replaced by a lingering resentment, but Lilly found it hard to maintain even that. It made sense, in a weird sort of way. But that left a big question to answer.

"Well, *I* know about you. Now what happens?" Lilly had a sinking suspicion she knew where this was going, but maybe, just maybe, she was wrong.

Selene looked back at Allona, who had recovered her composure. They stared at each other for a time, and Lilly had the feeling they were somehow communicating, even though neither spoke. Finally, Allona gave a shake of her head that, on a human woman, would have been rueful.

"There is no time to train another," Allona said. "It is no longer our way, but there is no choice. If the fugitive is allowed to succeed in her plans, the damage to our worlds, and to the possessed, would be too great." Her glowing eyes turned to look squarely into Lilly's. "Will you help us?"

That's what she thought Allona was going to say. "How?"

Selene spoke up. "You already know what you have to do. At your recital on Friday, a moment will come when the fugitive will attempt a spell. When that happens, just play the music I taught you."

"That's it?"

Selene nodded. "That's it. You already know the song; you've been bursting at the seams with it all week." She smiled apologetically. "That's why I had to take over today. If you had played the song fully, she would have learned how I mean to counter her, and alter her spell to avoid it."

Another shiver went up Lilly's spine. If the showdown was going to take place during the recital, and playing that song in rehearsal could reveal it, that could only mean one thing. "You're saying the fugitive has taken possession of someone in the band."

Selene shook her head. "No. I thought so at first, but now I am certain that the fugitive is taking refuge within your instructor."

"Mrs Quigley?"

Selene nodded gravely. "So. Will you help us, to save your teacher, and both our worlds?"

It didn't seem to Lilly there was much of a choice to make, putting it that way.

Mother gave Lilly a hug. Right there in front of everyone. Flushing with embarrassment, Lilly tried to squirm out, but Mother just tsk'd. She finished the hug with a quick squeeze then stepped back, grasping Lilly's shoulders lightly.

"Have fun tonight, kiddo," she said, here eyes glittering happily as she put on an encouraging. "Knock 'em dead."

Lilly returned the smile with more trepidation than she normally would have felt. Then Mother released her and turned away.

They stood just inside the entrance to the main auditorium in her High School. Other students, parents, teachers, and relations of all sorts mingled about, finding seats and chatting amongst themselves as they prepared for the recital. Most were dressed up, the men and boys in jackets and ties, the women and girls in dresses that were almost, but not quite, to black tie standards.

For her part, Lilly had on a simple dark blue dress with an off-white sash about the waist. She, or really Mother, had put her hair up in a bun at the back of her head that made her forehead feel as though it were being stretched halfway over her skull. But, she had to admit the results looked nice. She almost felt pretty.

Mother selected a row halfway down the room toward the stage. She turned back and waved quickly, then blew a kiss!

Lilly rolled her eyes and, clutching her clarinet case in both hands, turned toward the door. She paused to let an older couple —someone's grandparents probably—enter, then slipped out into the hallway with its endless rows of lockers between classroom doors.

She turned left toward the backstage entrance at the end of the hall, and found herself bumping into a boy. He staggered backwards, and Lilly realized it was Josh Harrington again. Like everyone else tonight, he was dressed up in a jacket and tie. The blue of the jacket went well with his eyes.

Her cheeks flushed red as he grinned at her. "Hey Lilly. Getting a little payback for the other day?"

"No, I... Uh... Sorry." She stumbled over the words, realizing she was sounding like an idiot.

He laughed good-naturedly and grinned a bit wider. "I'm just kidding." He stepped around her and toward the doorway to the auditorium, but paused before he went inside to look back at her. "Good luck tonight. You look great." He winked quickly, and then he was gone, leaving her to blush even brighter.

You should try actually talking with him.

Over the last day and a half, Selene had been popping those sorts of suggestions into her head seemingly at random. Apparently now that her secret was out, she felt free to do so, and it was becoming annoying.

"Shut up," Lilly whispered, and heard Selene's amused laughter in her head.

She put Josh out of her mind and hurried toward the backstage door. The show would be starting soon, and she still had a lot to do to be ready.

Everyone else was already in their places when Lilly stepped out onto the stage. The various musicians were tuning up and there was a feeling of anticipation in the air, stronger than Lilly could recall from any other recital she had played. Looking out at her bandmates, she had to swallow a growing lump in her throat.

She was letting her nerves get the better of her. She never did that.

But then, she had never faced a performance quite like this, had she?

Lilly forced herself to move, sliding past the oboes to reach her seat next to Henry. For once, his hair was under control, and he actually looked halfway put together in a grey suit jacket and red tie. He grinned at her as she got settled in place and started babbling something cheerful, but she didn't hear him as movement from stage right drew her eye.

Mrs. Quigley walked onto the stage, dressed in a clingy off-white evening gown that made her seem to glow in the bright stage lights that shone down on them all.

Or was it more than that? Was the being that had taken possession of her beginning to show itself?

It doesn't work that way, Selene said silently. *She will not reveal herself openly. That would ruin her plans. No one but you will ever know she was involved. If they do notice anything, they'll think it a fancy light show, nothing more.*

That was little comfort. Looking at her teacher—her opponent —she began to shiver. Their eyes met for a second and Mrs. Quigley smiled at her. Lilly felt a surge of adrenalin, and had to stop herself from bolting.

Easy.

She knows. She had to know. About Lilly, Selene and Allona, everything.

Doubtful. She suspects, nothing more. Be calm, and wait until I tell you. It will be alright.

Easy for her to say.

Lilly went through her preparations mechanically, assembling her clarinet and wetting the reed, then going through some warmup scales the way she always did. Usually, that calmed her nerves before a performance.

Not tonight.

She took a deep breath and forced her eyes away from Mrs. Quigley. She looked around the rest of her bandmates, and for a moment, her gaze came to rest on Katrina, wearing a very pretty pink dress and looking gorgeous as always, who was running through some scales of her own from the looks of things. Their eyes met, and Katrina looked away quickly, her lips drawing down into a little scowl of distaste.

Lilly felt an ache in her chest. Recalling those memories of the two of them when they were little, times she hadn't thought of in quite a while, added an extra twinge to the normal hurt of being snubbed. They had been so close once, but something changed around middle school. Katrina suddenly became the popular one. And then it was as though being friends with her was no longer convenient.

Lilly felt her eyes beginning to water as she remembered the early pain of that lost friendship. Over time, she had set that aside, but…

It hurt all over again, thinking about it.

She looked down at her clarinet, where it rested on her lap, and ran her fingers along it. Her only true friend. That, and Selene apparently, and she wasn't even real.

I'm as real as you are.

Not the same thing.

The silence in her head after that spoke volumes.

Mrs. Quigley stepped up onto her conductor's stand and said some words of encouragement, but Lilly paid them no heed. She was too miserable to care right then, and even if she weren't, it wasn't like she could believe anything the possessed woman said.

And then, the curtain opened.

For most of the first piece, Lilly lagged a half-count behind and missed notes and runs that she normally could have played in her sleep. She just couldn't get into it between her renewed heartache and the anxiety, bordering on outright fear, that she had been fighting all night.

When the song finally ended, and the audience, mostly hidden beyond the glare of the spotlights that shone from the back of the auditorium, applauded, she had a powerful urge to get up and run off the stage.

She couldn't do this. She wasn't good enough, pretty enough, smart enough. Her hair was bad, she was too chubby, she was sweating up a storm from the heat of the stage lights. She was scared. Miserable.

And she was quite sure the being within Mrs. Quigley knew it. She had lost before the fight even began.

No. Lilly. That's not true. You are wonderful, more special than you know.

Selene's feeble attempt at encouragement didn't help at all. She almost got up right then.

"Lilly, are you alright?" Concern shown through in Henry's voice. She glanced aside at him and saw the same in his eyes.

She shook her head, but had no words.

"Hey, it's ok. This is for fun, right?" He smiled that goofy grin and nudged her with his elbow.

Something about the way he said it, the playfulness of the nudge, brought up a half-bitter, half-desperate little laugh from within her.

"Come on, we got this."

She met his eyes, and all that silly enthusiasm that had annoyed her about him before felt right then like a buoy in the middle of the ocean: something to cling to to avoid sinking, She managed a little smile and wiped her eyes with the back of her free hand.

Right then, she could have kissed the goofy kid.

Mrs. Quigley raised her arms and the rest of the band brought their instruments up. Lilly sniffed back the tears that had started to run and lifted her clarinet again.

The second piece was Mozart. The same piece that she had gotten carried away in before. He had always been her favorite, and now, knowing that they had a shared experience, it felt as she began playing that she was playing with him. That he was there alongside her, giving her a little extra helping hand from across the centuries and the gulf between Earth and heaven.

Or maybe that was just some of Henry's enthusiasm rubbing off, or a subconscious boost from Selene.

Or all of the above.

Whatever it was, she felt herself drawn into the performance, finally. The notes flowed out of her, joining with Henry's perfectly as they played their part in the majesty of the whole. Losing herself in the music, her spirit began to soar and the earlier doubts began to slip away. This is what she was made for. The music.

And the magic.

Unbidden, she felt herself moving into the strangely familiar melody that she had begun the other day, the music that she now knew Selene had taught her over these many weeks.

No, not yet. We have to wait until she makes her move.

Her guide's voice in her head snapped her back to the moment and she faltered over the notes. She had to search on the sheet music for her place, and noticed Henry looking at her from the corner of his eye, his expression questioning and, again, concerned even as he continued to play.

She gave a little shrug and picked up the piece again. But as she played this time, she remained careful to stay in control, to not get too carried away.

And then, just like that, the piece was finished.

Again, the audience applauded. And again, Henry grinned at her and gave her a little nudge.

She grinned back at him, more genuinely this time.

Mrs. Quigley turned to address the crowd, and from stage left some of the backstage crew rolled a stand-up piano and player's bench out onto the stage. With a broad smile, the teacher walked over to it and settled down onto the bench. Katrina, as first violin, stood and moved to Mrs. Quigley's former position at the conductor's stand.

This is it. When she plays, the dark spell will begin.

So when do I...

You will know.

Ok. Here goes nothing.

Mrs. Quigley looked over her shoulder at Katrina and gave a little nod. And for just a second as she turned back to the piano, Mrs. Quigley's eyes met Lilly's. They flashed red.

Lilly's heart skipped a beat. It was real. Part of her had been doubting, despite everything she had seen and heard to this point. But it was real, there could be no denying it now. And knowing that, true fear ran through her.

Katrina turned to the rest of the band and raised her bow like a conductor's baton.

The rest of the band began, but Lilly remained rooted to the spot for three full beats before she was finally able to make herself play.

The piece was more modern than the rest of their repertoire, by Yanni. At first, Lilly had been leery about it, but after Mrs. Quigley had showed them a video of him playing it at the Acropolis with the London Philharmonic Orchestra, she was sold. The piano and orchestra parts blended together seamlessly, gently, and powerfully.

Lilly would never have thought that one of her teachers would introduce her to a new favorite modern musician, but Mrs. Quigley had done just that.

And now, she was going to use that man's lovely song to poison the well of magic in Lilly's world.

Not gonna happen.

She played, putting her whole heart and soul into it, watching Mrs. Quigley for the cue to slip into Selene's counter spell. Or whatever the right term was.

And then, toward the end of the solo interlude for the piano, the teacher's eyes flashed red again, and it seemed darkness began to swirl around her.

Lilly took a deep breath and began Selene's melody.

Right at that moment, Mrs. Quigley looked over at her, and a malicious grin, a grin of triumph, appeared on her face.

And then the teacher gave a little jerk and the red glow in her eyes went out. She slumped, her fingers stumbling over the piano keys, and shook her head, clearly confused.

For a second, everything stopped.

Lilly lowered her clarinet, confused. Had she just won? That seemed too easy.

A lone violin began to play.

All eyes turned to Katrina, at the conductor's stand. She had the violin solo part, which followed the piano's. She must have decided to start early, to cover for Mrs. Quigley's stumble.

But as she was turning to face the audience, she flashed Lilly that same, maliciously triumphant grin, and her eyes glowed red.

What? No, this can't be right.

There was actual fear in Selene's voice. Almost panic.

What's going on? It was supposed to be Mrs. Quigley.

It was her. The fugitive always claims a host, and sticks with it. Always! There is never a second. Never!

Well it looked like there was a second now. Ok, well if that's how it was going to be, Lilly could take on Katrina easily enough. She drew a breath and lifted her clarinet back to her lips, to play Selene's tune.

You don't understand! It won't work!

Lilly's blood went to ice. What did she mean, it wouldn't work?

I crafted the counter-melody to match the piano part, not the violin. Oh heavens above...

Katrina's solo started out just as the violin solo in Yanni's piece always did, but after a few bars it deviated. The audience, and the rest of the band, would think it an improvisation. But as she played, the darkness that had been gathering around Mrs. Quigley for that brief moment began to coalesce around her.

The dark spell had begun.

What do I do? Lilly shouted the question at Selene inside her head. What do I play?

I don't know I don't know I don't know.

Panic had given way to despair. To defeat. It flowed from Selene into Lilly so strongly that she dropped her clarinet. It bounced off her knees and fell to the floor at her feet.

Oh, all is lost!

Selene's cry became a wail that stretched on an on, drowning out everything else. Lilly's vision swam and she became light-headed as her guide's hopelessness crashed over her. It was a struggle to focus on anything around her.

Damn it, shut up!

The fury that she sent the thought with surprised her; she almost never raised her voice. But it seemed to have done the trick. Selene was quiet.

Lilly shook her head to regain her equilibrium, and Katrina's solo came back full-focus in her consciousness. It was brilliant. Katrina had always been a whiz on the violin, but this... Lilly had never heard her play anything like this. She listened in rapt attention for a few bars, amazed.

And terrified, for as the solo progressed, the darkness grow, becoming a sphere of deepest black hovering a few feet over Katrina's head. All light in the auditorium seemed to be leeching away, even the brilliant spotlights seemed to fade out like the colors in an old photograph: still there, but shadows of their former selves.

Lilly had no idea what that spell would do once released, but it had to be something awful. And she could do nothing but watch it happen.

For a moment, she felt like wailing the way Selene had been.

Then Katrina's playing shifted in tone, and the solo began to seem...familiar, somehow.

It was almost like...

Another memory rose to the surface, from the days when she

and Karina used to play duets together in the backyard. There was one simple duet for clarinet and violin...was it...yes, it was Mozart. And was she imagining it, or was that run Katrina just played lifted straight out of it?

Another three bars confirmed it. She was playing a variation on that Mozart piece.

Lilly knew what she had to do.

She bent over and grabbed her clarinet off the floor. If there's something you need to do to make this work, she thought at Selene, get ready to do it.

Confusion wafted back. *What are you going to do?*

Just get ready.

She lifted the mouthpiece to her lips and paused. It had been years since she last played that piece, but right then it was like she was reading the sheet music, she could see the clarinet part so vividly.

Maybe Mozart himself *was* helping, after all.

She licked her lips, then placed them around her mouthpiece and began to play.

Katrina whipped around as Lilly's notes joined hers in counterpoint, her fingers still flying over the strings even as her brows rose in surprise. Her eyes, glowing brightly red still, narrowed, and her lips compressed into a scowl.

Her other bandmates' eyes turned toward Lilly as well, one and all registering confusion.

"What are you doing?" Henry asked, from his seat next to her.

She paid them no heed. There would be time for explanations later. Assuming there *was* a later. Now she had to focus completely on the music.

From the start, she was playing catch-up. Katrina had the lead, and she was deviating from the baseline of Mozart's original in unexpected ways, and constantly. Lilly had to shift with her, but with no guide, no inkling of where she was going next, their two parts were disjointed, almost dissonant.

It wasn't working. They both knew it, and that smile began to reappear on Katrina's face.

Beads of sweat ran down the sides of Lilly's face, and doubts rose up within her all over again. It wasn't working!

Yes, I have it!

Selene's words filled Lilly with warmth, and suddenly, she felt sure she knew what Katrina's next note was going to be, and what she should do to match it.

Her clarinet line steadied out, becoming more in synch with Katrina's violin, and Lilly felt herself relaxing into the flow of the music more. Her spirits lifted, and she felt buoyed once again. Nothing existed but the music, nothing mattered but remaining in synch with her erstwhile friend, harmonizing with her.

And slowly, as she lost herself more and more, another light began to illumine the stage. Pink-white, like the nimbus Allona had stood within, it shown from everywhere and from nowhere, pulsing in rhythm with Lilly's harmony line.

Katrina noticed the new light as well, and her nostrils flared, the scowl returning, becoming more a snarl. She bore down on her bow, powering the notes from her violin's strings as her fingers flew all the faster.

Lilly pressed hard, taking her breaths quickly when she could and blowing harder to match Katrina's crescendo. But she could not keep the pace up for long. Already she was starting to become light-headed. She was going to have to take a real breath soon.

The light grew brighter, washing out everything except for Lilly, Katrina, and the sphere of blackness in the air.

Still they played on. Lilly's head swam, her lungs burned from the exertion of blowing so hard, for so long. Several strand of horsehair had broken on Katrina's bow. They flapped around with every bow stroke, waving like pendants from her bow hand.

And all the while, the light grew more intense.

It was almost painful to look at now. Lilly had to squint to avoid being overwhelmed by it.

She wasn't sure how much longer she could continue.

Everything became a wash of pink-white. She couldn't see a thing, except for those glowing red eyes.

And then, all at once, it all vanished. The glow, the black sphere, everything went away, with a POP that echoed silently through Lilly's brain.

Katrina swayed on her feet, the glow lost from her eyes. She stopped playing and looked around with wide, un-focused eyes.

"What?" she said, bringing her bow-hand up to her brow.

And then she collapsed.

Lilly stood up, her clarinet falling from her hands as a great gasp issued from the lips of everyone in the audience and the band both.

Mrs. Quigley shot up from the piano bench and rushed to the conductor's stand, where Katrina lay in a heap. Lilly pushed past the other woodwinds in front of her and moved to the teacher's side.

Mrs Quigley bent over Katrina. She checked her pulse, then glanced out at the audience. "Call 911," she said.

Oh no.

Several members of the audience had cell phones out. Someone was calling Katrina's name, and people were rushing forward. Her parents.

Please let her be ok.

Lilly knelt down next to Mrs. Quigley, who had taken hold of Katrina's shoulders, giving them a gentle shake. "Katrina," the teacher said softly. "Katrina, can you hear me?"

Katrina's eyes fluttered and she took a deep breath. Then she opened her eyes fully. Her gaze locked onto Lilly's for a long second.

"Oh." She blinked. "Lilly. Hi."

Katrina smiled, genuine warmth in that expression for the first time in a long while. And then she passed out again.

By the time the paramedics arrived, Katrina was awake again, and sitting up. She leaned heavily against the conductor's stand and sipped at a cup of water that someone had brought to her.

Lilly sat on her heels and watched in a daze as the medics checked her over, then maneuvered her gently into a wheelchair and pushed her out of the auditorium, her anxious parents following along after them.

It all seemed unreal, like some sort of waking dream. Everyone's voices were muffled, the milling masses a blur aside from her old friend. Even after she had gone, Lilly could focus on nothing aside from concern for her.

She'll be fine. Selene's voice carried calm certainty as she spoke within Lilly's head. *The casting requires a lot of energy, and she used more to fight against the fugitive. But after she's rested it will be as though this never happened.*

That was something, at least, and Lilly felt a weight lift.

You were wonderful. I never...

Selene trailed off, but Lilly had a feeling she knew what the guide was going to say. She never thought it would be as difficult as it had been.

That made two of them.

Lilly drew a deep breath and forced herself to her feet. She swayed for a moment after she stood up, feeling a wave of fatigue wash over her. Right then, she wanted nothing more than to lie down for a week.

She turned to make her way back to her seat, but a hand on her shoulder stopped her.

"Lilly."

She looked back into Mrs. Quigley's eyes. The teacher looked unsettled, confused. And irritated.

"What was that?"

Lilly shrugged slightly. "We always played together," she heard herself say, in a small, distant voice.

Mrs. Quigley's brows furrowed. "I wish you would have told

me you two had that cooked up." She stopped and drew a breath, then shook her head. "Next time - "

A man's voice interrupted her, and Mrs. Quigley looked to the foot of the stage, where the Principal stood. He beckoned her over, and Mrs. Quigley released Lilly's shoulder and went to him.

Lilly turned away and slipped past a trio of her bandmates, who were looking at her with strange expressions on their faces. She reached her seat and disassembled her clarinet. By the time Mrs. Quigley announced that the rest of the recital had been cancelled, Lilly had already left the stage.

Mother met her outside the school's main entrance, and greeted her with a big hug. Lilly returned it in kind. They stood there for several moments, and gradually, the daze that had filled Lilly's head receded and the full import of everything that had happened struck her.

Unbidden, tears began running from her eyes.

Mother pushed back and looked at her, concern on her face. "What's wrong?"

Lilly shook her head, unable to put it into words. The fear, the wonder, the despair, the loneliness that she had worked through that night was too much. She should be feeling triumphant, joyous at their victory. But she didn't. And she didn't know why.

Mother pursed her lips and put an arm around Lilly's shoulder. "Come on, let's go home."

She began to lead her toward the parking lot, where their car was parked.

From behind them came a chorus of male laughter. A group of three boys walked past, and Lilly shrank away as she recognized Josh among them. He stopped what he was saying to his two friends as he saw her and Mother, and paused, gesturing for them to continue on without him.

"Hey," he said, grinning as always. "That was awesome."

Lilly blinked, surprised.

"Never heard anyone play like that. How long had you been working on it?"

Mother gave Lilly a squeeze. "All her life," she said.

"It shows." He gave the two of them a nod. "Well, I'd better not keep Brad and Tommy waiting. See you around." He turned to leave.

Lilly recalled what Selene had said before the recital. Maybe some other time, when she wasn't feeling so ragged, she would not have done it. But right then, she couldn't find it in herself to be afraid any more.

She called out after him. "Where are you guys going?"

Josh stopped and looked back over his shoulder at her. "There's a party over at Scott McClendon's house later." He paused. "Why, do you want to go?"

A big part of her wanted nothing more than to just go home. She almost said no. She meant to say no. But instead, she nodded affirmative.

Maybe being alone, again, like always, wasn't the right answer. At least, not tonight.

He grinned again. "Great. Swing by your place in about a half hour?"

"Ok."

He walked away, and Mother gave Lilly a strange look. Then she smiled gently and led Lilly to the car.

Much later that night, Lilly returned to her bedroom and got ready for bed.

The party had been a revelation, in more ways than one. People were surprised to see her. The performance was on every-one's lips, and she received more compliments than she ever thought to.

But more than that, so many people told her they were glad

she had come, and were sorry she hadn't come out with them sooner, that it left her stunned. She had always assumed that she wasn't welcome.

Why would you ever have assumed that?

Selene had not spoken since immediately after the recital. Lilly paused in pulling on her nightgown and considered the question.

It just seemed a given that she wasn't wanted there. It's not like she had ever actually been invited before. People had given her the cold shoulder, by and large.

Uncertainty can make us see things not as they are, but as we fear them to be. You were unsure of them, and they were unsure of you.

Maybe so. Certainly no one had snubbed her tonight, so maybe all it really needed was for one side or the other to make a welcoming gesture.

A little courage can go a long way. I'm proud of you, Lilly.

She smiled as she laid down to sleep.

In her dreams, she played her clarinet with Mozart, and he wore a big smile on his face.

Facilitated
Interrogation

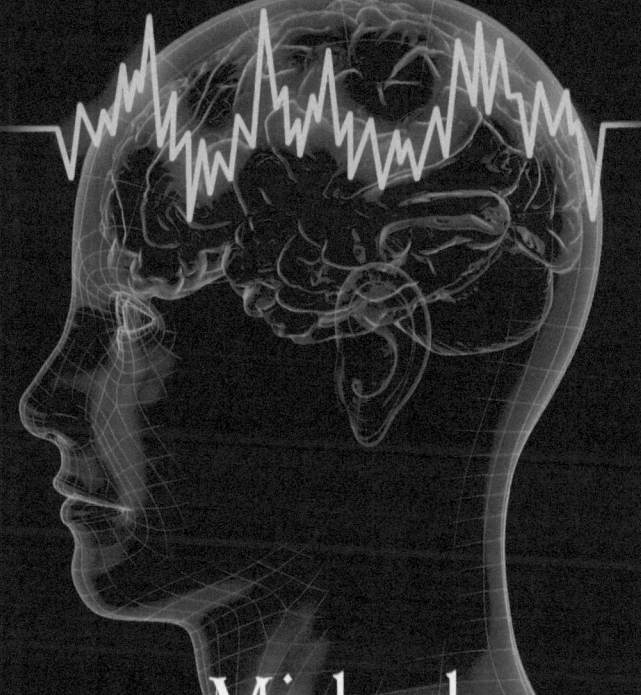

Michael
Kingswood

Author of the Dawn of Enlightenment Series

FACILITATED INTERROGATION

Drip.

Cain squeezed his eyes shut and tried in vain not to hear.

Drip.

It was not real. This was not happening.

Drip.

Stop it!

Drip.

Think of something else. Anything else.

Drip.

…

Drip.

Drip. Drip. DripDrip. Drip. Drip. Cain tried to impose the melody from "A Little Night Music" onto the sounds. They were coming in almost the right rhythm.

Drip Drip.

Damnit! It refused to cooperate.

Drip.

…

…

…

Was it over?

…

…

…

Drip.

Cain screamed. He screamed loudly until he ran out of breath, and then relished the fact that he could only hear himself panting. Gradually his breathing returned to normal, and for a moment he thought maybe he had escaped.

Drip.

Oh Lord, help me please. Please!

Drip.

No more, Lord. Please, no more.

Drip.

Make it stop!

Drip.

…

…

…

Thud.

The scream that followed overpowered Cain's earlier, feeble attempt. No human being could scream like that, that loudly and for that long. On and on it continued, threatening to shatter Cain's eardrums and leave him deaf and alone.

Then, all at once, the scream cut off in a choking gurgle that seemed to drag out forever.

Silence.

Cain sobbed in relief.

…

…

Drip.

Doctor Luisa Melendez leaned forward from her waist and brushed a lock of her dark-brown, almost black hair away from her eyes. Through the plexiglass window in front of her, she could see the subject: a man in his mid-forties, caucasian, about fifteen or twenty pounds overweight with receding brown hair and a scruffy beard. He lay strapped down to the facilitation table, secured by restraints on his wrists, ankles, waist, chest, and forehead. He was nude except for a white cloth that had been placed over his private area. His body twitched from time to time, straining against the restraints.

Embedded in the plexiglass, a holographic image of his face, from a camera in the ceiling directly over him, showed his eyes, wide open and darting to and fro, seemingly at random. His mouth gaped open and shut rapidly, and he had a look of absolute fright on his round, chubby face.

Another hologram below the image of his face showed his name: Chesterton, Cain R.

Bernard spoke from where he sat at the facilitation technician's station, to Luisa's left. "Respiration and heart rate are up by ten percent from baseline."

Luisa looked sidelong at him. African-American, with shoulder-length hair done up in a multitude of small braids that almost, but not quite, resembled dreadlocks, he wore a lab coat over jeans and a red polo shirt. He squinted at the display in front of him, more holograms embedded in the plexiglass that showed the subject's vital signs and the input settings for the neural shunt that overrode the subject's sensory responses.

Mr. Chesterton would see, hear, taste, touch, and feel only what they allowed him, so long as he lay strapped to that table.

"You dialed it back to resting state?"

Bernard nodded. "And he's still elevated."

Luisa smiled thinly, nodding to herself in satisfaction. She glanced up at the time display. 1037, Friday 22 April. This was shaping up to be a fast case. A few more hours of this and Mr. Chesterton would be ready to tell the truth, the whole truth, and nothing but the truth to his questioners. In the company of his attorney, of course.

She turned to the man to her right. Tall, two or three inches above six feet, he had broad shoulders and a heavily muscled chest, a square jaw on an equally square clean-shaven face, and close-cut black hair that was starting to go grey at the temples. There were squint lines between his grey eyes and frown lines around his mouth. He wore a plain navy-blue suit and black tie with a white collared shirt, the sort of outfit that screamed FBI.

"Looking good, Agent Gomez," Luisa said. "He'll be singing for you in time for Happy Hour."

Gomez nodded quickly. "Excellent."

Luisa turned back to her status displays, checking them over one last time. Then she nodded again. "Take it to level two."

"Will do." Bernard adjusted some settings on his controls. In the room beyond the observation window, Chesterton jerked more forcefully against his bonds. "What did this guy do, anyway?"

"You know I can't discuss the case, Mr. Samuelson," said Agent Gomez in a disapproving tone. "The guy has rights. You just get him softened up, and leave the rest to us."

Luisa reached out to turn the tactile gain down a bit. No sense overloading him, not yet. "Relax, Agent Gomez," she said. Looking back at him, she gave him a playful wink. "Have I ever let you down?"

Sure enough, the process got finished by three o'clock, and Luisa and Bernard were out the door in time for Happy Hour. They had made it a tradition of sorts to get a beer together at the end of the week. It helped to unwind, and they had similar tastes in brew, so it worked out nicely.

Coventry's Pub lay a block away from their office building in Southeast DC, in the refurbished area around the Nationals ballpark. It was everything you could want in a British-style pub: dark wood finish all over, leather-padded bar stools, deep leather seats at the tables, every sort of tasty ale or beer you could want on tap, and pub food in all its glory. Of course, they had the Union Jack hung up behind the bar, and soccer on the holoscreens. You did *not* want to be in there when Manchester United played Liverpool.

But on a Friday afternoon it was low-key and relaxing. Luisa and Bernard made it there quickly enough, without their lab coats of course, and ordered their usuals: for him, Guiness, for her, Bass. Then they settled down at a table halfway back in the room.

"Thank God it's Friday," Luisa said and raised her glass. Bernard obligingly tapped his against hers, and they both drank up.

Ten minutes later, Bernard had not said another word. He just sat there, sipping at his beer and staring off into space.

Luisa frowned and leaned forward over the table toward him. "Ok, what's up. You're sulking."

Bernard made a little half-shrug and ran one finger along the rim of his glass. "Does it ever bother you? What we do in there?"

Luisa leaned back in her chair and regarded him for a minute, trying to get a read on where he was going with this. He wasn't normally this pensive. "What do you mean?"

"I mean, doesn't it seem a bit…twisted?"

She chuckled softly and shook her head. Bernard gave her a direct look.

"What, you're serious?" She rolled her eyes. "Bernard, we're the good guys. All we're doing is helping get to the truth faster and more efficiently. I mean, it's not like we're torturing these guys." She took another drink.

He raised his eyebrows. "Aren't we?"

Luisa swallowed quickly. "No!" she said, and set her glass back down on the table. It struck the wood with a solid thud and she realized she had slammed it a bit harder than she intended. She took a deep breath. "Look. This thing's been studied to death."

"I know."

"It's been run up through all of the courts. The ACLU bought off on it."

Bernard rolled his eyes at that.

"Christ, even the UN Council on Human Rights approves of the process. What more do you want?"

Bernard snorted loudly. "The UN? You mean the International Brotherhood of Tin-horn Dictators? Luisa, fucking *North Korea* was on the Human Rights Council when they made that ruling."

Well, she had to admit he had a point there. "If it bothers you so much, why do you still work here?"

Bernard picked up his glass. "That's a question I've been asking myself a lot late…" He trailed off, his eyes moving from her face to something behind her. He mouthed, "Oh shit," silently, then said, "Don't look now, but here comes your Ex."

A moment later, Luisa felt a hand come to rest on her right shoulder. She looked up to see a man of about six feet. His roguishly handsome face was capped by blond hair that looked as though it had been professionally styled. He wore a light grey suit that looked tailor-made, with a blue tie that set off his eyes nicely and a white collared shirt. A gold watch was on his left wrist, and he carried a glass in his right hand filled with, unless she missed her guess, scotch on the rocks. Top-shelf scotch, of course.

"Bernard," the man said, jovially. "Luisa."

"Richard," Bernard said, nodding in greeting. "What's new?"

Richard took his hand off of Luisa's shoulder and moved around to stand more fully between them. "Oh the usual, you know. Fighting the forces of evil," he said, smiling broadly before he took a sip of his scotch.

"I hear you're some kind of high-up muckety-muck these days."

Richard waved off Bernard's remark with a (false) show of modesty. "Special Counsel to the Deputy Assistant Attorney General." Which meant he was one of probably a hundred mid-level underlings, but it sounded impressive enough. "But," he said, "I think I'll be moving up again pretty soon."

Bernard's eyebrows rose. "Oh? Big case in the works?"

"Well - "

Luisa cut him off. "Richard went to Cornell with the new guy." She smiled, sweetly, at him. "He's hoping for a bit of nepotism."

Richard looked at her askance, but before he could say anything Bernard piped up.

"They're really tearing into your boy in the confirmation hearings."

Richard waved a dismissive hand. "They have to do that. Part of the act. But it's all in the bag." He grinned again, but his gaze left them, meandering toward the door. "Well, I'd love to stay and chat, but it looks like Kim's here." He nodded in Bernard's direction. "Bernard." Then he turned to Luisa and gave her shoulder a little squeeze. "Luisa. Great seeing you again."

After he had departed, Bernard shook his head. "Never knew what you saw in that guy."

Luisa turned her head to look over at Richard and Kim. "He has his moments."

Kim was a leggy blonde, almost as tall as Richard and heavy in the bosom department. She wore a conservative grey sports coat and matching skirt that went almost to her knees, a white collared shirt and two inch heels. Like she needed to be any taller. The two of them walked to the far end of the bar and Richard pulled out a stool for her. They began chatting up a storm, leaning in towards each other like besotted teenagers.

"She's an attorney too, isn't she?"

Luisa nodded. "K-Street."

She could hear Bernard's eyes roll. "Must burn you up, him getting re-married so soon."

She turned back to him and shook her head. "Honestly, I'm happy for him. We're much better apart than we were together."

Bernard gave her a level look. "That's not what you were saying six months ago."

She chose not to answer that.

Bernard looked at the time and winced slightly. Then he downed the last of his Guiness in one gulp. "Well," he said, pushing his chair back. "I hate to drink and run, but I...have a date."

"Really?" Luisa felt her eyebrows lifting, and she grinned at him. "With whom?"

"Her name's Kelly, and she plays bass." He grinned. "Her band's playing at the House of Blues tomorrow night, if you want to come."

Luisa shook her head. "Wouldn't want to cramp your style."

"Come on," he said, spreading his hands theatrically, "I got no style to cramp."

She shook her head again, in amusement this time, and chuckled. "See you Monday."

Luisa strode into the facilitation control room Monday morning, just itching to talk to Bernard. Between his date and what she had seen on the news feed this morning, she didn't know where to begin. Her eyes swept past the plexiglass observation window and the control stations below it, to the server racks that were the heart of the system, to the plain wooden desk that sat against the rear wall, and she grinned.

"Morning."

Bernard looked up at her from where he stood next to the server rack. He wore his usual lab coat over khakis and a blue collared shirt, and held a clipboard in his left hand, the pre-startup checklist no doubt. He did not look happy.

Either the date had gone poorly or he was taking the news hard. Better not press the date first if that was the problem.

Luisa stuffed her hands into the pockets of her lab coat and casually moved toward him. "Man, it's been a bad year for your team, Bernard." He frowned, and she shook her head. "Senator

Robert Thompson, Republican, Pennsylvania, arrested over the weekend for involvement in a human trafficking and sex trade operation. Tsk, tsk."

Bernard's frown became a scowl. "It's bullshit is what it is."

Luisa couldn't help it. She laughed. "Oh come on, that's six Senators gone in, what, eighteen months? I know you're a Republican. Honestly, I think it's kind of funny that you are. But seriously, even you have to see that - "

He rounded on her, his nostrils flaring. "What's so funny about it?" he demanded loudly, very nearly shouting. He was gripping the clipboard stiffly and his right hand had made a fist, so hard that the pencil he was using to mark the checklist snapped between his fingers. "What, a black man's not allowed to have his own opinion about things? He's just supposed to blindly check next to D at every election because his masters say to? Is that it?"

"Whoa!" Luisa took a step back and raised her hands, palms open, between Bernard and herself. They had been teasing each other over politics for years, but he had never reacted like this before. "Where did *that* come from?"

Bernard gave a little jerk and took a breath, then visibly relaxed. He looked abashedly at her for a second, then turned away toward the desk at the back of the room. "Sorry. I'm just... tired of being called an Uncle Tom for how I vote." He trailed off as he set the broken pencil down atop the desk and opened up one of the desk drawers to get another. "Look, it's not about politics." He went to the facilitator technician's station below the observation window and sat down in his chair, then began checking off more items on his list. He glanced back at her, no doubt feeling her astonished gaze on him. "I know the guy, ok? No way he did what they're saying."

Well, that was unexpected, and it piqued her curiosity. She walked over beside him. "You know Senator Thompson?" She tried not to sound incredulous, but did not succeed completely.

Bernard checked off another item on the list then stopped. He sighed and put the pencil and clipboard down on the control panel, then swiveled in his chair to look at her. "Yeah. He and my dad were in the Army together during the war. When they got out, they both settled down in Pittsburgh." He managed a small grin. "I practically grew up at his house. We watched the ball games there. Barbecued there. When he ran for State Senate, my dad helped with his campaign." He half-chuckled. "Hell, I lost my virginity to his daughter, for Christ's sake. So yeah, I know him."

Luisa's eyebrows rose high onto her forehead. "Really." That was *very* interesting. "You fucked Senator Thompson's daughter?"

Bernard looked askance at her for a second, then grinned sheepishly and gave a little shrug. "Well, yeah."

She grinned her best impish grin at him. "You know. That is pretty awesome."

Bernard burst out laughing, and Luisa followed suit. After a short while, he got ahold of himself and nodded. "Yeah." Then his eyes went a bit distant. "Yeah," he said more softly, and a bit wistfully, "it was pretty great." He gave himself a little shake. "That's not the point. He's a stand-up guy, a family man. Totally straight-laced. No way he did that shit." He pointed at her with his index finger. "It's a setup job, I'm telling you."

Luisa raised her hands. "If you say so. But how long's it been since you saw him last?"

Bernard frowned thoughtfully. "I guess, right after I graduated High School."

"So about ten years."

"Pretty much. I mean, I've seen him a few times at the holidays, but never like before."

Luisa sighed. "People can change a lot in ten years." She made a sweeping gesture with her left hand. "Especially in this town."

"Not that much."

She gave him a level look. "Bernard. All joking aside, he's a politician. Doesn't matter which party he belongs to, they're all crooked. You know that."

Bernard's eyes lowered sadly, and he turned his chair back to the control panel. "Yeah well, he was one of the good ones." He paused. "Or at least I thought so."

Luisa laid her hand on his shoulder. "Sorry."

"Well," he said, straightening up and grabbing the clipboard again. "They're almost done in there. We'd better get ready."

Luisa was going to ask about his date, but glancing into the facilitation room, she saw he was right. The two techs within were just finishing hooking up the last of the leads to the day's subject: a thin asian woman who looked to be about thirty. But then, with asian women Luisa really couldn't tell, they tended to age so well. One of the techs gave a thumbs-up sign, and Luisa returned it with a wave. Then the techs left through the lone door in the facilitation room.

Something Bernard said earlier came back to mind. "Do people really give you shit for being a black Republican?"

He looked up from the checklist and rolled his eyes. "You have no idea." Then he went back to what he was doing.

A couple minutes later, the door to the control room clicked, and Luisa turned to see a short blonde woman walk into the room. She was heavy, but not fat. More like she had muscles and a bit of padding. She wore a dark blue pants suit with a very light blue shirt beneath, and a severe expression on her face.

She nodded in Luisa's direction. "Doctor Melendez."

Luisa smiled in return. "Agent Hopkins." She turned to her left and gave Bernard a meaningful look. He checked the last block in his checklist then gave her a nod. Luisa turned back to the FBI agent. "Ready when you are."

"Let's get started."

Two weeks later, Bernard quit.

On Monday, he was at work like normal. The two of them went about their business as they always did, talked as they always did. Joked.

On Tuesday, he was gone. Luisa walked into the facilitation control room to find a different technician running through the startup checklist, a chubby blonde girl who could not have been older than twenty, maybe twenty-two. When she saw Luisa, she grinned and stood up.

"Hi, I'm Shelly, your new tech." Shelly extended her hand for a shake.

Luisa looked at her in shock. "What happened to Bernard?" she said. It took her a second to register the girl's hand, and she flushed. "Sorry. Nice to meet you." She shook hands with the girl, who had a surprisingly firm grip.

Shelly raised an eyebrow at her. "Didn't he tell you he was quitting?"

No. No he had not.

The rest of the week, that lack ate at Luisa. Surprise turned to confusion, then to hurt, and finally to anger. They had worked together for three years. Sure, they were not bosom buddies, but they had becomes friends in that time. Aside from that one conversation at Coventry's, he had never even hinted that he was thinking about quitting. And he certainly hadn't told her he was actually going to do it.

What in the hell?

It felt like a betrayal, silly as that sounded even to herself. But by the end of the week, Luisa was flat-out furious with him.

His text, coming during her lunch break on Friday, only made her angrier.

"Conventry's. Seven o'clock."

Yeah, like she was going to just obey his...summons. Who did he think he was, running out on her and then expecting her to just come at his beck and call? It was just like... Just like...

She had to take a deep breath to calm herself before she threw her mobile across the room. Bernard wasn't Richard. He hadn't run out on *her*, he had left a job. Nothing more. It wasn't worth getting angry over.

That didn't help as much as she thought it would have.

She almost didn't go. But as the minutes ticked down until the time she would have to leave to meet him, she found she could not say no. At the very least, she would make him explain why he hadn't even told her he was leaving. She deserved that much after all the time they had spent together.

She found him seated at a table in the back corner of the pub, shielded from view from the front door by the curvature of the bar. He wore a light leather jacket over a dark t-shirt and faded jeans, and he had bags under his eyes as though he had not been sleeping. He smiled slightly when she approached and stood.

"I'm glad you came."

Luisa shot him a glare that carried all the conflicted emotions she had been feeling the entire week, and he blanched. He gestured toward the empty chair at his table and sat back down.

She took a moment to remove her own jacket, a lightweight affair for the evening's chill, and set it over the chair's back before sitting down herself. "So you quit," she said, intentionally putting an accusation in the tone.

Bernard didn't react to her tone. He leaned forward over the table and fixed her with a look that was all seriousness. "Yeah. I'm leaving town tonight, as soon as we're done here." His eyes flicked away from her, toward the pub's entrance. "I think someone's been following me."

That brought Luisa up short. Anger turned to confusion and she sat, speechless, for a moment. Why would someone be following him? That didn't make any sense.

Bernard either didn't notice the confusion on her face or didn't care, because he kept right on going. "I wanted to warn you before I left. There's some serious shit going down, and you need to get out of that place, too."

"What are you talking about?" Had he had a breakdown or something? This was not like him at all.

"Remember how I told you Senator Thompson was set up?"

Good Lord, not this again. She could understand him being

upset about it, but seriously. She kept her voice carefully level. "Yeah."

"I found proof."

"Proof? Proof of what?"

He shook his head. "I don't have time to explain, and you wouldn't believe me if I did. But he was set up, and we helped do it." He narrowed his eyes at her. "You and me."

"You're nuts." Luisa pushed her chair back and made to stand up. She didn't need to listen to this. He needed help is what he needed. But he shot his hand across the table and grabbed her by her left wrist in a vice-like grip, preventing her from pulling away.

"Let go of me!" That came out in a shout, and eyes from around the room turned to rest on them.

Bernard recoiled and released her wrist, looking about with uncertainty. The other patrons watched them for several seconds before going back to their business. When they had, he said, "Sorry. Please just listen to me."

He sounded tired. But also determined and, no kidding, scared. And there was a pleading look in his eyes that made Luisa sit back down again. But she didn't scoot her chair back in to the table, and she kept her hands resting together on her lap.

"Ok, spill it."

He took a deep breath. "The facilitation does something to people. More than we thought, more than anyone's been told. It makes them say or do things..." He trailed off, then shook his head. "Look, I can't explain it. I'm not sure exactly what it does. But I do know it was used to help set up the Senator, and *we* did it."

Bernard reached into the pocket of his jacket and took out a slip of paper. He set it down atop the table and slid it across to her.

"What is that?"

He took a quick breath. "It's the user name and password to a backdoor access from our facility into the Justice mainframe. It'll give you access to case files."

Luisa's breath caught in her throat. "What?" Incredulity, and no small amount of fright, flooded through her. That was a serious breach of security. What the hell had he done? "Where did you get *that*?"

Bernard shook his head. "That's not important." He leaned forward again. "What's important is what's in those case files. Look for yourself."

He slid his chair back and stood up, then glanced quickly around the pub before looking back at her. "I'll be in touch. Be careful," he said, "and do not use that from your office terminal."

He stepped away from the table, toward the small hallway leading back to the bathrooms and the pub's kitchen. And the back door, no doubt.

"Wait," Luisa said, and he stopped, looking back at her. "What are you going to do?"

"I'm going to help clear Senator Thompson's name."

She should have thrown out that scrap of paper.

All weekend long, she thought about it. She took it out of the little drawer in her desk and home where she had put it and stared at it. Several times she crinkled it up to throw it in the trash, but she always ended up flattening it back out again.

Keeping it was trouble. Big trouble.

But she couldn't get the look on Bernard's face out of her head. What he had told her was crazy, certifiable. But at the same time, he had seemed to certain, and so fearful... He had discovered something, that was for certain. Something that had scared him enough to make him take off.

Could he be right?

No, that was preposterous.

But all the same, on Monday morning when she went into

work, that little scrap of paper rested in the bottom of Luisa's purse, just waiting for her to take it out and make use of it.

It wasn't until Wednesday that she got the nerve to actually do it.

She brought a bagged lunch, and begged out of going out with her other colleagues, claiming a new budget plan. When most of them had gone, out to the deli down the street, she slipped out of her office and down to a small room at the rear of the building that housed a trio of workstations, one secure and two unclassified, and a printer. It was supposed to be used by visiting officials from other agencies, so they could access their email and information portals while visiting the facilitation lab. But she and her colleagues often used it for unofficial business like booking flights for vacation and the like, things that they strictly speaking weren't supposed to do from their work terminals.

The bosses looked the other way at using the spare room for those purposes. No harm, no foul.

That lax attitude suited Luisa's needs perfectly.

She slipped into the room and shut the door behind herself, then sat down at the secure workstation, which conveniently was positioned caddy-corner form the door, so she would have a second or two to back out of anything incriminating should someone else come in. Then she draw a deep breath and pulled out Bernard's scrap of paper.

It worked like a charm. Within moments, she was within the Justice Department's criminal database. But not just anywhere within the database. This place was bordered in yellow and marked top and bottom with TOP SECRET//OMICRON//. That made her pause, and she almost turned off the workstation right then and there. But she had come this far, and it would nag at her forever if she didn't see it through.

Luisa looked around the page for a clue as to where to begin. At first she was overwhelmed by the sheer number of links and choices she could make, each one presumably leading deeper into a top secret maze. But finally she found a little hyperlink on the left side of the page that brought her to a search function.

She typed in Senator Thompson's name and pressed enter.

It only took a minute of paging through the file to see what had set Bernard off. The Senator had been named by an accomplice, who had revealed his involvement after facilitated interrogation. The accomplice's name was Cain R. Chesterton.

But that didn't make any sense. They had conducted Chesterton's facilitation the Friday before Thompson had been arrested, and from what the file said earlier…

Luisa paged back and confirmed it. Yes, he had been under investigation for a month before Chesterton tipped the FBI to him. So what prompted the investigation?

She frowned deeply as she scanned the file. There was evidence found on Thompson's computer that corroborated Chesteron's story, and mysterious money had been deposited into the Senator's account. But the first instance of the deposit was the week before his arrest, on Friday.

That was awfully coincidental.

She closed the file and pulled up Chesterton's. The man had been booked three days before his facilitation on…charges of identity theft? What did that have to do with human trafficking?

Luisa's frown grew, as did her confusion. This didn't make any sense. No judge would have issued a warrant for a US Senator's arrest for something this flimsy. There had to be more to the story…

Her eye caught a tab at the top right corner of the screen, marked Public. She clicked it.

A different file opened, though it had all of Chesterton's vital information in it. This file lacked the classification markings of the first, and told a totally different story. A story of FBI surveillance going back for months. Of over two-dozen underage girls and boys found in a prison house in the basement of a building that Chesterton had been observed entering and leaving repeatedly. Of the raid that exposed it all, the week before Thompson had been arrested, and of Chesterton's facilitated interrogation, that linked the Senator.

Two case files.

One for the public, and the other the truth.

Luisa's throat clenched. She could hardly breathe, the shock of what she was seeing was so great. This could not be real.

Could it?

She went back to Thompson's file, and sure enough there was a public version of his as well. Of a last-minute investigation after he was named, and a hurried warrant issued before the Senate came back into session and the Constitutional provision forbidding a member of Congress' arrest could take effect.

Because if they had waited, he could have fled, of course.

The chill that went down Luisa's spine was more like a dip in Polar seawater. This...this was...

She swallowed, despite her throat being suddenly dry, and she recalled what she had taunted Bernard with before. Six Senators in eighteen months.

Five more searches confirmed it.

All five had been arrested during Congressional recesses, of course. All had been named by other defendants under facilitated interrogation. And all had been under extensive secret investigation beforehand, but the evidence presented against them bore no resemblance to anything shown in the secret files.

"Holy shit," she breathed.

Voices outside in the hall made her almost jump out of her chair. She glanced at the time; lunch hour was just about over.

She thought it over for a second, then printed out all of the files she had seen, public and private.

No way was she going to use that username and password again, but she wanted to be able to go over what she had found again later, if only to prove to herself that she had not gone insane.

Luisa did not sleep well that night. She sat at her desk at home, reading and re-reading the files she'd printed out, trying to find away around the conclusion she had come to. To no avail. Finally, well after weariness forced her to bed, she found herself lying in the darkness, her brain awhirl with the implications of what she had found. When she eventually dozed off, sometime deep in the wee hours of the morning, the blaring of her wakeup alarm interrupted a fitful slumber after what seemed only minutes.

She went through the motions at work the next day. Fortunately, there were no facilitation subjects on the schedule. She was not sure she could have actually performed the procedure, and not just because of her fatigue. After what she had learned...

She drifted off at her desk several times, despite multiple cups of coffee, and by the end of the day had accomplished next to nothing. And there was a scheduled facilitation tomorrow. A chill went up her spine and her stomach clenched in revulsion when she saw the schedule.

She couldn't go through with it.

Her supervisor's reaction when she begged off work the next day due to sickness was telling. He gave her a quick look up and down and nodded grimly. "Yeah, you look like hell. Don't worry about tomorrow. Murphy can handle it; he's been qualified for a month now and has been chomping at the bit to do one. Go take care of yourself, and we'll see you Monday."

So she left early, making a beeline for home.

That evening, she went over the files again, somehow hoping that they would contain something different, but again they did not. And again, the implications struck her hard.

After the last election, the Democrats had firm control of the House, but the Republicans, with fifty-six Senators, had held up all of the President's initiatives, not even allowing them to come to the floor let alone proceed to a vote. She had complained bitterly on all the networks about their tactics, pointing our, rightly, that the American people had elected her for her grand vision of the future, and the changes we had to make to get there.

Luisa had been right there with her. The changes were needed, and right.

And now, with the Senate down to 50-50, the Republicans could no longer obstruct the changes from going through. They had lost their majority position thanks to the Vice President's tie-breaking vote and could no longer dictate the Senate's docket. Sure, they could filibuster, but that tactic had been all-but emasculated in recent years; it was easy to get around.

It was a turn of events Luisa would normally have greeted with enthusiasm. In fact, she had done just that...until now. Elections were supposed to mean something. Even when she didn't like their results, they had to be respected. To blatantly, purposely subvert them like this...

It was just one step away from pure dictatorship.

She fell asleep on her couch, and had nightmares of jack-booted thugs marching in lockstep down the streets, to the sound of the President's campaign promises broadcast through loudspeakers that stood at each street corner.

Friday morning, Luisa awoke feeling gravelly-eyed, but more focused than she had been the day before.

Bernard was right; clearly the facilitation had played a part in what was happening here, but what? She had studied the process in medical school, and it was sound in every way, else she would not have gone into the field. Had it been corrupted somehow? Had something been missed?

She set to her computer and pulled up every professional journal she had access to. After a few hours searching, she found over a hundred articles about facilitated interrogation, stretching back over a decade.

It was going to be a long weekend of reading.

Facilitated Interrogation began as the brainchild of an obscure PhD student from Cal Tech named Johan Ferguson. Down through the years there had been talk of truth serums and the like, but few such things actually worked, and those that did give some results were unreliable, or had bad side effects. Ferguson theorized that it might be possible to lower, or eliminate entirely, a subject's capacity to lie through electrical stimulation directly to the central nervous system itself. By eliminating pharmacological effects, he claimed, the process would be more efficient and more humane.

His notion was, of course, ridiculed as impossible, and even if it were possible it would be nothing short of brainwashing, mind control, or torture. Not something a man with any scientific ethics to speak of should pursue.

Ferguson was not dissuaded. What that said about his ethical upbringing was open to interpretation for quite some time until, to the astonishment of all, he claimed success in perhaps the most widely read PhD dissertation of all time.

Published fifteen years ago, his paper set off a firestorm within the scientific community, and then soon thereafter, throughout the rest of society. The same cries of mind control, the accusations of corruption, flew from every corner. But then, study after study confirmed his findings. His technique could force truthfulness, and without unpleasant side effects. Every person who was subjected to facilitation, despite their reactions on the facilitation table, reported no discomfort or trauma at all afterwords.

The implications were profound, the applications of the technique obvious. Very quickly, Doctor Ferguson obtained venture capital from multiple firms and within two years his facilitation devices were being sold throughout the world to law enforcement agencies, courts of law, and other organizations of all kinds.

Prosecutors found their conviction rates skyrocketing, while at the same time the number of cases overturned on appeal plummeted. Because all testimony was true beyond any doubt whatsoever, innocent men were hardly ever sent to jail anymore.

It was a Godsend.

As Luisa read study after study, all of them backing up what she had always learned about facilitation, all of them in agreement about its soundness, she began to wonder whether she had just been imagining things. Whether Bernard had as well. There could be other explanations for the discrepancies between the files she had seen.

By the time she went to bed Saturday night, with dozens of studies still to review, she had mostly convinced herself to just let it go. Bernard was just upset, and overreacted to his old acquaintance's bad situation.

Sunday morning dawned bright and clear, with not a cloud in the sky. Luisa pushed herself out from under her covers and stretched, letting the sunlight streaming in through her bedroom window warm her skin beneath the cotton t-shirt and baggy knit pants that she used as pajamas. It was going to be a beautiful day, perfect for a walk along the Potomac. Maybe a visit to the rising giant over at Hain's Point, or to the Cherry Blossoms. They were not in bloom, but the basin there by the Jefferson Memorial was always lovely.

She sighed and managed to smile, feeling the cares that had been plaguing her the last several days slip away, and she resolved not to waste this day on any more paranoia.

After a long, hot shower, she donned a pair of dark blue stretchy pants, her favorite sports bra, and a wicking shirt that she'd received from the last Race For The Cure, then went down to the kitchen. Two slices of bread in the toaster while her coffee maker brewed a cup filled the room with soothing aromas, and her spirits buoyed even more.

No sooner did the toast spring up from the top of the toaster than the telephone unit that was set into the wall rang.

Luisa glanced at the clock. 8:30. Who would be calling at this hour on a Sunday? Frowning in curiosity, she stepped over to the phone and tapped the control pad beside it.

An elderly black woman's face appeared on the screen. She

was in her late 60s, with hair that had gone totally grey, almost white, and a pleasantly plump face with deep smile lines on either side of her mouth. Luisa recognized her at once, but she was not smiling now.

"Hello, Luisa," Bernard's mother said in her warm and ever-polite southern accent. She had been a transplant from Georgia, following Bernard's father north, from what Bernard said. "I am sorry to disturb you so early."

"Not at all, Mrs. Samuelson. What can I do for you?"

"I wonder if you know where Bernard is? He told me he was coming home almost a week ago and I haven't heard from him since."

Luisa's blood went to ice water, and she shook her head slowly, her muscles moving on autopilot as her mind reeled at the question. "No... No, I haven't seen him in over a week."

Mrs. Samuelson frowned deeply. "Oh Lordy," she said, sounding deeply concerned.

Luisa put on a brave smile. "I'm sure he'll be there soon," she lied. "You know Bernard. Probably met a girl and got distracted along the way."

Mrs. Samuelson sniffed in disapproval. "If you hear from him, tell him to call me, please dear?"

"I will."

After Mrs. Sameulson hung up, Luisa dropped into one of the chairs that surrounded her small breakfast table, all thoughts of enjoying the day forgotten.

What had happened to Bernard?

Her toast forgotten, she grabbed the now full cup of coffee and strode purposefully back into her office, where the printouts from the Justice files lay atop her desk and the multitude of journal articles about facilitated interrogation waited. She never thought of calling the police. If he had been right, and he had not made it home as a result, the police could not help him.

Calling them might actually make it worse.

She needed to find corroboration, something to show his theory as more than just paranoid delusion.

By three o'clock, she had it.

A small article in a third-rate journal, published three years ago and written by a researcher out of Denmark. He found that small modifications to the facilitated interrogation device could, if made exactly correctly, change the effects of the device from forcing truthfulness to inducing a state of complete openness to suggestion. It would leave the subject willing to swear to his dying day that what the facilitators told him to say was true, even after subsequent facilitation on the normal settings.

It was a bombshell, torpedoing completely the notion of facilitation's efficacy and safety.

So why wasn't it followed up? Luisa had never even heard of it before. If she had not been digging so deeply...

She paged through the journal database and found one mention of the Denmark article, from a trio of researchers in Cambridge. They lampooned the Denmark study, finding errors in composition, in statistical analysis, and accused the author of confirmation bias, because he had been skeptical about facilitation on many other occasions in the past. If his notion had any validity, it would have been selected for publication in a more reputable journal, and the trio were quick to point out that it had, in fact, been rejected by peer review on three occasions before finally being accepted in the "rag", as they called it.

Luisa frowned, then opened up the Denmark study and read it through again. She would have to spend some time analyzing it in detail to be sure, but offhand, she didn't see the huge, glaring discrepancies that the trio accused it of.

There did not appear to have ever been a response from the man in Denmark in any of the literature, either. That was odd. The trio had made some fairly serious accusations. Not the kind of thing that could just be ignored; surely he would have wanted to defend his reputation, if not the results of his study.

Why had he not?

Ten minutes of Googling showed her why.

Another small story, almost buried in a local Copenhagen news outlet: the researcher had been killed in a hit-and-run car crash.

Luisa pushed back from her keyboard, suddenly finding herself shaking all over as icy fear flooded through her.

It was mad, ludicrous. But she was certain, all the same: someone had killed him, to keep his findings out of the public eye. Killed him, and maybe paid off the trio from Cambridge to denounce him?

And now Bernard had vanished.

Luisa shivered.

She had to tell someone, but who? The media? Fox News would love to run the story. Democrats corrupting the judicial system, framing Republican Senators...it would be right up their alley. Love it? Hell, they'd offer to marry it to their daughters!

But could she trust that they would really look into it, that they wouldn't just run to get the headlines, and be sloppy?

She snorted. Not be sloppy? When had a journalist ever done that?

Luisa stood and tensed her muscles, to get the shiver under control. Then she tapped the phone control that was built into the top of her desk.

A short few moments later, the phone screen came to line, showing Richard's face. He blinked in surprise. "Luisa. Didn't expect to hear from you today." Or at all, his expression said.

"I need to talk to you about something important, Richard. Can I come to your office tomorrow?"

His brow furrowed. "What is it?"

"I can't tell you over the phone, but it is important."

He opened his mouth to talk, but she cut him off.

"Please, Richard."

He paused for a long moment, then glanced over at something to his right before nodding. "Alright. Come by at two."

"Thank you."

He nodded, and the phone winked out.

Richard's office lay on the fifth floor of the Justice Department headquarters. It was not a corner office; he didn't rank that high. And it wasn't particularly large. But he had a more than decent view of the surrounding buildings and the street below, and you could see a bit of green from a nearby park if you looked from the right angle.

He met Luisa at his door, dressed as usual to the nines in a dark grey suit and another blue power tie. His shoes were polished to a sheen and his teeth seemed to be as well when he smiled in greeting. It made her feel decidedly underdressed in jeans and a red t-shirt beneath her light leather jacket.

"Luisa," he said, gesturing for her to enter. He sounded as though he were greeting an old friend, not the ex he had left not even a year ago. "What can I do for you?"

She went into his office and took a seat in one of the two chairs that sat before his desk, and he took a moment to close the door and sit down himself.

They looked at each other in silence for a while, Luisa unsure how to even begin. She drummed her fingers on the folder lying on her lap, the folder that contained all of the evidence she had found for the conspiracy, or whatever it was.

Richard raised an eyebrow at her quizzically.

Might as well just get to it.

"I've discovered something horrible," she said. And then it all came out in a rush. Everything, from the secret database to what she'd found in the journals to the political ramifications of it all. She laid it all out, flopping the folder down on his desk and showing him each page in its turn. Finally, when she had said it all, she sagged back in her chair, feeling completely drained.

Richard's jaw had dropped open a minute into her dissertation. He only closed it about ten seconds after she finished. For about ten seconds more, he just looked at her, speechless. Then his eyes turned down to the documents on his desk.

"Jesus Christ," he said.

She nodded emphatic agreement.

Richard pressed his right palm down onto the pages as though they were going to fly away on their own if he did not. "How did you find all this out?"

She looked at him askance. "Bernard. He found the backdoor to the database."

His eyes narrowed. "He knows about this too? Where is he now?"

"I don't know." All of a sudden, the chair felt too cramped and she stood up, moving over to the window. She looked down at the people walking along the street below and shuddered. "Richard, tell me I'm crazy. Please. This is all so unreal, and now Bernard's disappeared...." She looked back at him, and said, more softly, "I'm scared."

Richard looked directly in her eyes and shook his head. "I don't think you're crazy."

For some reason, that made her feel better. She smiled, thankfully. "Thank you. I didn't know where else to go, who else to talk to about this. I thought about going to the press - "

"Jesus Christ, no," Richard said, fairly jumping out of his chair. "Don't do that."

Luisa blinked. "Why not? This needs to come out into the open."

His lips compressed. She could see the wheels turning behind his eyes as he walked around his desk to come stand next to her. "If you go to the press, one of two things will happen. One," he gestured at the evidence, "if this is what you think it is, they'll go to ground, cover their tracks. They'll make Arthur Andersen look above-board and transparent. Or two, if it isn't, it'll stir up a huge pile of scandal and innuendo that will tarnish the administration forever, no matter that it wasn't true."

"But - "

"And that's not all," he said. "It won't be hard for people to figure out who leaked this. You'll be ruined."

She shook her head. "No, there are whistleblower laws."

Richard chuckled mirthlessly. "Do you really think that will stop it? They won't have to punish you, or take any action that would trigger those laws." He stared hard into her eyes. "All they'd have to do is discredit you. A few anonymous leaks about your job performance. Maybe some rumors and innuendos about your character. Nothing that can be traced back to anyone specific, but enough to ruin your reputation, make it really hard for you to get any kind of decent job once you decide to resign your position."

Luisa flinched away from his gaze, swallowing hard. She wanted to believe he was wrong, but she knew better. She'd seen that sort of thing happen more times than she could count. That icy ball of fear that had been growing in her gut all weekend long just grew heavier, more frigid.

"So..." She stopped, the tremor in her voice giving her pause. She swallowed, squared her shoulders, and looked back at him. "So what do we do?"

"We," he said, "don't do anything. You go back about your business and try not to draw attention to yourself. I will start an investigation. Quietly. This sort of thing has to be handled very carefully, or we're both screwed, and the country with us." He made a little smile, one that Luisa thought was supposed to look confidently determined. And maybe to someone who didn't know him as well as she did, it would. But she could see the uncertainty, near fear, hiding beneath the facade.

"Are you sure? I can help."

He shook his head emphatically. "You did the right thing

bringing this to me. Now let the pros handle it." He smiled again, more genuinely this time. "Trust me, this is what I do."

He was right about that, at least. He had made his name at Justice by taking on some powerful people in the past. But this was whole new territory, and they both knew it. Still, Luisa couldn't think of who else could do it.

She nodded. "Ok. Thank you, Richard."

He placed his hand on Luisa's shoulder and turned her toward the door. "No, thank you. Now, I've got a meeting in five minutes, and then I'd better get cracking on this."

She saw the dismissal for what it was, but he was right. It was best she get out of there, and away from this so he could do his job. That fear diminished, a glimmer of relief replacing it. It was out of her hands, and she was glad to be getting away from it.

"Let me know what you find out?"

Richard's eyes twinkled mischievously and he gave her a little wink. "You'll be the first to know. Well, you and three hundred million others."

As she left his office, she could not help but chuckle.

The door closed behind Luisa and Richard went back to his desk. He sat down and stared at the documents that she had brought.

This was bad. Very bad.

He rubbed at his temples as possibilities washed over him, none of them good. This was the sort of thing that could make a guy's career. Make it, or break it beyond all repair. An investigation would be tricky at best, dangerous at worst, and what it could uncover...

He shivered.

Richard turned it over and over in his mind, playing through his every possible course of action. In the end, it always wound up with his ass dangling in the breeze, vulnerable.

No matter how he played it, he was going to need top cover. He made his decision.

Richard stacked Luisa's papers and pushed them to the side, then tapped the controls to his phone. After a few seconds of electronic beeping, the image of a grey-haired woman appeared in the phone's display.

"Yes?"

"Richard McCandless for the Attorney General."

"One moment."

More waiting, and then his old friend appeared on the display. He had aged, but then they both had. But the Attorney General still retained that ambitious glimmer in his eyes he always had.

"Richard. What's up?"

He took a deep breath. "Caleb. You've got a serious problem, brother."

Luisa took the escalator up from the King Street Metro station and stepped out onto the sidewalk. She paused for a moment, breathing in the evening air before she turned and walked east toward the Potomac. Dusk had given way to full night, and the streets of Old-town Alexandria were thronged with people going about the business of DC's nightlife. Mostly young people from the looks of it; from what she could see, the scene was vibrant, healthy.

Any other night, the sight of all those people just out for a good time would have lifted her spirits. But not this night.

Despite Richard's assurances, she could not help but feel a creeping dread as she turned off King Street and walked toward home. It was unthinkable, what was going on.

If it really was.

She gave herself a little shake and tried to force herself to stop dwelling on it. It was out of her hands now. Richard and his people would investigate, and if there really was wrong-doing he would stop it and bring the bad guys to justice. That was why he went into law in the first place, and why he took a position at Justice. Richard was many things, but beneath his outer mask he always had a firm desire to see wrongs righted. It was one of the things she admired about him.

It was going to be ok.

Luisa arrived at her brownstone and paused, reaching into her purse to find her keycard.

She didn't notice the man standing in the shadows adjacent to her door until he spoke.

"Doctor Melendez."

She froze, her heart racing immediately as she rotated her head to look his way. He was tall and bulky, wearing an overcoat. But his other features were obscured by the darkness, and she felt a sense of menace wafting from him.

Luisa took a step back and opened her mouth to ask who he was.

In that instant, someone pressed into her back and a hand clamped over her face, pressing a rag over her mouth and nose. A sharp, almost metallic odor filled her nostrils, and she quickly grew light-headed. She tried to pull away, but all the strength left her limbs.

Her vision darkened, narrowed.

As she lost consciousness, she heard the man say, "You should have left it alone."

Time passed. It could have been a day or five minutes, but she could not have said which if someone held a gun to her head.

All around was blackness, and silence.

She felt...nothing.

Smelled nothing.

Tasted nothing.

What was going on? She tried to move, but could not tell if she was successful or not, because nothing changed. She could not even feel whether her arms or legs had responded at all.

Silence.

It stretched for a small eternity, and she thought for certain she had gone insane.

Drip.

...

...

Drip.

What - ?

Drip.

...

Drip.

...

...

...

Drip. Drip.

Realization hit her, and Luisa screamed. She screamed until she should have gone hoarse, but there was no feeling. She kept on screaming until she could not scream any more.

On the other side of the observation window, the facilitation technician started in surprise and consulted his readouts. "Wow, that was fast."

Standing at his side, his supervisor, a middle-aged man with thinning black hair atop a gaunt face, nodded. "No kidding." He turned his head to the right and grinned. "This one's not going to take long at all."

In the back of the room, in his navy-blue suit, white shirt, and black tie, Agent Gomez stood with his arms crossed over his chest. At the supervisor's words, the corners of his lips turned up slightly.

"Excellent."

The Beast And The
God-Woman

The worst terrors come from within.

Michael
Kingswood

Author of the Glimmer Vale Chronicles

THE BEAST AND THE GOD-WOMAN

The beach stretched forth as far as the eye could see, a blazing strip of white sand that returned the sun's touch with a fire of its own as though daring the sun to burn hotter. Small crabs, barely larger than a thumbnail, dug their way up from beneath the scorching sand and poked their claws out, tentatively testing the air before scurrying down to the water's edge. Many never made it there, instead getting snatched up by seagulls that winged overhead, watching the sand and waves for prey with sharp eyes and making their calls to each other in an avian symphony.

A strong offshore breeze made the palm trees lining the beach sway, their long green leaves rubbing against each other like lovers caught in a passionate embrace. The same breeze drove rolling waves that collapsed over hidden breakers well over a hundred paces from the beach, leaving only small ripples to lap ashore and cool the few grains of sand lucky enough to be within their reach.

In the nearly still water, colorful fish danced around coral beds and through forests of swaying seaweed, content and sheltered from harm in their gentle lagoon. Or so the fish thought, but the breakers that created such peaceful conditions for them also allowed the gulls easy view of their prey in the water. On occasion, one of them would plunge toward the water instead of the sand and emerge with a fish that happened to swim too near the surface held in its talons. Crying out in triumph, it would bring its meal to the sand and consume it there for all to see.

Yili liked it when they did that because gulls were easier to take on the ground than in the air. He would crouch under the palm trees at beach's end and watch with a stone loaded into the cup of his sling, and when a gull landed unawares within his range he would whip the sling around his head, casting the stone at the bird and taking it before it knew danger was lurking nearby. Then he would dart onto the sand, his bare feet long since calloused against the sand's fire, grab the bird, and retreat back to the cover of the vegetation.

He often felt the call of the sun in those brief excursions onto the strip of fire, and felt the desire deep in his bones to stay and lay himself down, nude save for his loincloth made from the hide of a boar, on the burning sand and wait for the Sun God to take him away to paradise. But he dared not remain on that beach too long; that way lay danger, a danger that threatened to take him away from the Sun God's protection and drag him screaming into the darkness, where torments beyond imagination waited for those unwary or unlucky enough to be caught.

He had never seen it happen, but the elders assured him it was so. And Yili had learned long ago the elders were wise, far wiser than he. They knew these things.

Sitting beneath the palms that day, Yili watched the gulls and thought of Jola, dead two years now. He had scoffed at the elders' teachings, proclaimed that it was the people's birthright to dance under the sun. Worse, to ride upon the waves, to see what lay beyond the breakers.

Madness. Nothing lay past the breakers. Nothing that could serve the people, in any account. And if it could not be of use, what good was it, even if it was there? No, better to not think about such things. So the elders said. And after what happened to Jola, Yili knew it for truth.

The memory of his brother's corpse, burnt, twisted, and broken, what was left of his mouth locked open into a soundless howl of agony and his eyes wide from the horror of his final moments, still haunted Yili. Jola had been a good man. A kind brother, a dutiful son to their mother, a loving husband. It grieved Yili that his brother had not lived to see his twin sons born.

That was what came of defying the Gods' decrees. Men were meant to remain within the trees, away from the sand of fire. And certainly man was forbidden the sea.

A gull's cry pulled Yili from his reverie. He lifted his eyes in time to see as it dove earthward, its eyes fixed on a small crab that was meandering its way toward the surf. It would be just close enough to snatch. Yili set his sling to spinning and loosed the moment the gull's talons latched onto the crab. It had hardly began to launch itself back skyward when the rock struck it on the side of its head. The dull squish of the impact was punctuated by the soft crack of breaking bone, and the gull fell to the sand, dead.

Yili smiled in satisfaction. Two queries with one stone. Once there had been a time when he could not have dreamed to take such a prize so easily. He laughed inwardly at himself and his early, clumsy ventures with the sling. But Jola helped him learn; it fell to him since their father died when Yili was still little. Jola would have been proud to see Yili make this shot.

Yili felt a momentary pang of loss, but shoved it aside. It had been long enough; to dwell on a matter so far in the past was counterproductive and did Jola's soul no honor. He would prefer Yili to be strong and provide for his—for their—family without letting himself be laid up by regrets.

When he stepped onto the sand and felt the burning sun over-heard, Yili felt no such thing, only a surge of ecstasy as he felt the Sun God's touch upon him. As always, the temptation to stop fell heavily upon him, but he did not give in. In mere moments, he crossed the short expanse of sand, snatched up the gull and crab corpses, and darted back beneath the palm trees. There he stopped for a moment, to gather his breath and his wits.

He could have sworn he saw something out of the corner of his eye as he darted back. Something long and dark, nearly black in the blazing sunlight and the glare of the sand. But when he looked around from his position of safety, he saw nothing.

A shiver of fright surged down his spine and Yili had to stop himself from turning away and fleeing back to the village as fast as his feet could carry him. It was the Beast. It had to be. And yet, when he looked around he could see no sign of the thing. The only tracks on the sand were his, and where the dark body lay on the beach there was not the slightest disturbance.

It was nothing, just his mind running ahead of him.

Yili felt another impulse to flee to the village, but he forced himself to remain. He always took the time to pluck feathers from his kill and people would remark upon it if he did not do so this time. No sense in opening himself up to awkward questions. And even more, it was far better not to worry Caeli excessively. She was due for her third child—his this time—any day now. So Yili sat down and began pulling feathers from the gull's corpse.

He spent some minutes - some hours? - there, preparing the evening meal for roasting, before he noticed it.

At first he thought he was imagining things again. There had never before been anything to see on the sea other than waves, with their gentle lapping and their occasional whitecaps. But sure enough, after Yili blinked his eyes and looked away for a half-minute, the thing remained there, bobbing along the waves as it made its way toward the island.

What was it?

It was white, like bleached driftwood, and had a tree growing out of it. Except the tree did not have palm fronds like trees normally do. This tree was bare except for a loose white thing that flapped around in the breeze. It reminded Yili of the time Samo had stolen Gil's favorite loincloth and tied it to the end of a palm. It had flapped around just as that loose white thing did. But Yili had never heard of a tree growing a leaf like that.

His kill forgotten, Yili watched, heedless of the lengthening shadows, as the strange object drew ever closer. Only when it reached the breakers did he actually come to believe it was real. And then only the sound of it impacting the reef, the twangs and crunches—and the shout of dismay—convinced him.

It was the shout that really did it. Yili had heard all manner of wildlife before. But man...

Man made distinctive sounds. And the sound emanating from that thing as it broke apart on the breakers was definitely made by a man. A man in fear.

But men are forbidden the sea. It had always been thus, and always would be thus. So how had a man managed to get on that...whatever it was...and become endangered on the breakers?

He watched as the strange object split in two, and then split apart further under the force of the waves against the reef. From the distance, he saw two man-like shapes struggle to remain onboard even as the thing broke apart. Finally, they fell into the crashing waves, and Yili thought for sure that was the last he would see of them. Nothing got through the breakers; the Gods had placed them there to protect the island and its people, and they did a fine job of it.

Yili felt a flash of sympathy for the two men. Drowning did not seem a pleasant way to die, though in reality he could not think of any way that was. Except perhaps how old Beru had passed: in his sleep, peacefully. And yet Yili could not also help feeling a certain relief, almost satisfaction. The Gods protected his people well. Surely those two only looked like men. Man was not for the sea, therefore those two were more likely demons, servants of the Beast, and come to the island for no good.

He smiled slightly and turned to finish plucking the gull; only a few feathers remained. But more movement in the water, within the lagoon, grabbed his attention once again.

A single dark shape - it was difficult to make out any details from the glare of the lowering sun against the water - bobbed there, moving closer to shore. Wait. It was not a single shape; it was two, but so close together they just seemed as one. Curious, he squinted his eyes, trying to see better. The objects drew nearer, and it became clear one of them was moving, swirling the water ahead of itself in a way that appeared random at first. But quickly, Yili realized there was a purpose to that swirling as the objects continued moving in toward shore, against the retreating tide.

All at once, Yili realized what he was seeing. The two men were moving through the water, propelling themselves somehow with their limbs. Another thing that was unimaginable, perhaps even heretical. They drew closer, and it became obvious that only one of them was actually doing the swirling. The other bobbed limply, only accompanying the first because he had his right arm wrapped around the limp man's body, pulling him along.

Amazing.

They should have sunk there beneath the relatively calm surface of the lagoon, but after just a few moments the pair reached the shallows near shore. The injured one continued to lie limply while the other pulled them both up onto the sand. But he only managed to get them a few feet above the small surf's lapping waves before collapsing in a heap next to his injured companion.

Closer now, Yili could see more details about them. The one who had pulled them ashore was tall, probably head and shoulders taller than Yili, and pale. He was colorful, much more colorful than anyone Yili had ever seen. His torso was a swirl of bright colors and flowers, except for his arms from just above his elbows. His legs were white above the knee and almost as pale below. It made no sense. How…

It took a moment for Yili to realize that the colors were clothing of some sort. But it was like nothing he had ever seen before; it certainly was not fur or tanned hide.

More amazing still, the man's hair was golden! Yili had never seen anything but black hair on a person before; what sort of being was this?

All at once, he felt a rush of excitement, and more than a little fear, beneath his growing curiosity. Perhaps this man and his companion were Gods themselves. It would explain a great many things. But if so, why would they have crashed, had such a hard time of it?

Yili sat still for a long several moments, thinking. Then, setting his kill down again, he maneuvered slowly toward the edge of the tree line. He glanced back and forth down the beach; no sign of the Beast. Perhaps the golden man's presence frightened it off. Yili shook his head quickly. Small chance of that. The Beast did not fear the Sun God; small chance it would fear these men, even if they were Gods themselves.

They needed to get off the beach before it was too late.

Drawing a deep breath, he stepped from beneath the palms' protective canopy and hurried over to the two prostrate forms. As he drew near, though, he realized he had made a mistake. These were not two men. The smaller of the two, the one who had bobbed limply along behind the man, was a woman.

It was obvious from up close. She was curved in the hips like the other women Yili had known. But she was lush and toned in a way that other women were not. There was something intensely alluring about her: the strength of her cheek bones, the magical golden locks that so resembled the man's, the muscles of her arms and legs, the way her rounded breasts moved with each shallow breath she took. The fact that her breasts were so nearly revealed; she wore only thin scraps of some strange material over them, with thin straps that rose above her shoulders to keep the scraps in place. Quite a bit different from the tunics the women of the island wore.

Unbidden, he felt himself reacting physically to her, and he forced himself to look away. It was not proper to think of a God so, and now that he had seen them up close, what else could these two creatures be? Surely no man and woman had ever appeared as they did.

Just then, the man made a surprised sound, and Yili jumped. His heart pounded in his ears as he lost his balance and fell onto his bottom. He winced at the feel of the hot sand on his skin, more tender there than on the soles of his feet, and looked over at the man.

He had awoken, and pushed himself up onto his elbows, looking quizzically at Yili with deep blue eyes. He was clearly exhausted, but determination shone from his features as he took Yili's measure.

The man spoke in a deep voice, saying something that Yili could not understand. But he could understand the question in the man's eyes. Who was he?

Yili swallowed, then tapped his chest and said his name slowly.

The man stared at him, then slowly sounded out the word as though tasting it. Then he nodded and pushed himself up to a sitting position and began to speak again. But again it was unintelligible except that the man sounded weary, frightened, angry, ashamed - all at once.

Yili shrugged slightly and opened his mouth to say how pleased the others in the village would be to meet two Gods travelled from so far to visit. But something stirred at the edge of his vision and his breath caught in his throat.

All at once he became fully aware of the Sun God's heat beating down, diminished as He approached the horizon but intense all the same. Of the movement of the crabs and gulls. And of the sudden silence. The gulls were not calling as they normally did, and even the lapping waves seemed muffled.

Again there was movement at the corner of his eye and he whipped his head around to see. But there was nothing there except a vague impression of darkness fleeing from the range of his vision.

The Beast.

Yili's blood ran cold and he sprang to his feet. After a moment, he realized he was babbling, words spilling from his lips in a rush that left the man's eyes wide in confusion.

They had to move. Get off the beach.

Yili pointed at the man, then the woman, then the palm trees. More like stabbed with his fingers toward the trees as emphatically as he knew how. The man just looked at him in the way the people had looked at poor Seera when her mind left her.

This time the movement was not just at the edge of his vision. Something dark flashed across the beach on the other side of the strange man, distant but obviously moving closer.

There was no time. They had to get off the beach immediately.

Yili bent down, took hold of one of the woman's wrists, and began pulling her toward the tree line.

A flash of bright light overwhelmed his vision as something struck the side of his head, hard, sending him sprawling to the sand. Nausea surged upwards, and he almost vomited. His ears rang and his vision swirled haphazardly for several seconds. When he finally righted himself and managed to prop himself up, the man was standing over him, his great hands clenched in fists and a fierce light in his eyes.

Gods, he thought Yili was trying to make off with his woman!

Slowly pushing himself to his feet, Yili shook his head emphatically and tried to explain. He gestured from the woman to the trees, then from the man to the trees, all the while saying how important it was that they leave, and leave now. He could hardly believe they had lasted so long, now that he thought on it.

The man's scowl only grew more deep as Yili spoke and gestured. He almost thought the man was going to attack him again.

Then, suddenly, the man's face went slack, his eyes wide as his gaze moved from Yili's face to something over his shoulder. Then the slack expression turned to one of fright.

He *saw.*

The man let out a little whimper, bent over, and scooped his woman up into his arms. Either she was lighter than she looked —she was slightly taller than Yili and though without excess fat her toned muscles would add to her weight—or he was very strong. Not sparing Yili a glance, he began hustling toward the tree line.

Not a moment too soon. Yili turned to follow him, trying to hold down the growing terror that clamored at his mind and thanking the Sun God that they were finally moving.

Then something black as night whipped past between Yili and the man. It moved too quickly for Yili to see anything except for the darkness of its presence. But whatever it really was, it struck the man at the ankles. He screamed in sudden pain, lurching forward and falling to the sand. His woman tumbled from his arms as he fell, landing in a heap next to him.

The man screamed again, louder.

Stunned, Yili saw that the man's feet were simply gone below the ankle. Only stumps remained at the bottom of his legs. Stumps that did not bleed; they were charred like overcooked meat. But unlike cooked meat the odor they gave off choked the breath out of Yili's lungs and threatened, for the second time in as many minutes, to send him stumbling away to find a place to vomit.

But he did not; somehow he knew that if he gave in to that impulse it would be the end for him and the woman, as well as the man.

Yili stumbled over next to the man and squatted down.

He was all but mad with pain and terror, but he grasped at Yili's arm and gestured toward the woman. Then to the tree line. Just as Yili had. Satisfaction threatened to overwhelm compassion for the man as part of Yili's mind scoffed at the man's desperate request. Had he but listened when Yili tried to help, they would all be safe now, not -

Movement off to the left, and a flash of blackness, helped Yili get control of himself. Forcing the shamefully scornful thoughts down, he nodded to the man and clasped arms with him. Then he turned and, grabbing the woman by her wrists, began dragging her away.

The man tried to follow, dragging himself across the sand with his arms. But the end was never in doubt.

Yili wished he could not see. But he was dragging the woman and had his back to the trees to get the most leverage. He could not help but see as a wave of black rose out of the sand and engulfed the man. His scrabbling fingers were not able to prevent himself from being dragged away. Down he went, into the darkness. His final scream was blood-curdling, horrid.

And then there was nothing but the sand and the lapping of the waves. Even the man's tracks had been wiped clean by the passing of the Beast.

Yili stumbled into the village, his burden grown so great that he could barely place one foot in front of the other.

The shadows had long since grown into giants that quickly fled before the onset of twilight. The fires were lit in the pits, the torches placed in their holders around the village's perimeter, beating back the growing darkness. Everyone would be gathering for the evening meal, followed by games and songs, or perhaps stories from one of the elders.

The thought of that pleasant company, the joy of family and friends, was all that had kept him going these last hours.

He halfway expected to be devoured as the man had been, but somehow he made it to the tree line, where the Beast could not touch them. It did not take long to decide that he could not simply drag the woman all the way back to the village. It was too far, and she would likely be injured in the process. So he had, mustering all his strength, scooped her up.

She was not as heavy as he had feared, but nor was she light. But he quickly found that he was able to travel more readily with her draped over his shoulders.

That was, until he reached the path up the island's central mountain.

The people had good reasons for locating their village up on the mountain's flank, not the least of which was it placed them far enough from the beach, and the Beast, that there was no worry of accidentally wandering too close. But the path was steep, difficult enough while not carrying a burden. Several times, Yili thought he would fall, sending he and the woman both tumbling down the path and probably causing grave injury to both of them.

But he made it. As he stepped into the circle of firelight that marked the village's boundary, his spirits lifted. For a moment, he almost forgot what had happened down on the beach.

That did not last.

Yili's return sparked an outburst of interest. At first because he had returned, and so much later than normal. Caeli led the crowd of villagers rushing toward him, relief and joy on her face. But she stopped before reaching him, almost skidding to a halt as she beheld his burden. The others did as well; no one came within a half dozen paces of him. They all just stood there in a loose half-circle, staring in surprise, curiosity, and fear at him, and what he carried.

Finally the elders came forth. The crowd parted before their withered, powerful forms, younger men and women making respectful half-bows as they allowed the village's leaders passage. The wise ones looked at him severely, their eyes narrowed such that he could not read their expressions, but said nothing.

Yili swallowed. It was always thus when something was done that needed explaining. The elders never questioned. They simply watched with their eyes that missed nothing and waited for an explanation. Some of the youngest men among the people played a game: who could hold out the longest beneath their gaze before confessing the truth. When he was younger, Yili had played that game too, fool that he was. To his knowledge, no one had ever lasted beyond a slow count to thirty.

After reaching forty-five—part of his mind screamed to Yili

that he was perhaps even more foolish than he had been those years ago—Yili told the tale of his encounter on the beach.

The people were taken aback, as he would have expected them to be. Had he not been there himself, he would not have believed such a turn of events possible, either. And yet they happened; he was living proof of it, and so was his burden.

The elders frowned, all of them, their expressions troubled. Then they retreated to confer amongst themselves, pausing only to tell him to place the strange woman down on a pallet in the hut nearest the central bonfire. The hut belonged to Pao, Neela, and their small daughter Teya, but they did not complain. If anything, they seemed honored that the elders had deemed their home worthy of such an honor.

Yili did as instructed and then finally embraced his wife. Caeli was trembling, the anxiety of her evening finally letting loose now that he was there. It did not help to hear of the terror he had endured, Yili was sure.

As he drew her close, he felt a deep shame. She had been through so much, losing her first husband the way she had. As Jola's younger brother, it was his duty to look after her after he passed, but nothing forced him to take her as his wife. It would have been completely within his rights to take another, so long as he provided for Caeli and his brother's children. But he had always felt affection, more than affection, for her. It had not taken long before, in his brother's absence, that affection had grown into much more. He could no more have taken another than he could have cut off his own arm.

When she accepted his offer, he felt a relief and a joy that he never thought to experience. The imminent arrival of their first child together was the only thing in his life that surpassed that feeling.

And yet…

And yet as he held her, felt her arms clutch him tightly, he found himself looking back at the God-woman who lay within Pao and Neela's hut. The magical gold of her hair, the curve of her legs, her hips, her breasts. And he felt a longing that he had not felt with Caeli before.

The elders liked to tell the tale of Armsrung, who dared fly from the world's embrace, far away until he touched the moon itself, and returned to Earth a God in his own right. Yili had never understood such an impulse before, but now... What would it be like to touch a God, and be touched in return? Would that not import Godhood onto the man who dared such a thing?

Yili shook himself, willing his thoughts back to the present. The now. Caeli was his woman, his beloved. The mother of his children, who had only ever treated him with warmth and deepest respect. He owed her better than that.

And then the elders returned, their faces, if possible, even more troubled than when they left to confer. In hushed tones, they decreed that no one was to interact with the God-woman except themselves. To even approach her hut was to invite the Sun God's kiss.

Yili shuddered at the thought, but voiced no protest. Their decree made sense.

The elders then gestured for the crowd to disperse, to go back to their homes. There would be no stories this night; the evening had brought enough ancient legends to life as it was.

Yili could not fault them for that decree, either. Suddenly weary, and no wonder considering all he had witnessed and done that day, he walked with Caeli back to their hut, where the twins were already fast asleep. He wasted only the half-moment it took to strip off his loincloth before flinging himself down into his and Caeli's furs. He barely felt her snuggle in next to him before he drifted off into a deep sleep.

Two days later, the God-woman awoke.

The elders were not sure how long it would be, or whether she would ever awaken again. But Yili knew she would come around.

It was a certainty, as far as he was concerned. The likes of her do not just roll over and die so easily.

He stayed as close to her hut as he could, for as long as he could, each day. He almost let his work for the village slip. He would have, had Caeli not been on hand to direct him back onto the right road. And so he did his job, and did it well, collecting fruits as well as a couple trapped rodents each day for the evening meal.

But when he was not off doing that, or assisting Caeli with the young ones, he was near the hut. Sometime during the first night, the elders selected guards for the hut and ordered them to be... severe...with anyone who strayed too close to the God-woman. But they recognized Yili as the one who had brought her in from the wild, so they did not question the fact that he remained so close. And so he was close at hand when she awoke.

The first sign was the shrill shriek that emanated from the hut as she came to in unfamiliar environs. After that came the words of the woman appointed to watch over and care for her. They were carefully chosen words, meant to be comforting. But her shrieks only became louder.

Yili did not wait to be asked. He darted forward toward the tent, cursing the women, and the elders, Gods help him, for idiots. He had told them she would not be able to understand them, but had they listened?

The guards did not stop him. They were too absorbed by the small drama going on within the hut, and anyway it was not like he intended harm to the God-woman or any of the normal women who cared for her. He arrived just in time to see the God-woman, sitting on the ground, shove Guona away with so much force that she stumbled backwards and bounced off the side of the hut.

Guona was more tough than her slender build let on. She shrugged off the pain of her impact and drew herself upright, ready, no doubt, to give the God-woman a piece of her mind.

Yili would have loved to watch, or rather listen, to such a discussion if he were not so wearied by the concept of waiting.

And so cynical - he chose the word himself - about how such arguments would never amount to anything. So instead he raised his voice to get Guona's attention, then directed her to exit the hut.

She glared at him as she left, and Yili knew he was going to be in trouble, incredible trouble, with the elders as soon as she gathered her wits and complained to them about what had happened. But he knew he was right. He was there on the beach when she arrived. He had seen her companion - her husband? - die. It must be he who explained matters to her.

As Guona left Yili and the God-woman alone together, Yili was again struck by her physical presence, her appeal. He had never seen a woman to equal her before. Ever.

He shook himself slightly to recover his wits; he must have said that same thing to himself any number of times over the last couple days. It was silly, and besides, a God would have no use for a mere human such as he. And.... And, he was married. Yili gave an inward start of surprise when he discovered he had to remind himself of that fact.

Before he could chastise himself properly, the woman spoke, less shrilly than before, with less obvious panic. She was someplace good and helpful. Why else would they have taken the time to fish her out of the sea? Or at least, Yili presumed that was what she thought. It was obvious they were just trying to help her, after all.

Yili squatted down next to her and smiled. Pressing his hand to his chest, he said his name slowly, as he had with the man.

The God-woman just looked at him for a long moment, then nodded slowly and pointed at herself. "Care-ul," she said. She paused, looking down at the dirt floor of the hut. When she spoke again, it was in a near whisper. "Air-ick?"

Yili had no idea what she was trying to say, so he simply shook his head.

The God-woman - Care-ul - spoke again, more forcefully. Demanding. "Air-ick!"

Yili retreated a half-step, remaining in a crouch. Something about her tone was disquieting. Again he shook his head, adding a gesture of confusion in the hopes she would understand better.

She was growing frustrated, he could see it on her face. She rolled her eyes and forced herself to her feet, nearly falling back to the ground in the process as her knees wobbled. As she caught herself, her hand landed on her hip, and her eyes widened. Yili had not noticed before that the strange loincloth - it was larger and at the same time more tight than a loincloth, going down to mid-thigh on her legs - had pouches built into its sides. She fished her hand into one of the pouches and, with a small grin of triumph pulled a strange object out. It almost looked like it was leather, but it flipped open easily. She worked around in the thing for a short time, then pulled out a small, thin object and held it out to him.

Gods above! Her companion, the God-man, was there, trapped within the thing she held!

Yili jumped backwards, landing on his feet as a sudden fright sped through him. What strange magic was this?

Care-ul flinched at his sudden movement, but did not put the thing away. Instead, she stepped forward toward him. With her free hand, she pointed at the trapped man and said again, "Air-ick?"

Suddenly it became clear. Air-ick was the God-man's name. Yili sighed and dropped his eyes. He shook his head and made a cutting gesture across his throat.

Care-ul's breath caught and her eyes went wide. Her lips began to tremble; Yili saw tears beginning to well up. Then she dropped down onto the ground and began to sob, in loss. In despair.

Three weeks passed.

For most of the first, the elders limited the people's contact with Care-ul for fear of frightening them - or her - more than necessary. And because they did not know how she would react to so many new faces at once, especially being unable to communicate with them. Only a select few women, the elders themselves, and Yili were allowed to see her. Yili suspected had he not been the first one to get her to open up at all, he would have been excluded as well. That notion caused him far more consternation than he would have thought.

By the end of the first week, though, Care-ul seemed to accept that they were not going to hurt her, and that they had not killed Air-ick. Or at least, she stopped looking at them with tearful, half-frightened eyes. And so the elders allowed her the run of the village. She began walking amongst the people, in company with one of the more familiar women or Yili.

By the middle of the second week, she began helping with some common chores around the village and trying to learn the language. The men were all amazed at her skill with knots; she could take a vine and bind branches together in ways that no one in the village had ever considered before. Before long, using the new knotting techniques she taught, the people began making some much-needed improvements.

Because of her contribution, and the fact that she was quickly picking up at least a smattering of the language, the people lost their initial unease around Care-ul. By the end of the third week, she was like a familiar friend. Not family, obviously; she would never be truly one of them, as different as she was. But she was no longer the other, to be feared and watched. And for her part, she seemed more comfortable with them as well.

All the same, Yili noticed she would often stare off into nothing with a haunted look on her face. And in the evenings she would cry herself to sleep.

Then, some of the hunters found Air-ick's body.

Three men brought him into the village at noon. His body was decaying, rank. Putrid even. But the elders had decreed that he be found, if possible, and returned for a proper burial. After Yili described where on the beach the event had occurred, some men were sent each day to search. Yili had gone himself the first several days, even though he knew there was no hope of finding anything; the Beast had taken him away to the netherworld, and mere men could not travel there.

But in the end, the elders were right. They always were right.

The hunters related that they had found a mound of sand not far from the tree line about a hundred fifty paces from the place Yili specified, and that crabs were swarming over it. It was in that mound they found him.

He was almost un-recognizable, except from his golden hair and large size. But Care-ul knew him at once, and rushed to his side before the hunters had lowered him to the ground. There she wept for what seemed an hour, the pain and loss that Yili had thought dampened by the passage of days apparently still sharp.

He stood there, watching her in her grief, for a long time before he realized Caeli had come to stand next to him. She watched Care-ul with eyes that reflected the God-woman's grief, and Yili recalled how long it had taken her to move past Jola's death. It had been months before she was able to give herself to him fully, even though they had been married only a few days after the cremation.

Yili put his arm around Caeli's shoulder and drew her close. She snuggled close, rubbing against him in that comfortable way that was her want, and he thought she sobbed a little.

"You should become friends with her," he said softly, and she stiffened. She shook her head quickly, and he continued. "It might help her to be with a woman who has also known loss." Caeli looked up at him for a long moment, then nodded. She looked almost nervous, but when she left his grasp and turned toward Care-ul, her back was straight.

She walked over to the weeping woman and sank down next to her. Slowly, as though wary to touch her, Caeli reached out and placed her hand on Care-ul's shoulder, then gave it a gentle squeeze. Care-ul looked up at her in surprise - she and Caeli had hardly interacted at all during her sojourn in the village. Then, seeing something in Caeli's eyes, perhaps a reflection of her own pain, and understanding, she grabbed Yili's wife in a fierce embrace.

Soon they were both crying together.

They did not delay, but held the ceremony and cremated Air-ick at sunset. Normally there would be a day devoted to remembrances of the deceased, words said in his honor, and a grand feast. But no one knew Air-ick except for Care-ul, and he was so far decayed that to delay would have been to risk scavengers and sickness.

And so there was just a simple ceremony, the elders taking a short while to intone the blessings of the Gods on their returning brother, and then the funeral pyre was lit. Most of the people filtered away quickly after the body was fully ablaze. After all, the trail from the promontory overlooking the northern beach, where they held final ceremonies for the dead, while not particular steep, was narrow. And it would be better to not navigate it after dark.

After a few minutes, only Shumay, the wisest of the elders, Yili, and Caeli remained with Care-ul beside the fire. Caeli stood at Care-ul's side; it looked as though she was whispering to the God-woman. As adept as Care-ul had proven at learning the language, Yili would not have been surprised if she understood a fair amount of what Caeli was saying. Yili and Shumay stood apart, giving them space.

Shumay stared at the fire, a deep frown on her lips, and was silent for a long time. When finally she spoke, it was in a low tone that would not carry to the two women.

"I am troubled, Yili."

He nodded. "We all noticed."

Shumay sniffed. "First Jola and now this. The Beast had not

attacked anyone in my lifetime until your brother. And now another victim, so soon afterwords…"

Yili frowned. Two years was hardly soon. But then, when one is looking back from the span of fifty years, as Shumay did, two years must seem just a blink. "What are you saying?"

"This woman and her man were sent by the Gods. That is obvious. But for what purpose?" She drew her shawl, made from the hides of two boars, tight around herself as though to ward off a chill, even though the evening was far from cold even without the bonfire.

"You think the Beast means to thwart their mission."

"Is it not obvious?" Shumay shook her head. "I worry that, with that woman here among us, the Beast may not keep to the beach any longer."

Yili recoiled as though smacked. "What?" The import of her words struck him, and he shook his head. "No, that is impossible. The Beast walks the sand to thwart man's rebellion against the Gods. To keep us from the sea." So it had always been said. The Beast was the Gods', and particularly the Sun God's, opposite and thus always worked against them. But its nature was such that it also did the Gods' will without realizing it, by hunting men who would stray to places they were not meant to go.

"I wonder…" Shumay's words trailed off and she was silent again for a long time, just staring at the blaze. Finally, she rolled her shoulders and stepped away from the pyre, toward the path back to the village. But before she left, she placed a slender, bony hand on Yili's shoulder. "Watch her closely, Yili," she said. "If she becomes a danger to us…"

Shumay left the rest unsaid, but Yili understood. Sent by the Gods or no, if Care-ul brought the Beast down on the people, they would have to move against her, to stave off their own destruction.

It was like a dagger through his heart.

The next morning, Caeli and Care-ul spoke for a long time near the outskirts of the village. Yili noticed them together as he was preparing a snare that he intended to set later that day. He was struck, again, by how different they were. How radiant Care-ul was, even with her eyes sunken and dark from a night spent weeping. And how plain Caeli was by comparison, like a wilting flower. He hated himself for thinking of her that way, but he could not shake the comparison from his mind.

He needed to focus. He turned away from them, putting all his attention on the snare he was constructing.

A few moments later, Caeli's voice, from behind his back, intruded. "She wishes to go to the beach. To where Air-ick died."

Yili felt a chill. Dread seeped into his bones as he turned to look at his wife. "Are you sure?"

Caeli nodded. "Her speech is still difficult, but," she swallowed and managed a half-smile, "she was very clear about that."

A number of curses that were so foul no one every gave them voice, at least not in public, sprang to mind. Taking her to the Beach... That would potentially be bad. Very bad. What if the Beast came for her? But even as he thought that, he knew he could not refuse her this thing.

He nodded. "When?"

Caeli looked at him askance, and he sighed. "Alright. Let me finish this last lashing. I was going to set the snare down near the base of the mountain anyway."

He stood, hefting the snare; it was not very heavy, but it was bulky, and took some adjusting to carry comfortably. Then he followed Caeli through the foliage at the edge of the village until they met Care-ul, not far from the path down the mountain. As always, she was enchanting to behold. His eyes were drawn down to the scraps that covered her breasts before he could control them. As quickly as he could, he forced them to her face, lest she sense his vulnerability. His shame, feeling something like that for a woman besides his wife.

For a heartbeat, he thought she smiled slightly, a knowing

smile that said his ruse was easily detected. Surely not; she was still in mourning.

And yet Caeli went to him after mourning for much less time than Care-ul had spent. A woman wants to feel desired, does she not?

Yili shook off that thought - it was not appropriate - and led the women on the path down the mountain, and from there to the beach. He only paused to set his snare near a small game path that had yielded good takings in the past.

It took a long time to reach the beach where he had observed Care-ul and Air-ick's arrival. The whole way, he remembered the fear that drove him upwards with Care-ul over his shoulder, the weight of her pressing him down and making every footstep an effort, the nagging feeling in the back of his mind that by saving her from the Beast he was interfering in a divine play that man was not meant to take part in.

Unbidden, and despite his efforts not to look back at her, the image Care-ul as he had first seen her, unconscious and unashamed on the beach, the Sun God beating down on her toned arms and legs, the chill of the sea making her nipples rise against the strange fabric that covered them...

Yili stopped, forcing himself to think of something else as he realized he was reacting with desire for her. For someone other than his wife. It was not right, all the more since she was from the Gods herself.

From then on, he increased his pace to the beach, almost leaving the women behind completely until finally he reached the pair of trees he remembered from that day. He stood there panting for a long time, or at least it felt long, before Caeli and Care-ul caught up. Plenty of time to get himself under control again.

He turned to look at them - at Care-ul - and pointed out past the line of palm trees, past the burning white sand, toward the lagoon and, beyond, the breakers where, even now, the top of the tree that had grown out of the thing she and Air-ick had arrived on still protruded from the water.

Care-ul turned her head to follow his extended finger. When she saw the tree, she gasped and hurried out onto the sand, heedless of the way the Sun God turned the sand to fire in the early afternoon hours. It sometimes even made Yili's feet hurt, calloused as they were.

And yet Care-ul seemed not to notice. She ran down the beach at full speed, plunging into the lapping surf of the lagoon and wading ever deeper until the water was up to her hips. Then she lunged forward, her body lying atop the water somehow, and pulled herself forward toward the breakers and the strange tree with rhythmic pulls from her arms that were similar, but not exactly the same, as those Air-ick had used to get himself and her to the beach in the first place.

Yili stood there, stunned, and could only watch as she did it. His rational mind could not keep up with what she was doing. He had witnessed Air-ick moving through the water naturally, as though he had been born to it, but Yili had presumed that was because of the life or death nature of what was happening. Several times in his memory men had found themselves able to do amazing things when their lives depended on it, after all.

And yet, apparently, Air-icks ability to move through the water was not specific to him, or only driven by severe danger. It could not be, since Care-ul had the ability as well and she was certainly not threatened before she reached the water.

Was she?

Yili felt a sudden surge of fear and cast about quickly, searching for any sign of the enemy. The Beast. There was no sign, not even a hint of a shadow at the edge of his vision.

He breathed a sigh of relief. Beside him, Caeli looked more curious than frightened as she followed Care-ul with her eyes. But then, she had not seen what happened before. What Yili would not give to be to pure of sight again. He found himself taking her hand as he stepped out onto the beach, following Care-ul's footprints. She followed with only the slightest hesitation.

They stopped a few feet above the highest reach of the surf, small as it was. In spite of his nerves, Yili found himself reveling in the Sun God's touch upon his skin. It had been too long since he last allowed himself to really feel His warmth. It was like returning home, somehow.

Ahead, Care-ul was nearing the constantly pounding surf that marked the breakers' location. She stopped moving forward and instead bobbed there for a time. How she managed that, Yili could not guess, and yet she did. Her head moved from side to side; she was clearly surveying the scene and weighing her options. Smart. Finally, she seemed to roll over herself and sank beneath the waves, her feet kicking out of the water for just a second before vanishing completely.

Beside him, Caeli gasped. "Is she..." She broke off. The distress in her voice was matched on her face, which had grown pale, though not as pale as Care-ul's.

Yili shook his head. "I do not think so. The Gods did not bring her here so she could die in the water."

No sooner had his words left his lips than Care-ul re-appeared, her head breaking the water in a rush. Again she bobbed for a time, and then she went back under.

And again. And again.

Yili lost count of the number of times she went under. At first Caeli was nervous with each disappearance. In truth, so was he, though he chose to not reveal it to Caeli; better only one of them be afraid. But after a few trips, even she became calm. After all, Care-ul always came back up.

Finally, after more times diving beneath the waves than Yili cared to count, Care-ul rose form the depths and turned around, then began pulling herself toward the beach, and them. As before, when he watched Air-ick pull himself and her from the water, Yili found himself entranced watching her. The way she was able to turn the water to her will...that alone spoke of her divine origins. He forced himself to stop thinking of the other reasons she belonged in the heavens above. It was not fitting.

All the same, when she found her footing in the shallows near the beach and rose to her full height, Yili found himself gaping. The water streaming down her toned body, reflecting the light from the Sun God in ways he had never imagined... It was difficult to avoid becoming entranced.

Fortunately, when he glanced aside at Caeli, he saw she was similarly impressed, and had to force her eyes away from the God-woman to meet his. She smiled shyly, as though she were a newly-flowered woman flirting with a man she thought might make a good husband. What thoughts went through her mind to make her act like that?

Care-ul's voice drew both their eyes back to her. She wore a broad smile and held up a strange object for them to see. It was long and round, like a piece of wood. But it wood it was not, colored like the sky at sunset the way it was. And it had a bulbous end, sheathed in see-through material of some kind. Yili could see another bulb-thing below that material as well.

What was that? He found himself retreating a half-step. Caeli did the same.

Care-ul's grin became wider and she laughed before speaking. Her words were unintelligible, but when she gestured toward the object, Yili thought she said something that sounded like "EE-perb."

He just stared back at her and shrugged in confusion.

Care-ul opened her mouth to speak again.

And, just then, Yili saw it. A flash of darkness at the edge of his vision. Oh Gods....

He had feared the Beast would come, but after so much time waiting for the god-woman, he had dared to hope it would not. Yili turned away from Care-ul, casting around the beach quickly as he tried to locate the Beast. Nothing.

And then another flash of black. To the right this time.

"RUN!"

His shout caused Caeli to jump. From the corner of his eye, he saw her look at him with confusion mixed with fear.

"The Beast," he snarled. He reached out and pushed her shoulder, sending her stumbling forward toward the tree line. 'RUN!"

Caeli ran, and Yili followed. Behind him, he heard Care-ul exclaim in surprise and, he thought, anger. But after a few seconds her footsteps followed in rapid succession: she was running. Thank the Gods. Yili turned his head quickly left and right, but again he could not see anything concrete. The occasional flash of darkness, but never the dark mass he had seen when the Beast killed Air-ick.

And then they were beneath the palm trees.

Caeli stumbled to a halt a few steps past the safety of the tree line, then fell to her knees, her breaths coming in gasping heaves. She was not used to running that way. Then again, Yili found he had to lean against the trunk of a palm tree for support, his heart raced so.

Care-ul, though... When she broke through the tree line and stopped next to them, she was wet, but probably that was still water from the sea. Her breathing was only slightly more rapid than normal, and she looked calm. No, that was not right. She looked enraged. The glare she cast Yili's way contained daggers. Why?

Caeli noticed the glare as well and rose. Rather, she forced herself, painfully Yili thought, to her feet, and walked over to Care-ul. The two women had a long and hushed conversation. To spare his ears, Yili was sure...but also probably because of Care-ul's limited vocabulary.

Finally, Caeli stepped back from Care-ul, looking up at her and nodding, a small smile on her face. Care-ul still frowned, but it was more speculative than angry. She looked at Yili and their eyes met.

Her eyes had depths he had never dreamt a woman could have. Intellect, confidence, courage, knowledge...all those things and more were contained in her gaze. All of a sudden, Yili felt unworthy, ashamed. He lowered his eyes and breathed a soft apology, for what he was not sure; it just seemed the appropriate thing to do.

He looked back up in time to see Care-ul's nod of acceptance before she turned away.

Shumay's frown would have been enough to darken the sun, had cloud cover not already accomplished that feat. "You are sure of this?"

Yili nodded. "We got away just in time."

They sat within Shumay's hut, out of the way from the others at the uphill edge of the village. Unlike many others of the village huts, Shumay's had the feel of having been lived in your ages. And no wonder; by tradition it passed to the wisest of the elders when the previous wisest passed on. Generations of the wise had left an indelible mark on the place. Tokens of power hung from the ceiling, and the walls were painted and carved with the history of the people. Regardless of what happened to the other huts in the village - and for one reason or another most were replaced periodically - this one stood inviolate. Permanent.

Just like its occupants. The individual might fade away to take its place with the Gods, but the position of wisest would always be there. Would always live on.

Shumay licked her lips and turned away from Yili. She stepped over to the wall carvings to the left of the hut entrance. Reaching up, she ran withered fingers along the carvings as though reading them through her fingertips. And who knows, she may have been doing just that. The wisest possessed abilities and insights that the rest of the people did not.

"Did Caeli see it?"

Yili shook his head. "No." He paused, replaying the event in his mind. Finally, he added, "But she has never been to the beach before. She may not have known what to look for. Or she may have convinced herself she was imagining things." Shame made him lower his eyes. "I know I did, the first time I saw it." Not so long ago, that. Would Air-ick still be alive had he recognized what he was seeing? Had he acted sooner?

Yili could only tell himself all would have happened the way it did; that it had been the will of the Gods. But he was not so sure he believed that.

Shumay nodded slowly, her lips pursed in thought. "And the woman?"

Yili noticed Shumay never called Care-ul by name, and wondered about it. He knew better than to ask, though. He shook his head. "She was confused, and angry at me. If she had seen it…" She would not have been angry if she had recognized the danger. That did not need to be said, though.

Shumay nodded, then let out a breath that Yili had not realized she was holding. "So long as it remains confined to the beach, it is not a problem. Hopefully." She was silent for a time.

Yili eventually took the silence to indicate he was dismissed, and he turned away from her, toward the hut entrance. He was just about to exit when Shumay spoke again, stopping him in his tracks.

"What is this thing, this…EE-perb…she recovered from the site?"

Yili looked back at Shumay and spread his hand helplessly. "I tried to ask her, but she did not have the language to explain. She seemed happy to find it, though. Ecstatic."

Shumay nodded again, noticeably more slowly this time. Then she waved Yili out with a dismissive gesture of her hand. Yili took no offense.

Over the next week, Care-ul began acting strangely.

At first, her spirits were up, buoyed high by her find, whatever it really was. But then, on the morning of the third day after the discovery, she emerged from her tent distraught. Her eyes were baggy, with dark circles beneath them as though she had not slept, and her cheeks were smudged, the ever-present dirt streaked below here eyes by what could only have been tears. She carried the EE-oerb in her hand like a club, and wore her usual scrap of a top and tight loincloth that came down to her thighs.

Care-ul stalked across the village, past the fire pit and the multitude of huts surrounding it. Past the tanning tent and the cooks' preparation area to the edge of the village. There she stood for a short while, her breath initially rapid but slowly becoming deeper, more normal.

Then, with a shout of frustration and…despair?…she curled backwards then hurled the EE-perb out of the camp, toward a steep drop-off that plunged several hundred feet to the base of the mountain. It was practically a cliff.

Yili watched as the object flew away, but remained silent. He simply walked toward her where she stood breathing slowly in and out. She did not acknowledge his presence for a long time; her eyes stared down the drop-off, looking but not seeing. Finally, after may minutes passed, she shook herself and turned away, her head erect and her lips compressed into a scowl, the kind of scowl that said she intended to fight to the end.

But fight against what?

Yili thought he knew, but what he suspected… It could not be.

Care-ul stalked away from him, never acknowledging his presence. She passed through the outskirts of the village, ignoring the tents, the firepits, the latrine holes, the stares of the people who had seen her outburst and now watched her the way a person watches a venomous snake: wary, ready to flee or fight in a heartbeat.

Then she disappeared into the woods beyond the village's edge, her lean form quickly lost amongst the tree trunks.

Caeli would not see reason.

For whatever reason, she had grown attached to Care-ul over the last week or more. Barely half a minute had passed after she disappeared into the woods before Caeli pushed past the woman she had been working with and began rushing toward the forest where Care-ul had gone.

Yili managed to catch up to her and stop her before she got too far, but she fought against him. Actually pulled away with an angry shout. He tried to restrain her, to talk to her, but all she would say was that Care-ul needed help. That she was her friend, and she had to be there for her.

In the end, Caeli had squirmed free and dashed off into the woods after the god-woman, leaving Yili standing there, stunned.

It was Shumay's voice that stirred him to action.

"You must go after her."

Yili nodded. "Caeli does not know…"

"No." The correction was blunt, almost harsh. "The woman." Shumay's tone was severe, cold. "She is grown unstable."

"She is upset."

Shumay did not reply. Though she stood behind him, Yili could see the doubt on her face. He sighed.

"What must I do?"

"What you have always known you must. Protect the people."

Yili closed his eyes and took a long deep breath. Protect the people. Against the Beast that was an eternal threat to their well being. Against the god-woman who threatened to set the Beast free.

But she had not done anything to suggest she could, or would, do that.

"And if she waits until we are not prepared?" How had Shumay known his thoughts? "Then it may already be too late."

The pain in his heart as Yili considered her words was as real - as agonizing - as the time he burned his leg in the fire pit. It had been weeks before he was able to walk again without living in a world of pain. If he did this, how long would it be before his heart healed?

He sensed Shumay about to say something more, but before she could, he hurried from the village into the woods.

The two women left little sign of their passing, but Yili did not need any. There was only one place Care-ul would go, and Caeli would follow her.

He ran to the beach, leaping past rocks and boulders along the mountain path and using palm trunks as support to prevent himself from overbalancing as he raced downward. He made it to the beach where he had initially seen Care-ul and Air-ick in record time.

The women were already there, at the tree line. Caeli spoke softly, urgently to Care-ul. The golden-haired god-woman simply stared out at the breakers, so far off shore, her eyes filled with longing, with loss. Yili looked at the two of them and wondered why he ever settled for Caeli, so dark and withered she seemed next to Care-ul's radiance.

His brother.

Jola had forced him into it. If he had not died, leaving Caeli without husband, with twins to care for... It was his duty to watch over her and his brother's children. Yili had welcomed the duty; Caeli was beautiful, far above the other women of the village. All the same, it had been difficult to change his thinking from that of a man alone to a man with a family and responsibility.

But oh, now that he saw what was possible, how that duty grated on him. Almost as much as knowing that he must remove the source of that possibility; she was too much a threat to the people. Wasn't she?

Yili shook his head muttering something unkind about Shumay under his breath.

Caeli and Care-ul turned in unison, blue and dark brown eyes coming to rest upon him at once, with equal accusation in each pair.

"What do you say, Yili?" asked Caeli. Her voice was hard. Why?

In a moment of shame, Yili realized he must not have spoken the curse against Shumay as quietly as he thought. He flushed and lowered his eyes, shaking his head. "Nothing. I am just relieved to find you both well."

"Well." It was Care-ul who spoke this time. Her quick mastery of the language was amazing, but she did not need to speak the language to convey the bitter sarcasm of the single word.

Of course she would not be totally well, after all she had been through. Yili flushed again, embarrassment filling him. He looked up.

And froze.

Behind the women - within the palm forest, not on the beach - a flickering darkness swept through his vision and was gone.

Yili stood frozen, dread turning his bowels to water as the realization of their predicament struck him.

Shumay was right. The Beast was loose.

He opened his mouth to scream, to tell them to flee to the safety of the village.

The darkness swept past again, closer this time, stealing the strength from his lungs before he could speak.

Yili stumbled backwards, but his heel caught on something and he fell down onto his backside. The impact was mildly painful, but he hardly noticed the ache. He managed a whisper. "Run."

The women's stern, almost wrathful, expressions moderated, becoming merely angry, but also confused.

"RUN," Yili cried again, managing some volume into the warning this time.

Care-ul's face remained confused, but Caeli's took on an expression of stark terror. She knew well what dwelled on the beach, what the people dreaded would gain a foothold on the island proper, and doom them all. She shoved Care-ul forward, all the strength of her thin arms and wiry torso combining into a shove that was irresistible to the other woman, however powerfully built she may have been.

Care-ul stumbled several steps forward, looking confused, hurt, and infuriated. But when she righted herself, she saw. Just as Yili saw as the Beast's darkness circled around them again. Care-ul's anger turned to mortal fear, and, with barely a moment's glance at Caeli and him, she turned and fled into the forest.

Caeli watched her depart from her position next to Yili. As the god-woman faded from view, she turned to him and he could see that regardless of her fear, and it filled her to overflowing, she trusted him to get them out of it. Part of him screamed in agony at the blind, almost rapturous trust she placed in his love while he lusted after another, an outsider who had only recently come into their midst. She trusted him; how could he betray her so?

Yili forced a confident smile to his lips. "Follow me," he said as he grabbed her hand. Then, turning away from where he had last seen the Beast's darkness and praying that It would chase after the god-woman and not them (and Gods did his heart burn to pray for such a fate to fall on to Care-ul's fair form), he ran, pulling Caeli along behind him.

His heart would burn even more before they reached the slope leading to the village.

They found Care-ul crouched behind a tree near the start of the path leading up the mountain to the village. At first, Yili could not understand why she did not just continue up the path. At least there would be some safety, some shelter if nothing else, in the village huts.

But then he saw a flicker of darkness further up, along the path. The Beast had circled ahead; to continue that way would be suicide.

He dragged Caeli to a halt behind a clump of bushes, gripping her hand as tightly as he ever had. What were they going to do?

"By the Gods," Caeli said softly, between gasps as she gulped down air. "The village?"

Yili shook his head. He could not know if they were safe or not, could not worry about it. For now, the village was beyond his ability to care for.

Caeli's face broke, and he knew he had made a mistake. He saw tears welling up, and he realized she must have meant he thought the others...their children...were already dead. Cursing himself for a fool, he took hold of her shoulder and turned her so she looked him in the eye.

"They are safe," he said in a fierce whisper, hoping he was not lying to her. "But we can't worry about them right now. If we - "

A rustle of leaves drew his attention, and he saw Care-ul shifting from the tree she hid behind to one closer to them. But she was making far too much noise; a twig broke under her feet before she reached her goal. A heartbeat later, darkness flickered between the trunks of the trees up the mountain.

It was heading toward Care-ul. Toward them.

Yili waved his hands frantically, gesturing for her to run away. But she either did not understand or was being bull-headed, because she only paused to take a breath before she left the shelter of her tree and sprinted toward their hiding spot behind the bushes.

The streaking darkness of the Beast drew her up short, in the open.

It was coming. Yili saw it clearly, or as clearly as he ever had. She could not escape.

He acted without thinking, standing and throwing himself at the god-woman. Her eyes widened in shocked surprise, then his shoulder made contact with her belly, and they both fell to the ground. Something - the Beast - raced through the space they had just vacated. Yili felt the air stir in its passage. It was both terror and adrenaline that brought the shiver up his spine, but he payed it no mind.

They had to keep moving.

Yili rolled off Care-ul and pushed himself onto his feet. She did the same, gingerly. But she wore a grateful expression. An improvement, and something that brought a brief smile to his face.

Caeli's shriek drove the smile away. He turned around in time to see the Beast's shadow sweep over her, sending her sprawling to the ground in a heap.

His heart lurched to see it. Then he went cold with terror as he realized the Beast was heading straight for him next. He braced himself for the blow, knowing it was futile, that he could not avoid it, or survive it.

But then the Beast was no longer there.

He blinked in confusion. What was going on?

The sight of Caeli's sprawled form drove the question from his mind. He sprang forward, to her side. And had to avert his eyes. The blood. The way her head was twisted around so that her face looked over her back. It was too ghastly to look at.

Oh, the poor children. His poor boys. They were too young… There was no way to explain this to them; they were unready for such a blow.

Just as he was not ready for the blow that landed on the back of his neck. Surprised, shocked, stunned from the sudden explosion of pain, he collapsed to the ground. His vision was a blur of shapes and flashing stars, but he managed to blink the worst of it away and look up.

Care-ul stood over him, horrified contempt on her face. What was she doing?

"You!" she growled.

The last thing he saw was the bottom of her foot as she kicked him in the face. Then it all went black.

Pain was Yili's companion as he awoke. Pain in his neck and head where Care-ul had struck him. But another, different pain as well. The muscles in his arms and shoulders burned, as did his wrists. It was confusing, until he opened his eyes.

He was in the village, within the hut they had used to house Care-ul when he first brought her there. But he was given no furs to sleep in. His hands were bound with ropes made of vines and stretched above his head to two of the ceiling corners. He had been asleep standing up, his weight on the ropes. No wonder his arms and shoulders hurt, and his wrists.

The confusion only grew stronger. Why was he tied like this? What was going on?

Sunlight streamed in the hut's entrance; not too much time had passed. There would probably be a guard outside. He had to warn whomever it was. The village had to prepare in case the Beast returned.

Before he could say anything, a figure stepped into the entrance, blocking out the sun. It paused for a short time, considering him he thought, then moved within. As it left the sun's glare, Yili could make out its features more clearly.

Shumay.

The old woman stood still, silent, looking at Yili as though at someone she had never seen before. More than the vines binding his arms, her stare made him uncomfortable. Fearful even.

Finally he could bear it no more. "What are you doing to me?" he said, his tone harsh, more harsh than he intended, than he ever would have dreamed to use with the wisest.

Shumay's lips compressed slightly, as good as a scowl from another person. But she did not answer. She merely watched him, her eyes narrowed. He got the impression she was trying to stare right through him.

"Let me go!" Why was she doing this? "Shumay, the Beast - "
"Silence."

She spoke quietly, but then she always did. But her tone carried an edge of command that screamed in its intensity. In spite of himself, Yili found his jaws snapping shut, the CLACK of his teeth meeting seeming to echo in his head.

Shumay stepped forward, stopping within arms-length of him. She had to crane her neck to look up into his eyes, but she nevertheless seemed to be looking down at him from the heights.

"Never in my lifetime has the Beast actually taken anyone," Shumay said in a near-whisper. "Until Jola. And then the god-man, Air-ick." She paused, her stare, if possible, growing more intense before she added, "And now Caeli."

Yili had almost forgotten Caeli's fate, so focused he was on his predicament. His heart lurched to remember, but not with hope-less pain, as he just a year ago imagined it would have had he lost her. It was more like a faint regret.

Shumay sniffed. "You are as un-phased now as you were with Jola's passing. I thought then you were being strong for his widow and children. Now I am not so sure."

"What are you saying?"

Instead of replying immediately, Shumay turned away from him and took a step toward the hut's entrance. She drew a deep breath.

"You were very quick to marry Caeli after Jola died." She was making a statement, but Yili could hear the question behind her words.

"It was the right thing to so. The twins…"

"You never had feelings for her before then? You never wished she had married you and not your brother?"

Yili recoiled. As far as he could, anyway. Yes, he had wanted Caeli. Wanted her more than any other woman in the village. But she had only ever had eyes for Jola, and who was he to get between her and his brother? But what did that matter?

Shumay waited in silence for his answer. When he did not reply, she turned back to him, an eyebrow crooking upward knowingly. "I thought so." Her eyes flickered from his face to his hands, where they were bound, as though assuring herself he was secured. "The god-woman is beautiful," she said, looking back into his eyes.

The change in topic confused him. Where was she going with this?

"Everyone has seen you staring at her, watching her. You always are there to do things for her."

"I found her. It was a duty."

Shumay nodded. "And I agreed with it. As did your wife. But in the last few days, even she began to wonder."

Wonder? Wonder what? That he would be unfaithful? Never! He opened his mouth to protest, but Shumay beat him to it.

"What happened to the god-man, Air-ick?"

"What? I told you. The Beast - "

Shumay made a dismissive gesture. "Yes, the Beast. You said. A being of darkness that never truly shows itself. And only *you* have ever seen. And that, within the memories of everyone in the village, has only ever taken someone who had something…someone…that you wanted for yourself."

It was like falling from a tree and landing flat on his back. Yili felt as though the breath was forced from his lungs despite the fact that he had not been struck, so strong was the impact of Shumay's words. "You cannot mean - "

Shumay held up one finger. "You wanted Caeli, but she was married to Jola. Jola is dead." A second finger. "You became enamored with the god-woman, but she was with Air-ick. They were strangers to everyone. Air-ick is dead." A third finger. "She became more appealing to you than your wife. Your wife is dead. And you seem not to mourn at all." Shumay closed her fingers into a fist. "The pattern is clear, Yili."

"That is crazy! The Beast! It killed Air-ick on the beach. It followed us through the woods and killed Caeli. It's loose! If it comes to the village - "

Shumay made a soft tsking sound. "Ah, but it is already here." Her index finger extended, pointing at Yili.

A chill of fear, somehow greater than the fear he had felt when facing down the Beast on the beach and in the woods, crawled down Yili's spine. He shook his head in denial.

"The god-woman - "

"Care-ul."

Shumay sniffed, then continued. "Care-ul has become rather skilled with the language, Yili. She told us what she saw."

The fear faded a bit, replaced by a sudden hope. If Care-ul could tell it well, everything would be alright. Shumay and the other elders would see the danger and release him, so he could help defend the village. Somehow. But…wait. Why did… "Why do you trust what she says? You told me she was unstable. A threat."

Now Shumay looked surprised. Shocked. "I told you to watch her, Yili."

"No, no. Just today, when Caeli followed her into the woods, you told me…"

"These are the first words I've spoken with you today, Yili. The other elders and I climbed the peak early this morning, to commune."

That was impossible. Who had he spoken with then?

"Would you like to hear what Care-ul saw?"

Yili nodded, unable to fully process what has being said. It made no sense.

"Caeli had just accused her of cavorting with you when you found them. You were frothing with rage, made no sense. You kept babbling about the Beast, as you had on the beach. She grew afraid and ran. Later, near the path up the mountain, she saw you holding Caeli down behind a bush. She looked terrified, so Care-ul decided to help her." Shumay's voice turned cold and her eyes seemed to glow with an inner light. Indignation, maybe. "You saw her coming and knocked her over, and then brought the stone down on Caeli's head."

"What? No. The Beast… It was coming for us, and I… I saved Care-ul's life!"

Shumay just looked at him, condemnation in her eyes.

"How can you take her word over mine? You don't even trust her."

Shumay made the sign that invoked the Gods and inclined her head slightly, her eyes never leaving his. "When we spoke at the funeral site, what did I tell you?"

Yili frowned and tried to remember. The days…weeks?…since then were a blur. It was difficult to recall. Odd, that. He had always had a good memory. He felt sweat beading on his brow, and not just from the day's heat. "You…" He could not recall. What had she… Ah! "You said she and Air-ick had been sent by the Gods, and that the Beast may try to thwart them. That I should watch in case she became a threat to us."

Shumay's eyebrow quirked upward. "I do not recall thinking she may become a threat, let alone saying it." She drew breath and crossed her arms over her chest, in the manner the elders did during the prayer to ward off evil. "I said she might bring danger to us, because of the things the Beast might do in its battle against her and Air-ick. I wish that I had not been right." She sighed, shaking her head ruefully. "Or that I had seen the truth of the Beast's plotting sooner. If I had, all this may have been avoided."

She saw the question in Yili's eyes before he could voice it. Accusatio—no, contempt—in her eyes, she spoke again, clarifying. "You are the Beast, Yili. *You*."

With that, Shumay turned and left the hut. Yili shouted after her, denying her words. Denying the accusation, but no answer came back in response.

Yili lost count of the number of days he remained there, tied within the hut. From time to time one of the village women would come in, bringing water or some food, or to clean up his mess, though that was less frequent. And of course the sun set and rose. All the while he expected to perish at any moment, because surely the Beast would come to the village, seeking Care-ul. Surely it would not cease its designs, and they would all pay in blood.

But that never happened.

Once, he thought he saw the flickering darkness that he had come to recognize as the Beast's presence. It happened during one of his feedings. He thought sure Sala was going to be the first of many to die. He fought against the vines binding him, desperate to free himself so he could try to defend her, and the others. He fought so hard that she fled, shrieking in fear. But the darkness never re-appeared.

Even when two of the village men came in and thrashed him for, as they said, scaring poor Sala and never mind that he saw her in danger and was trying to help, the darkness never came back.

Through the pain of his chastisement, Yili nevertheless said a prayer of thanks that the village had been spared, somehow.

And yet, all those countless days passed without incident, except that he became ever weaker despite the food he was fed. It got to the point where he could barely raise his head to eat and drink. His shoulders and arms had long since gone through agony into numbness, and he seriously doubted he would be able to move them for a long time once he was released, assuming he ever was.

And it seemed he never would be.

Yili's days became a blur of discomfort and despair, his nights a terrifying return to memory and fear-dreams brought on by his uncertainty and the accusations against him. Or at least that was what he told himself.

In his dreams, he killed Jola himself, breaking his brother's knees with a rock and then roasting him alive over a pit of coals that he had prepared for that very purpose. He broke Air-ick's ankles using a heavy stick he had brought with him from the beach. Then he bludgeoned the god-man to death with the stick and buried him in the sand before dragging his woman off the beach. And Caeli... The dreams of Caeli were the worst. Her looking up at him with trusting eyes, believing him when he told her the Beast was coming. The faith in him only fading finally when he raised the rock against her.

Always he woke with a shout of denial. And then he cursed Shumay, cursed Care-ul, cursed all of them for making these false accusations against him. And worse, for making him doubt himself. Making him begin to think maybe they were correct, and he really was the monster they claimed.

No answer came. And no visitors save those who tended to him, and they said nothing.

Until finally it all changed.

Not long after he awoke, he could only guess how many mornings after he had been imprisoned there, three men entered the tent. Two of them went to his hands and began working the vines that held them up while the third stood before him, a scowl on his face. Yili knew all three men, of course. He had grown up with two of them and had been mentored by the third. But for whatever reason, though he knew their faces he could not recall their names. It was as if they had become strangers to him, as he had seemingly become to them.

The vines loosened, then released completely and he slumped to his knees. Only the men's quick action to catch him prevented him falling all the way to the ground. They boosted him up, one on each shoulder, and shifted around for a moment until they had him in a comfortable position ;comfortable for them, at least.

It struck Yili that he could escape rather easily, since they had made no move to tie him up again; they simply draped his arms across their shoulders. But he found that he could not move his arms at all, as he had feared would be the case; there was no need for them to bind him again. Of course, they had known it before he did.

The third man, the older one and the one in charge, nodded and said gruffly, "Bring him."

They began a long trek down the mountain. Not long in the sense that it was any great distance; he had made the journey many dozens of times in the past. But never had he been so weak, so helpless, so crippled during the walk down the path. Even with the two other men's support it seemed to take forever.

At the base of the mountain, they surprised Yili by turning left, away from the beach the people most often visited, the beach where Yili had met Air-ick and Care-ul. Instead, they circled around the mountain to the leeward side of the island, where the shore was more rock than sand and the breeze hardly ever blew except during the rainy season.

Finally, after a longer walk than Yili imagined possible given how short a distance it really was, they arrived at a small cove. Flanked on one side by outcropping rocks and on the other by a spur of sand that contained a few hardy palm trees and little else, the cove was familiar. Yili had come here with Caeli and the children many times before to watch the sunset. At the outset of the rainy season, all of the people gathered there for the feast to welcome the changing of the winds.

Indeed, Yili was surprised to note the winds were coming from the south, blowing past the outcrop of sand and creating a steady chop in the water. Had he been in that hut so long that the seasons had turned without his noticing?

Impossible, and yet the winds said otherwise.

All the people of the village were gathered in a loose arc at the cove's central beach. The arc opened to admit him and his escorts —guards—and Yili found yet another surprise waiting within.

At the water's edge was the strangest thing he had ever seen. Resembling the wall of a hut, it was a collection of logs that were lashed together with vines, but it lay flat just above the sand, supported by three larger logs beneath the wall itself. From the center of the flat wall, a single larger log stood straight up. Vines were tied from the corners of the flat wall to the top of the erect log, holding it in place.

Yili blinked, unable to comprehend what this thing was. But whatever its purpose, the three men guiding him dragged him toward it. That meant it could not be good. Yili tried to fight against them, but they were much stronger than he, and the battle was over before it was fought. Before long, he stood—was held—in front of the strange thing.

Shumay's voice drew his attention to the side, where she stood along with the rest of the elders.

"This is a day we have spoken of for some time now. And though we disagreed at first, I believe we all agree this is how it must be if we are to purge the Beast from our midst while remaining pure ourselves." Shumay's eyes swept the crowd and Yili followed with his own gaze. He saw no sign of dissent. If anything, he saw admiration and agreement when people looked at Shumay. When they looked at him...only condemnation, derision, and beneath it, fear.

"Yili," Shumay went on. He looked at her, giving her his full attention. Why not? "Many here thought you should be put to death for your crimes. But we decided your fate should be decided by the Gods." By the Gods? How would the Gods... And then Shumay answered him. "Care-ul is building a thing, she calls it a raft, to bring her back to her lands. We have been assisting her, and it was from learning what she has taught that we built this for you." She gestured toward the strange thing at the edge of the water. What was it she called it, a raft?

Yili looked incredulously at the thing. How was it supposed to interface with the Gods?

Again Shumay answered him. "Here the breakers are the weakest on the island. Here Care-ul will depart in two weeks' time. And here you will depart today."

Two men broke off from the crowd and carried objects to the raft. Coconuts, smoked meat from boars, a blanket made from boar's hide. Waterskins, several of them. They set those things on the raft and tied them in place next to the erect log using vines that were laid out for that purpose.

If Yili had felt despair before, it was but a shadow compared to what he felt now. They could not be serious. He opened his mouth to appeal, but all that came out was a croak.

Shumay spoke again. "You have food and water for a week.

Two if you are careful. Care-ul says it is possible you may find aid in that time, from other god-people who ride on the waves." She crossed her arms over her chest, and the other elders followed suit. "If it is the Gods' will that you live, that your punishment has been sufficient, you will. If not..." She left the rest unsaid.

This could not be happening.

The two men holding him up moved forward and dumped him onto the thing, the raft. The logs were rough, and he felt several stabs as protrusions from the bark dug into his exposed skin. He tried to push himself up. To push himself off the thing. But he could not move, only squirm ineffectually.

He felt the raft begin to move under him and turned his head. A half-dozen men were pushing it off the beach and into the water.

No! How could they do this? Man was forbidden the sea!

But they did not think he was a man anymore, did they?

A rustling from behind him drew his attention. He looked up and saw a single man standing on the raft with him. He was hoisting away on a vine that was tied to the top of the erect log. As he pulled, a triangular shape unfurled from the other side of the raft. It took Yili a moment to realize it was a collection of boar hides that had been sewn together, like a woman's blouse except larger. What was it for?

The man—Toram his name was—finished hoisting and tied the vine off, then dropped the loose end. Then he jumped off the raft, landing thigh deep into the water. Was he already that far away from the beach? Yili was going to turn and look, but then the triangle made a WHOMP and filled with the wind that was blowing form the south. Almost immediately, the raft began moving faster, toward the breakers.

What a wonder was that?

From behind—far behind it seemed—Yili heard Shumay's voice again. "May the Gods watch over you, and guide you to your fate."

He glanced back and his stomach lurched to see how far away he was from the beach now. Fifty paces? Seventy-five?

The breakers were closer now, their continuous surf growing ever louder. Yili forced his hands to grab onto the vines holding the raft together. Perhaps he would not be thrown off. He did not want to be thrown off; he could not pull himself through the water the way Air-ick had.

He shuddered to think of drowning.

He looked back at the beach again. The people remained there, watching him drift away. No one moved to assist, to try to bring him back. Then, behind them, he saw something. A flickering of blackness.

The Beast. It had come finally.

Despite his dread, his heart leapt. They would see it. See that they were wrong about him. And they would come rescue him before it was too late.

"How?" said a voice in his head. He refused to listen to it.

The blackness danced across the beach to the people's left, but they paid it no heed. Yili tried to call out to them, but again only a croak came forth.

Then water covered him. The breakers!

He held on to the vine, terror giving him strength he did not realize he could muster.

Again a wave hit. And again. But somehow he kept his grip.

And then the breakers were behind him. The raft was still afloat, the boar hide triangle still intact, and he was still making progress away from the beach. From the island.

The blackness flashed through the people now, but none of them moved. No one cried out, or even seemed to notice. It streaked over the water, crossing the lagoon and then the breakers.

Oh Gods, the Beast was coming for him! It was the Gods' punishment personified, or perhaps their mercy. A quick death instead of starvation or dying of thirst.

Yili found that was little comfort.

The blackness swept closer and Yili cringed away, bracing himself for the blow he knew was to come. He closed his eyes, not wanting to see.

But the blow never came.

After a moment, he slowly opened his eyes.

There, sitting on the raft beside him, was a man. Except that he was a man made from the blackest of darkness. And yet somehow Yili could make out features beginning to form within that darkness. Gradually, the man's face became clear, and Yili's bowels turned to water.

He knew that face. He had seen it countless times when he looked into the water of the drinking pool.

The face was his own.

He screamed then, a scream of denial, of despair, of acknowledgement.

And the Beast, the darkness within him, his only companion left in the world, smiled at him as they sailed away to meet their fate together on the waves of the sea.

What Lurks Between

From a place beyond reality, it comes to consume the world

Michael Kingswood

Author of the Glimmer Vale Chronicles

WHAT LURKS BETWEEN

I t came from outer space.

Well...sort of.

It actually came out of my lunchbox. But I brought my lunchbox into outer space that day, and trust me, it was *not* in that lunchbox before I went up. That's how come I can say it came from outer space.

What was it? Long story, but it starts simply enough.

So there I was, and this is a no shi—

Erm...sorry. That's the Navy in me coming out. But trust me, this really happened. Really.

Like I said, it started out as just another day on the job...

"Barry!"

I turned away from my locker to see Clark Haberman, the very last person I wanted to deal with, walking toward me. As usual, he wore his light-gray work coveralls, cinched at the waist with a black web belt that supported a number of tool pouches, and a scowl on his weathered face. Christ, what had I done now? I couldn't think of anything I'd screwed up lately, but Clark never got that look except when something had gone seriously wrong.

"Yeah, boss," I said, inwardly wincing as I anticipated the diatribe to come. I was amazed when it never did.

"You've been reassigned."

I blinked.

"You hear what I said? You're not working here anymore."

So that's how it was. I sighed and lowered my eyes. I had been fired before, lots of times, but at least the other bosses didn't screw around trying to make nice about it. "We don't need you anymore." "You messed up one too many things." "Get lost, loser." I had heard them all. But never reassignment. That was rich.

I let out a bitter laugh before I was able to catch myself. From the corner of my eye, I saw Clark's eyebrows twitch upward in...confusion?

No way.

"I ain't joking, dude. They want you up on Ketcham Station, starting today."

Clark held out a printout as he spoke. Expecting yet another pathetic joke at my expense, I snatched it away and began reading. As I did, my bitterness and fatalism faded, replaced by amazement. And maybe just a smidgen of hope.

"Congratulations," the note began. I could not recall the last time anyone had congratulated me for anything. It continued, "Your application for service aboard the Ketcham Station has been accepted. You will begin work on 27 April. Report to shuttle station seven at 0930 for transport. Welcome aboard!" The note was unsigned, but it came on company letterhead, and the office code at the top indicated it was from Human Resources.

"I didn't apply for duty on Ketcham Station," I murmured.

"I applied for you," Carl said, his scowl becoming more like a sneer. "You're always talking about how you should have stayed in the Navy. Ketcham's a ship. Sort of." He cleared his throat softly. "Anyway, I figured it was time you moved on to something better."

Better. Right. The Ketcham Station was a hole, and everyone knew it. Old, dilapidated, and about ready to de-orbit any week now, if the rumor-mill was to be believed. So yeah, I *was* getting fired again. So much for that smidgen of hope.

Oh well. At least this time I got to keep a paycheck. And, truth be told, if Ketcham Station was as run-down as they said, it would probably have plenty of work to keep an electrician like me busy for a while. Maybe I could rack up some more overtime on this gig.

"Great." I tried to sound like I meant it. Then I saw the clock: 0900. The shuttle station was a twenty minute walk from the locker room. Crap.

Wasting no time on chit-chat, I turned back to my locker and pulled out my duffle bag. It did not take long to pack all of my stuff; I only kept my lunchbox, a towel and soap, and the clothes I wore to work - jeans, a t-shirt from a trip to the Alamo, and a pair of beat-up sneakers - in there. Other guys kept their lockers full; I guess I never expected to stay all that long.

"Well," Carl said as I packed up, "good luck up there. Been nice working with you."

I knew he was lying, but it was nice of him to say it. Maybe he wasn't a total schmuck after all.

I stepped back from the locker and stared at it for a minute. I had not worked there long, but I had hoped that maybe this time would be different. Seeing the locker empty like that gave me a weird feeling. You know people say it was like someone was walking over their grave? Sort of like that.

But I did not have time to dwell on that if I was going to make the shuttle. With a grunt, I shouldered the duffle bag. Then I tugged the front of my gray work coveralls to smooth them out and turned away. My work boots made hollow echoes as I walked out of the deserted room.

When I returned to my apartment three days later, I was exhausted. The kind of tired where you see spots and talk to someone only to realize you are totally alone. I barely had the energy and wherewithal to kick my shoes off and drop my duffel before I collapsed onto my old threadbare couch.

Then I slept the sleep of the dead.

I came to eighteen hours later. It took a long moment to figure out where I was. I looked one way, then the other, and it was like I was staring at a foreign land.

Well, almost.

The pictures on the walls, the stuffed leather chair in the corner, the oversized video display unit on the wall, the kitchenette tucked into the rear corner, the door to the hall off to the left, a small door on the opposite wall leading into the bathroom, and behind me the double-doors that housed my pull-down bed were all familiar, but I could not place them at first. I was still that tired, even after that much sleep. Plus, I felt like hell; I had a sour taste in my mouth, like I'd been sucking on a lemon or something, and I ached all over.

Eventually it clicked. Home. A crappy little studio in a crappy portion of town.

No place like it.

It took a minute to push myself up off the couch. My aching muscles protested all the way. At least that made sense; I had worked hard on the station, though strangely my memories of what exactly I worked on were foggy. I chalked it up to my earlier exhaustion. Add to that the weird transition from full gravity to zero g on the shuttle to .5g on the station to zero g back to full gravity again and I was not the least bit surprised about the soreness.

I stumbled over to the little bathroom - it was the only separate room in my apartment - and, resting my hands on the sink, stared at myself in the mirror for a moment.

I *looked* like hell, too. Hair tussled, shadows under my bloodshot eyes. It was almost like I had been out drinking, except for the lack of headache.

"Get it together," I told myself, and pulled my toothbrush out of the medicine cabinet.

I was in the middle of brushing when I heard it. A rattling, or a scratching really, out in the main room.

More roaches? Sonofa... I just had the place fumigated a month ago. How could they be back so quickly? Muttering angry nothings under my breath, I dropped my toothbrush into the sink and stalked out into the room.

It was not roaches.

Whatever it was was shaking my duffle bag, almost as if something was inside and trying to get out. I gulped. I did not want to go see what this was. Killing bugs was one thing, but to make the duffle shake like that...was it a rat?

I used to play baseball in high school, then for a while in a local league. Though I don't play anymore, I kept my bat, a genuine Louisville Slugger. They are hard to find these days, and it was probably worth a bit of money, so it would have been a shame to get rid of it. Besides, I always told myself I would get back into baseball at some point; I used to be pretty good. In the meantime, the Slugger made for a handy home defense weapon from time to time.

I darted over and snatched up the Slugger from where it lay propped up against my stuffed chair. It made me feel a bit better to hold the solid wood in my hands. Rats ain't got nothing that can handle this.

Drawing a deep breath, I eased my way over to the still shaking duffle and, grabbing it by the zipper handle, dumped its contents.

The items from the bag tumbled out and I retreated a step, the Slugger held up, ready to swing. The clothes and towel landed in a heap, but the lunchbox rolled a foot or so before landing on its side. There was nothing else.

Ok...what was going on?

The lunchbox lurched and actually bounced a centimeter or so off the ground. I had to bite back a little yelp of surprise - not sure how well I succeeded - as I retreated another step and ran into the side of the couch.

The lunchbox lurched again. The rattling and scratching sound was louder now. The top of the box shook, and the latch holding it shut seemed to strain.

Inwardly, I willed the latch to hold. Whatever was in that lunchbox, I did *not* want it coming out. I should probably wail on it with the Slugger. I could probably bust the box up pretty good; that would at least knock silly whatever was inside it, give me time to figure out what to do with it. The food macerator under the sink drain sprang to mind, but I shoved that thought down. Too gross.

But I could not bring myself to move. I watched, Slugger held impotently at my side, as the top lurched and strained against the latch again. And again.

Then the latch broke and the lunchbox top flopped open, hitting the floor with a tiny metallic thud.

I gulped again.

Another rattle issued from the lunchbox and out crawled...a bunny rabbit?

What the hell was a bunny doing in my lunchbox? It was silly. Ludicrous.

But hang it all, it was darn cute.

A little white bunny, right out of an Easter Egg commercial. It hopped over toward me, its ears flopping in time with its hops in the most adorable manner. I'm no pansy, but I couldn't help it. Nothing that cute could be bad. So I dropped the Slugger and squatted down.

It hopped over to me and I scooped it up in my arms. Its hair was smooth, soft, just the way you envision a bunny's should be.

Its ears were perky, but flexible, and it had little white whiskers growing from its snout. Its eyes were pinkish-red; that made sense. The all-white coat meant it was probably an albino, the eyes just confirmed it.

The bunny snuggled in against my body and I pet it. It shivered, almost the way a cat will shiver when it purrs, and I could not help smiling. Questions of how it got into my lunchbox faded beneath the pleasure of cuddling it next to me. I sat down on the couch and activated the display. The bunny slid off my lap onto the cushion next to me, still vibrating soothingly.

The news was on. God, I hate the news. I glanced over at the timepiece on the wall. The game should be starting soon. Better to watch that than...

"Tragedy on Ketcham station," said the anchor, a severe-faced man in his early middle years who dressed like an undertaker, and I sat bolt upright, a chill going down my spine.

I could not have heard that right. I gestured for the display volume to increase, certain I was mistaken.

But I was not.

An image appeared on the display, clearly shot through a high-power lens, showing Ketcham Station's distinctive egg shape tumbling erratically through space. Gasses were streaming from several holes in the hull and the exterior navigation lights flickered on and off at random intervals, as though the circuitry or power supply had been compromised.

The anchor continued, his deep monotone speaking over the video. "Middle Earth Orbit Traffic Control lost contact with the station late last night after receiving a number of disturbing transmissions, followed by a distress call. While they struggled to regain contact, a nearby tug was vectored in and shot the video you are now watching. So far Traffic Control has been unable to link another craft with the station, and there is no word on the status of the two hundred and fifty scientists and support personnel who worked onboard. Family and friends of Ketcham Station employees can direct inquiries to..."

I slumped back against the couch, stunned, and let the rest of the anchor's words slide past without taking note of them. What the hell happened up there? I could not remember anything going seriously wrong. But then, I could not remember much of anything at all. I racked my brain, trying to think. There was the shuttle up, the young woman who greeted me at the airlock, and then...nothing. It was all a blur. Then something else sprang to mind, something that made the earlier chill in my spine turn into an icy feeling of dread.

How the hell did I get back home?

The bunny, still sitting next to me, squirmed. The little vibration it was making changed, becoming less soothing and more jarring, almost like when a musician hits the wrong note in a harmony part. I looked down at it, and dread turned into sheer terror.

This was no ordinary rabbit.

It crouched there on the sofa cushions, staring right back at me. Its irises, which before were albino pink, were now blood red, and its pupils were slits. Its ears were stiffer, their tips more pointed and also tinged with red. I became aware of something digging into my thigh through my pants and slid away. The thing's right front paw dropped down onto the cushion, leaving three little puncture wounds in my leg from long, sharp claws.

Run! Get up and run, jackass!

I felt like I was screaming that at myself, but I could not make my muscles respond. The best I could do was push as far away from it as I could, right up to the edge of the couch.

The thing just stared at me for a second. Then its lips drew back into a vicious little grin.

It had big, sharp, pointy teeth.

My muscles finally obeyed my mind's frantic pleas, and I bolted. I was off the couch in a heartbeat and heading toward the door. But the thing was faster. It snarled - a much louder snarl than I would have thought it capable of - and a second later it landed on my upper back, between my shoulder blades.

Pain flared from a dozen locations as the claws at the ends of its paws dug in. I thrashed around to try to get it off. Then a new, more intense pain came from the side of my neck.

I passed out.

I awoke to an awful pressure on my chest, as though a couple of burly guys were laying atop me. It was hard to draw breath. Very hard. As I slowly came around, I found myself wondering if my ribs would give way.

And then I opened my eyes.

I found myself staring straight into the bunny-thing's blood red gaze. I was lying on my back and it was sitting on my chest, staring at me. That's it. No big burly guys, just that little bunny-thing. It was a hell of a lot heavier than it looked. It noticed me waking up and grinned again. Its fangs were still there. More disturbing still, the fur around its mouth was stained red.

The ache in the side of my neck registered, and I flinched away as the source of the stains around the bunny's mouth became clear to me. Well, I tried to flinch, but the thing's weight prevented me from moving very far at all.

The thing's grin grew wider.

There's no point in trying to flee, Barry.

I heard the words in my head, but knew that the thought was not mine. Oh dear Lord it could read my...

Your blood is mine. I own you.

Its tongue caressed its fangs slowly, seductively. I had seen women use their tongues similarly, licking their lips while flirting. The display was quite a bit less arousing on this thing.

"What..." I cleared my throat, the tried again. "What are you?"

I am your master.

193

There was more than a hint of annoyance in the thought's tone. As though to accentuate its point, the thing dugs its fore-paws into my chest, sending lances of pain radiating from the area. I gritted my teeth, but groaned at the renewed discomfort.

"Stop."

Stop please, master.

It dug its claws in a bit deeper. It was as though someone was dripping molten metal onto my chest. For an instant, I had the notion of swiping it off of me. I was a strong guy; I should be able to do that. But the pain just escalated when I thought it. Worse, I found I could not move my limbs.

I had no choice. My ego rebelled against it, but I could not stand the pain any longer.

"Stop. Please." I had to draw a breath to get the last word out. "Master."

All at once, the pain ceased.

Good. The voice in my head sounded satisfied, pleased. *You learn quickly.*

I could not suppress a snort. *That* was something I had never been accused of before.

"What..." I cut off as the claws began digging in again, and the pain returned. I found myself groaning, and forced it down. Through gritted teeth I managed to mumble, "What do you want?"

The pain faded again, as quickly as it came. The bunny-thing looked at me for a long moment, its cat-like pupils narrowing in consideration. Another impulse to just shove it away came through me, but again it was as though my thoughts were disconnected from my body; I could not move a muscle.

Finally, it "spoke" again.

What I want... The creature's fangs seemed to lengthen, and I noticed little red stains on their tips. *I want food.*

I got a hollow feeling in my belly. Oh Lord, it was going to eat me.

It made a little coughing sound. Laughter?

You are not enough. Not for what I have to do. You will help me find more.

I somehow managed to swallow, despite having no saliva in my mouth. It could not mean what I thought it meant.

But it did.

I hugged my arms tight against my chest. Or as tightly as I could with the bunny - or whatever the hell it was - tucked into my trench coat with its nose poking out from the little V where the two flaps of the coat folded over each other.

I walked slowly down the street, a few blocks from my little apartment. The late autumn chill made my breath freeze in the night air in front of my face, but it was not the cold that made me shiver so.

It was the company.

The bunny monster had been insistent that we go out. I knew what it wanted, but I could not say no. Even when it was not digging its claws into me, I felt a...force...bearing down on my mind when it projected its desires into my head. I found myself doing its bidding before I realized what was going on.

I did not know how, but it had ahold of my mind. That was scary enough. The suspicion - no, the certainty - of what it sought was terrifying.

I went. Unwillingly, but I went trudging past the boarded up storefronts, the broken windows, the trash-laden streets. My little corner of Boston had never been the best neighborhood, but the last few years had been especially unkind. Businesses closed every week, or left for fairer shores despite the "best efforts" of the local officials to entice them to stay. I suppose all the promises of kickbacks and tax incentives in the world don't matter worth a damn if you can't enforce the basic rule of law.

Who would have figured?

My mind whirled as I picked my way past the detritus of a

failing city, and I could not help but feel it was appropriate to bear the bunny monster with me down the dark streets. If any place would feel like home for it, this would.

Then I felt that pressure in my head again.

There.

I stopped abruptly, glancing around in confusion. What was it...

That one.

The thought came accompanied by pain as its claws dug into my chest. I grimaced to hold back a scream and stumbled forward, nearly bending over double. What was it talking about? Where...

Then I saw, and a new chill spread down my spine.

I knew. I knew without it having to tell me, but I did not want to believe the bunny monster really meant it.

But when the bunny monster's claws loosened their grip as I finally noticed the homeless man slumped against the wall of an alley ten meters ahead on the other side of the street and I felt that pressure in my mind again, I could not deny the truth.

We were out to get food.

I could not stop myself. My feet seemed to move of their own accord, jogging across the street in the wake of a passing Yellow Cab, then turning left toward the homeless man's alley. Against my chest, the bunny monster began purring, or whatever it was, again.

As we approached, I saw the man's features as clearly as if it were noon, and never mind that it was approaching midnight. Curly brown hair that hung in unwashed strands from his head. A matching beard, complete with bit of paper - or food? - caught in the long whiskers. High cheekbones and dark, defeated eyes. A ratty overcoat with several holes in it that he held close about his thin body, trying to preserve what little heat the thin garment would retain.

On any other night I might have thought about giving him a buck.

When I stopped in front of him and gestured into the alley, his eyes narrowed suspiciously. "Wha chu wan, buddy?"

Just as my feet had moved on their own, I found myself speaking before I realized what was happening. "Want to earn some money?"

The homeless man's eyebrow quirked upward, then he spat off to the side. "I don' turn tricks."

I felt the bunny monster's purring change, and I felt, faintly, a wry, almost derisive amusement seeping into my mind.

"No tricks. Job pays two hundred."

Both eyebrows climbed high on the man's forehead, and he suddenly grinned. He had several missing teeth and breath that would knock a moose over at twenty meters. It was all I could do not to gag. But then I found myself gesturing into the alley again.

This time the man nodded and, licking his lips, began walking in that direction.

As I followed him and the light from the street faded, it was like I was watching someone else. My heart pounded in my chest, and I could acutely feel every pulse through my my neck; the sound of my heartbeat was like a bass drum in my ears. My mouth grew dry and I found myself beginning to tremble. Was I really going to let this happen?

But I could not stop it.

The nameless man rounded a corner in the alley, taking us completely out of view from the street, and turned to face me. Before he completed the movement, the rabbit monster shoved itself off my chest and, springing from the low neck of my trench coat, landed on the man's chest.

He had enough time to voice a wordless shout of surprise, then the beast was on him. Its little head darted upwards, toward the side of his neck, and I heard as much as saw its fangs penetrate.

The man's eyes widened, and his shout became a rasping gurgle as he staggered backwards, his hands going reflexively to his neck, and the creature latched on there. He tugged at the bunny monster, but it did not budge. He stumbled back again, turning to the side as he did so, and slammed his back into the side of the building to my left. He beat on the bunny monster with his fists.

But it was all in vain. After maybe thirty seconds, he slumped to the ground. His eyes lost focus and rolled up in their sockets. His limbs began to spasm, his feet drumming against the alley's cement paving stones. Then, finally, he lay still.

I watched this happen, my feet glued in place. Though part of my brain shouted, "Run, you idiot!", another part was, unbelievably, fascinated.

I had never seen a man die before.

By the time we returned to my apartment, self-loathing consumed me.

What had I done? I let this...thing...kill that poor man. I did not even try to stop it. Worse, part of me had enjoyed it, or at least was not completely repulsed by it.

I slammed the door shut and flung my wallet and keycard onto the small table standing next to the door, then made quick work of removing my trench coat and hurling it into the corner. Then I stumbled over to the couch and collapsed. I pressed my palms against my forehead and felt myself on the edge of tears.

The bunny-monster, whatever it was, hopped slowly across the small room toward the couch from where it had landed when I took off the trench coat.

Rest. More tomorrow.

I found myself sobbing as I shook my head in denial. "No," I whispered. "I can't."

The pressure came crashing down on my mind again, and I felt its weight upon me as it hopped up onto my abdomen. Pain lanced through me as it landed and dug in.

Were its claws longer? It felt like it.

You will. You cannot stop me.

The pain grew greater, and I heard myself scream. Thankfully, I lost consciousness soon after that. But the monster's final words echoed through my mind as dreams took me.

It continued that way for the next week.

When I was not asleep, or engaged in biological necessities, the bunny monster rode me out onto the streets. And every time we went out, it took another victim. I lost track of the number of nameless schlubs the bunny monster killed, but it was a lot. And a slideshow of faces, all dead now, were emblazoned on my memory.

I saw them when I slept. I saw them in the bathroom mirror when I brushed my teeth and shaved. When the monster let me do those mundane things, anyway, which was not often. I could not escape the memory of those poor people.

At some point during the week, it struck me that I needed to go into work. Clark had not actually fired me, after all. He might not care, but presumably the company would care that I was alright, not dead on Ketcham Station.

And how exactly had that worked out, anyway?

I had no idea. I still could not remember what happened up there, though it was improving. Instead of essentially a big black blur of no memory at all, I slowly began to get flashes. Just individual images, an occasional face, a spoken word. Not enough to make any sense of. But it was something.

The point was moot, though. No sooner had I voiced the thought about returning to work than the bunny monster put the kibosh on it. I was not to go anywhere without it, and it was not going to my place of employment.

For a moment, before the pain began, I had the impression it was actually afraid of where I worked, for some reason.

Then I learned never to think on such things again.

By the end of the week, I began to notice a change. The bunny monster was larger.

But not all over.

Its claws had definitely grown - I had felt them too many times to not notice that. As had its fangs. The rest of its body, however, remained the same size it always had been.

Except for its belly.

At first I thought I was imagining things. It moved more slowly around my apartment, and when we went out and it pounced on a victim. But it was always a small enough difference that I could not be sure.

Then, one night, a week and a half after we first met, the bunny monster almost missed a meal. The poor schlub it picked out ducked its initial attack and ran away, screaming. For a moment, I thought he would actually get away, as difficult as the chase appeared to be for the monster. But finally, get him it did.

When it forced me back home, I looked at it - really looked - for a long time. There could be no doubt, now that I concentrated enough to really note the differences.

Its belly was most definitely larger. At one point, I swore I saw part of its belly move, even. I shrank back, swallowing hard. I thought I was past terror after the last week being held prisoner by that thing, but I felt a new, icy feeling of dread in my gut as I considered what I saw.

The bunny monster turned its head toward me right then. Its catlike eyes narrowed, seemed to grow more brightly red for a moment. Then it ran its little tongue over its lips and sniffed the air.

Soon.

The intruding thought echoed in my mind, its intensity making me rock back for a moment. The thought contained a deep, grim satisfaction, coupled with a primal eagerness that was barely contained. Were I that eager for something, I would be bouncing off the walls, but the bunny monster simply sat there, gazing at me with its unsettling eyes for a moment.

Then it smiled.

They will come soon.

That dread became sheer horror as I suddenly understood.

The creature was female.

How do you kill something that has complete, or near enough that it makes no difference, control over you? Something that you know from experience can kill *you* with little effort, and will if given the slightest cause to do so? Something that seems to know what you are thinking before you do?

That was the question that ate at my soul. Assuming I still had a soul, after what I had seen it do. What I had *allowed* it to do.

But I knew, sure as I was sitting there when the full meaning of the bunny monster's projected thought became clear to me, that this was what I had to do.

Under no circumstances could I allow that...thing...to give birth.

I could tell it sensed my revulsion as realization came over me. It's little lips turned upwards into a feral grin and it made a short, mocking, purring sound. Then it turned away and hopped over to its favorite side of my couch, where it nuzzled into the corner and went still.

The thing slept. It was a living creature, so of course it slept. Problem was, it usually slept when I did. On those few times when it had fallen asleep before me, it had been tempting to try something: to leave, to bash its brains in, something. Except that the very first time it slept in front of me, I did try something. Something so ridiculously minor it almost did not bear noticing.

Its rear paw was resting on one of my comic books. I tried to pull the comic out so I could read it. The bunny monster almost killed me.

Since then, I feared doing anything more than sitting or lying still. Even going to the bathroom in the middle of the night was a terror. I was tempted just to wet my bed and clean up later, except that I had no idea when later would be, since when the bunny monster was awake it allowed me to do nothing except bring it out for food or feed myself.

The apartment was beginning to stink bad enough without adding *that* sort of mess to it.

That afternoon, after the bunny monster's revelation, was the first time it had fallen asleep so early. Was it possible that I could find an opening somewhere?

I thought back over my life, back to when my mom was pregnant with my baby brother. I was ten, and I had no idea where my father was, but lo and behold here was a little brother, due for the world in a few months. When she told me, my feelings were mixed, but as time moved on I became more and more excited to have a brother, even one so much younger than I. That eagerness faded a bit when Mom grew - how do they put it? - "great with child". She was uncomfortable - hell, miserable - all the time. And she had only a fraction of the energy she normally did. I remember her sleeping a lot, and being damn hard to wake up.

It was that memory that convinced me I had a chance, even just a small one, to stop this thing before it got out of hand. And for some reason I was certain once that thing gave birth, that was exactly how things would become. Officially.

That just left figuring out how, exactly, to do it.

Seriously, how does one kill a vampire? I knew beyond a shadow of a doubt that was what the bunny monster was. Hell, I had seen it drink more blood than I ever thought possible.

I racked my brain, trying to recall all the little clues from vampire lore, but found nothing helpful.

More often than not, I cooked spaghetti for myself. It was quick and easy, and fit with the bunny monster's demanding schedule. I tried putting more than the usual amount of garlic in the sauce, hoping that the cloves would induce the bunny monster to leave. If anything, the smell of the garlic seemed to make it lick its lips with appetite.

Holy water? I did not have any, and I had no means to get any. But one night we walked past a church and I veered inside, just to see what would happen. The bunny monster's claws dug into me painfully, as expected, but no more or less than any other time I did not do exactly what it said. In fact, aside from its chagrin at my disobedience, it seemed perfectly comfortable within hallowed ground.

From that I deduced that holy blessings or other spiritual things mattered little to the bunny monster. And besides, in every story I could remember you had to believe - really believe - in that stuff to make it work. That was not me.

So much for trying to ward it off with a crucifix.

What to do? Staring at it, its chest rising slowly with each inhalation as it slept, I just wanted to grab a butcher knife from the block in my kitchenette and stab it to death.

But what if that didn't work? I shuddered to think of what it would do to me if I tried and failed. If it sucked me dry, like it did with those homeless men and women, would I live to feel the last drop leaving? Would part of me be trapped within it and its offspring, living - if you could call it that - in terror forever?

That was asinine, but I could not get the thought out of my head. So I sat there, impotent in my fear, and drifted off to sleep while I had the chance.

I awoke a short while later, sitting upright with a start. My heart was pounding, and I was wet with sweat.

The dream must have been a doozy, but I could not remember any of it. That was odd; I normally remembered most of my dreams. Going back over them helped ease the drudgery of my work days, a lot of the time.

Wiping the sweat off my brow, I decided it was probably just as well that I did not remember. Any dream that left me in such a state was best cast aside as quickly as possible. Besides, whatever the waking world, and the bunny monster, had to throw at me would be so much worse...

I glanced aside and did a double-take. The bunny monster was still asleep.

That was odd. Ever since it first arrived, it had awakened before I did. Most times, until the last couple days as its pregnancy grew more pronounced, it had been awake when I fell asleep as well. Oh, I had caught it napping a time or two, but rarely. This...this was unheard-of.

Moving carefully to avoid disturbing the bunny monster's cushion, I boosted myself up from the couch. As I reached my feet, I was struck by the urge to flee. Just run out the door and get the hell out of there. Go to the nearest police station and tell them what happened, so they could come in force and take the bunny monster down.

No sooner had I thought it than I recognized how stupid that thought was. The police would not believe me. Best case, they would ship me off to the funny farm. Worst case, they would lock me up and charge me with all those homeless people's deaths. Or both. By the time they realized I was telling the truth, the bunny monster would have given birth, and so, maybe, would have its offspring.

And then it would be too late.

No, there was no shoving the bunny monster problem off on someone else. I had to deal with it. And quickly.

But first, I needed to brush my teeth. They felt like they had a year's worth of accumulated gunk on them, but it had only been a week or so since I last managed the time to take care of that little chore, and I had a horrible metallic taste in my mouth.

I trudged over to the bathroom, scratching at an itch on my forearm, and tried hard not to notice how I smelled. I was sure I probably put those homeless people to shame.

I looked even worse.

The person brushing his teeth in the mirror was almost unrecognizable. Unkempt brown hair that was...going grey? When did *that* happen?...at the temples, a scraggly beard that also bore its share of silver, sunken eyes with dark half-circles below them. A stained green t-shirt with some obnoxious logo or other on the breast. All in all, I looked like hell boiled over.

I could not imagine why.

I swished and spit, and found myself transfixed by the sight of the water from the faucet as it took hold of the foamy residue from my mouth and swirled it down the drain.

I blinked, then spat again and watched it flow away. There was something about it...

An image flashed through my mind, like a single frame inserted into a movie, and I almost fell over. I had to grab the sides of the sink to keep my feet.

What the hell was that?

It came again, and I found myself sagging forward. My forehead touched the mirror, and I remembered.

I *saw*.

I was back on Ketcham Station, repairing some fried wiring in the rear of a backup lighting switchboard. They had experienced a minor malfunction that managed to knock out their primary lighting a couple days earlier. The backups had engaged automatically, of course. But several of the backup lighting strings failed, hence their urgent need for an electrician, once the initial malfunction was resolved.

The wiring in that particular switchboard was mostly intact, so I quickly finished, closed up the switchboard panel, and moved on. Or tried to move on.

The switchboard was directly opposite one of the station's research labs. What exactly they were doing was beyond me, and well above my pay grade, so I made sure not to pay too much attention. Easier to avoid trouble that way.

But something in the lab caught my eye, and I found myself stepping toward the large plexiglass window that separated the lab from the corridor where I was working. I glanced around, but none of the white lab coat wearing people noticed me. Their attention was fixed on some device toward the rear of the lab. I could not see what it was, but clearly it was important.

From another room, off to the left, a burly scientist entered the lab, carrying two wire mesh cages, one in each hand. Each cage held a cute white rabbit.

The bunnies seemed relaxed and content, even when the guy dropped their cages - quite abruptly - onto a countertop near the center of the room. Only when a couple of other researchers opened the cages, reached in, and yanked them out by the scruffs of their necks did the bunnies react, kicking and squirming in their captors' grips.

The researchers turned their backs to the window - to me - and carried the bunnies further back, toward the device I could not fully see, and I got a hollow feeling in the pit of my stomach. What were they doing to those little rabbits?

"What are you doing?"

The gruff female voice made me jump in surprise. I turned to see Dr. Liu, one of the more senior researchers on the station, glaring at me. She was in a white lab coat, like all the others, though her security badge had several more stripes of color than almost everyone else's did; she could go pretty much anywhere in the station she wanted. Her hair, still mostly black despite the fact that she was certainly in her mid fifties at least, was pulled back into a neat bun. All in all, she was not bad too look at...except for that glare.

I said something inane about just finishing up what I was doing and she grunted.

"Don't linger..." her eyes lowered and narrowed as she focused on my security badge, and my name, "...Barry. This is a security area. I'm sure there is more work for you elsewhere, yes?"

I nodded and, gathering up my tool kit, hurried away.

I blinked and came back to the present. Glancing out of the bathroom toward where the bunny monster lay waiting, I felt a surge of adrenalin flow. The image of the researchers manhandling those rabbits - they were so similar to the bunny monster - would not go away.

I shook myself to ward off the chill that was traveling up my spine. Whatever it was that was going on aboard Ketcham Station had no bearing on my problem: how to take down the bunny monster and free myself, while at the same time saving the Earth from an infestation of the buggers.

I pushed myself away from the bathroom sink and stepped back into the main room of my apartment. Again I looked over at the kitchenette, to the small block where I kept my cooking knives. Maybe it would work.

A rustling from the couch drew my gaze away, back to the bunny monster as it slowly stirred. It would be awake soon. Once it woke, I would have to put such thoughts out of my mind. I did not know how far the monster could go, whether it could just implant its own thoughts or read all of mine. But if it detected any hint of a plan to do it harm...

Things would get ugly, very quickly.

I hurried over to my corner of the couch and sat down, slumping back against the cushions as though I were still asleep. It would not do to have it wonder how long I had been awake, and what I had been doing. A small voice in the back of my mind whispered that it likely did not care, that it knew it had me cowed and was satisfied in its superiority. I forced that voice down, irritation mixed with disgust - at its sentiment as well as the fact that the sentiment was true - lending me extra strength to get my thoughts under control.

I waited.

At some point, I drifted back off to sleep. I did not realize it had happened until the bunny monster woke me with a pair of rough scratches along my forearm. That was how it always went in the morning; if I was not awake soon after it rose, I got a scratch. Never enough to draw blood, but enough to sting for a while and get me up.

It had never before had to scratch me twice.

I bolted awake, clutching at my arm and cursing softly, but the words died on my lips as I saw the bunny monster staring at me, its blood-red eyes narrowed into dangerous slits. If it were human, I would have said it wore accusation on its face.

Too much sleep.

I blinked; it also bore accusation in its thoughts. Had I given myself away somehow?

"Sorry. I..." I shook my head and rubbed at my eyes for a moment, then glanced at the clock. An hour had passed since I sat back down on the couch. It felt like five minutes. "I had an intense dream."

The bunny monster stared at me for another long moment, the turned and hopped off the couch, apparently satisfied.

Come. We hunt.

Obediently, I stood from the couch and went to my coat rack to retrieve my jacket. As I prepared to go on another ghastly journey, I shifted my thoughts back to the short nap I had taken. Intense dream. That was an understatement.

I was aboard Ketcham Station again. It was vivid, every detail as plain and real as if I were actually there.

I was taking a coffee break, sitting at a table in the corner of the station's small cafeteria, and nursing a steaming cup of what almost passed for a decent brew. In that respect, it was a far sight better than the coffee in most workplaces I had been in since leaving the Navy. Just three scoops of sugar and a couple dollops of cream was all it took to make the coffee drinkable. That was one thing about the Navy; those salty guys really do know how to brew a mug. I tried to remind myself of all the bad things, the reasons why I had gotten out. But right then, sipping on that barely tolerable mug of Joe, it was hard to remember.

I was not alone in the cafeteria, though I sat alone at my table. A pair of men in researchers' white lab coats stood on the other side of the room, in front of the stainless steel of the service station, and gave their orders. They would likely sit together and leave me alone. One other table was occupied, by a woman in workman's coveralls, but she had her back to me and was watching the latest ball game streaming on the live feed from planetside.

So while I was not alone, I had my privacy, which is the way I wanted it. Get in, do my thing, and get out. That is how I preferred to do business, and this day was no different.

I turned my gaze away from the other in the room and stared down at my coffee, my thoughts drifting forward to rest of the morning's tasks. There was a faulty solenoid in the actuator on an emergency bulkhead seal door on deck three, a set of malfunctioning lights in the female berthing area on 01 level - that would be no fun; the hoops I would have to jump through just to get in there, let alone while I was in there working, saw to that - and a new fan to install in fan room six. It was a lot to do in one morning. But then again, the station was getting up there in years, and even without the recent malfunctions there was plenty to do to keep up the aging infrastructure.

"...very promising results."

Nearby voices drew my eyes from my mug. The two research men were settling down into plain white plastic chairs at the table next to me. They each held a bagel on a small plate in one hand and a cup in the other. Their security badges were only slightly less striped than Dr. Liu's had been. That meant they were high in the chain, though I did not recognize them. Which was hardly surprising since I had just reported aboard.

The research man who spoke wore a large grin on his face. His companion was less cheerful.

"How can you say that?"

"It almost worked, and the data we got will help us refine the settings. Next time..."

The glum researcher waved off his colleague's comments. "Data, shmata. Did you see what happened to that rabbit? The portal..."

He stopped talking, seeming to notice me for the first time. His mouth shut with an audible clack of teeth striking teeth and he scowled.

"This does not concern you," he said, looking right at me. His tone became cold, biting. As the man spoke, his cheerful companion followed his gaze with a stare of his own. His lips, turned upward a moment ago, compressed into a scowl.

I recognized what that meant. Part of me wanted to protest that I was here first and they were intruding on my private time. But I knew that would do no good and likely land me in trouble besides, so I stood up. "Sorry, gents. I was just leaving."

I slipped around their table, trying not to feel my head being ripped apart beneath the weight and economy of their combined stares. The coffee sucked anyway. I walked over to the trash can near the doorway and tossed it, plastic mug and all. Then I took a minute to sling my tool bag over my shoulder. Before I left, I heard the researchers begin speaking again, more quietly this time but still loud enough to easily carry to where I was standing.

"...Just a few setting changes and the quantum tunneler will be operational. And when that happens, who cares what happened to a couple of stupid rabbits..."

That was the cheerful one again. His voice cut off abruptly as the door slid shut before me. I was happy to hear it go; I had work to do.

The Quantum Tunneler.

The bunny and I were walking the streets again, looking for the bunny monster's next victim. I hardly noticed where it was taking me, the people around me, or the time of day. Which was unusual; it - she - had almost never taken me out during the day, let alone on a hunt at that time. And yet there we were. She must really be hungry to throw caution to the wind like this. But I did not care. Maybe I should have, but I did not. My mind kept going back to those words.

The Quantum Tunneler. That was important, and I could have sworn I had heard those words before. But from where?

That one.

The bunny monster's insistent thoughts intruded rudely into my head, forcing me out of my contemplation as it directed me to the right, toward a woman sitting alone on a bench a half block down the street from where I stood.

I hated when the bunny monster took women.

As we approached, I saw that the woman was not like the other victims had been. She was young, with red-gold hair and a lovely face. Her clothing and jacket were inexpensive but not in disrepair. There was no odor of alcohol around her, and she did not seem beaten down by the world. Rather, she appeared cheerful. Not at all like the others.

She saw me coming and quirked an eyebrow upward. "Spare some change, mister? I'm on the road," she said. Her voice was clear, strong. Optimistic.

I shook my head, a negative meant for the bunny monster, not for her.

Not her; the monster could not have her. I tried to veer away, but I felt the claws dig in deep. Deeper than usual; deeper than they ever had after that first day with the monster. I had to bite my lips to keep from crying out from the sudden agony.

"Mister?" The girl sounded concerned. "You ok?"

I curled my arms over my chest and tried again to turn away. Maybe I could keep the monster form reaching her...

But, despite its increased bulk, the bunny monster remained more than limber. It squirmed against my chest, digging its claws in with each move, and forced itself out of the V in my trench coat. There it paused for the briefest of moments, casting a baleful look at me that promised pain and worse.

The girl saw it. Her concern became confusion, followed by enchantment. "What a cute bunny..." He words were lost in a shriek of sudden terror as the bunny monster bared its fangs and leapt at her.

It should have got her. Should have killed her and feasted on her blood, just as it had so many others. But somehow, in that one moment, I was the faster. As it leapt, I lunged forward, stretching my arms like a wide receiver going for a pass that was just slightly overthrown, but never actually expecting to catch the thing. When I felt soft fur in my hands, I almost let go in surprise and shock. Hell, the bunny monster froze in shock as well; or at least I presume it was in shock. Regardless, it did not move in those couple seconds I had it in my grasp.

I did not stop to wonder at the turn of events. Instead, I turned and hurled the bunny monster away, as hard as I could. It flew through the air, tumbling head over fluffy tail in a way that, in different circumstances, would actually have been funny. Then it struck an overturned trash can at the entrance of a nearby alley.

Part of me wondered, hoped, that the impact had killed it, but I knew better. At most it would delay the bunny monster's attack, only now it would come after me as well as the girl. We had to get out of there, and fast.

I turned back to her. She was looking at me with wide, fearful, but confused eyes and her mouth was agape.

"What... What..." she stammered.

But this was no time for explanations. "Run!" I cried, and shoved the back of her shoulder, turning her around and propelling her away from the bunny monster's landing spot before she could raise a word of protest.

Amazingly enough, she ran. I could not understand it at first. Maybe it was because the whole situation was just too weird. Maybe I managed to put enough fear and command in my tone that she decided it would be better to do what I said, at least for the moment.

Or maybe it was the roar - an actual honest to God roar - of fury that the bunny monster made before it set out after us.

I had seen how quickly it could move. Its small body was deceptive, and I knew it could catch us easily if we did not get out of there, and fast. Problem was, get out of there to...where? All up and down the street, shops were boarded up. The few that were not were open for business, their entrances standing wide open to admit customers. Not exactly an ideal place to run, where the bunny monster could easily follow.

There were cars, though. A steady stream of cars flowed down the street, and every so often a cab. If I could flag one of them down, we could... I shelved the thought as soon as it reared its head. In the time it took to get a cab, the bunny monster would be on us. And besides, I had no money on me and I doubted the girl did either. She *had* just been begging for spare change.

"What is that thing?" the girl asked in between gasps. She was getting winded quickly, a bad sign.

"Long story," I said, knowing it was a lame answer. I cast around, looking for something, anything, and then I saw it. At the corner of the next block, across the street: a T station. If we could get down there and onto a train... "Come on," I said, and picked up the pace. I was already running at well beyond a comfortable pace, but now that I had a goal in sight, there seemed no point in holding back.

The girl opened her mouth, to protest I thought, but just then the bunny monster roared again and I heard a crash from astern. Looking back over my shoulder, I saw that it was rapidly closing the distance; it was maybe twenty yards behind us now. The crash was from another garbage can. The bunny monster must have knocked into it, because it lay on the ground in the monster's wake, rolling away slowly as it spilled its contest onto the sidewalk.

Gross.

But it spurred the girl on to greater speed.

We charged down the street. I heard the bunny monster behind us, but I did not dare look back again. It would cost too much speed. The T-station was only a short distance ahead, and I began to think we might make it.

Then something solid and sharp struck me in the center of my back and I stumbled forward, landing face-first on the sidewalk.

It had me. I could hear its breathing, feel its claws digging in as it scurried up my back toward my neck. Briefly, I thought it would just punish me and that would be it; everything could go back to the way it was. Or maybe I hoped that. But deeper down, I knew that was not the case. It meant to drink me dry, then have the girl as well. After all, it did not really need me anymore; it had had its nourishment and was about ready to deliver its babies. Whether it killed me now or in a day or two was immaterial at this point.

I squirmed, trying to roll over and slam my weight into it, but again the bunny monster seemed to weigh more - much more - that it should have. And when it thumped down on my shoulder blades with its front paws, I found myself slammed into the sidewalk again.

Fool.

Its thought entered my mind, and with it images. Horrible images. The things it planned to do to the girl after it finished me. And then to others once its babies were born. I had always known it would be bad, but to *see* it... I screamed then, and not just because I feared for myself.

But then, suddenly, I heard an impact above me, felt a lurch, and the bunny monster was gone.

I looked up in time to see the girl following through on a kick. The bunny monster's excessive weight must have been a trick of the mind, because it sailed through the air and landing hard in the street. Right in the path of a delivery truck.

The driver tried to hit the brakes, but the bunny monster landed too close. The squeal of skidding tires and the smell of burning rubber reached us at the same moment as the, softer, sound of the bunny monster going SQUISH beneath the truck's left front tire.

I rolled over and pushed myself up onto my elbows, ignoring the pain in my back and chest for the moment as I stared at the truck's tire. I could see one of the bunny-monster's rear legs sticking out from under it, unmoving.

My mind screamed out in protest. Seriously? It could not be that easy. I had lived in terror and guilt for how long, fearing to lift a finger to that thing and letting it do all the things it had done, and in the end it was *that* easy to kill? All at once, my disbelief turned into guilt, and disgust at myself. I had been such a coward.

I flopped back onto the sidewalk - the new wounds in my back screamed in protest, but I ignored them - and pressed the palms of my hands to my eyes, trying to ward back tears of remorse and pain.

The girl's voice interrupted my self-pity party. "You ok?"

I lowered my hands and found myself looking up at her face, which was only a foot or two above mine; she was crouching down next to me. "Been better," I said softly.

She looked me up and down quickly, then nodded agreement. "Hope so." Gee thanks, lady. "What was that thing?"

I groaned and forced myself into a seated position. "You wouldn't believe me if I told you."

She snorted. "Try me."

Just then I heard a creaking, from over by the delivery truck. I turned my head, and saw the impossible.

The truck's tire was moving, bulging out in places and then returning to normal, as though something was squirming around beneath - or within - it, trying to get out.

"Oh no," I said as cold dread filled me. I began pushing myself to my feet. "We gotta get out of here."

"What?" asked the girl. "Why?"

I found my feet and pointed at the tire. Her eyes widened in renewed fear.

The bunny monster was still alive.

A small crowd had gathered, people dressed in everything from dirty clothing little more than rags to tailor-made suits. They clustered around on the sidewalks, staring at us, at the truck, but most of all at the tire as it squirmed around. They were all in danger from that thing, but I couldn't worry about that. The bunny monster's first desire would be to get me. And the girl, whoever she was. It wanted her, above and beyond the others - there were surely many others - that we had passed on the street that morning.

I grabbed at her arm, half expecting her to push me away when my fingers closed. But for wonder, she did not, transfixed as she was by the sight of the bunny monster struggling to free itself.

"We have to get out of here," I said as fiercely as I could while still keeping my voice low, so it would not carry.

She was trembling intensely. Her eyes were fixed into a terrified stare, and she did not respond.

I snapped my fingers in front of her face and she jerked.

"We have to go. Now!"

She nodded quickly, in fearful jerks.

That was enough for me. I grabbed her arm more firmly and pulled her along behind me as I made a beeline for the T station, now only a few tens of meters away.

The train door slid closed and we slumped down onto the plastic seats, drained. A few seconds later, the train began moving down the track in the direction of Alewife. Not that I intended for us to go that far. Downtown Crossing was just a few stops ahead; we could get off there with all sorts of options while I figured out what to do next.

As the train's acceleration picked up, the girl shook herself as though rousing from a daydream. And perhaps she thought she was; all power to her if she found that comforting.

The look on her face said she did not.

"Alright, what the hell *was* that?" she asked, her voice still trembling.

I shook my head. "You wouldn't believe me."

"You said that before. Tell me."

I looked at her for a moment. She was obviously shaken, afraid, but she was gathering herself quickly. More quickly than I had, the first time I met the bunny monster. In fact, she looked... I blinked. I had not really noticed before how good she looked. I mean, I had noticed, but not *noticed*. And really, she was a looker.

I suddenly became aware of how God-awful I probably looked, in clothes that had not been washed in who knows how long, to say nothing of how I probably smelled. I looked away, feeling the heat of an embarrassed blush creeping onto my cheeks.

I heard her sigh, in exasperation I thought. I was going to lose her in a second. So, I spilled it.

All of it.

From getting "transferred" to Ketcham Station, to winding up at my apartment, to the bunny dominating me for all this time. I told her all of it, and it was like a weight had been lifted. Just to tell someone else what the hell was going on felt good, comforting. The fact that no one else was sitting anywhere near us did not hurt. She, at least, stood a chance of believing me, after what she had seen.

I finished and she responded with only silence.

I looked back at her and saw that she was chewing on her lip thoughtfully. She still did not say anything.

"Well?" I asked, when I could bear the silence no more.

"You were really on Ketcham Station? I heard there were no survivors."

I blinked. I had never seen any news updates about the station's status, but then I had been a bit distracted. I suppose I had just assumed they rescued everyone. To hear differently was...

Wait a minute.

"No survivors? None?"

She shook her head.

"Holy Cannoli," I breathed. Now *that* was something I had not considered. Hell, for all I knew, they probably had me listed as deceased, since I had no idea if I checked in with anyone when I left the station or arrived planetside. Hell, I *still* did not know how I managed that at all.

If I was officially dead, that opened up whole realms of possibilities. For later.

The girl looked at me with a quizzical expression. "So you think this thing came back with you from the station." It did not sound like a question, but the way her eyebrows rose as she said it spoke volumes about how much she doubted I was correct. Or telling the truth. Or something.

I nodded, spreading my hands helplessly.

"So what the hell *is* it? Cause it sure ain't a bunny rabbit."

I shook my head. "I really don't know." My thoughts flashed back to the dream from the previous night, and the things I remembered yesterday. "I... I think they were doing some kind of experiments up on the station. They had rabbits...and a device of some sort. I think whatever they were doing went wrong and..." I made a vague gesture toward the rear of the train. "Now it's like it's a vampire or something. At least that's how it acts. All I know for certain is it's going to have babies soon, and once that happens..." I left the rest unsaid.

The girl nodded slowly. "So what, it wanted to eat me next?"

I nodded. She was remarkable calm about that part.

"Why didn't you let it?"

"What?"

"You let it eat the others. Why not me?"

"I... I didn't *let* it! I..."

She just stared at me levelly until I dropped my eyes to the floor, all the guilt and shame I had felt the last several days welling up again. She was right, of course. I stopped it from getting her; I could have stopped it with any of them. Or figured a way to kill it. Something. Anything, besides being a passive vessel for that damned thing.

Everything that had happened was my fault

I felt tears - of shame, of guilt, of accumulated stress - welling up, but I refused to let myself cry. Instead, I sniffed and wiped them away, and forced myself to look back at her.

She had asked a legitimate question. But how to explain that she alone of the bunny monster's chosen victims was not one of the dregs of society? That she was, well, pretty. Too pretty for me to allow her to come to that end. Just thinking it made me cringe at how shallow a reason it was.

Instead, I just shrugged. "I'd had enough of it." That much was true, at least.

She nodded slightly. "Fair enough." Her tone said she suspected there was something more, but thankfully she did not press. "Well." The next station was coming up; she stood and held out her hand to me. "Thank you, I suppose."

Surprised, I took her hand. She gave mine a quick shake, then turned toward the train door.

"What are you doing?"

She looked back at me, confused. "I'm getting off this train and then I'm calling the cops."

"Uh...miss, I don't think..."

The train came to a stop and the door opened. The girl turned her back on me and stepped down the stairs and off the train.

Something small and white jumped off the top of the train and crashed onto her back, and she went down.

It had followed us.

I stood transfixed for a second. In shock. In disbelief. In horror. How? *How* had it followed us, staked out the very car we were riding in? Not that I should have been surprised at all; the thing was nothing if not relentless and effective when it set itself to a goal. That much had become abundantly clear in the time it kept me prisoner.

But...damn...

The sound of the girl's scream broke me out of my reverie, and I bounded forward. The chimes that announced the doors would be closing sounded, and I threw myself out of the train. If I did not make it out of the train to help her, she was done. I knew that without question.

I felt the door tug at the sole of my shoe, and for a moment I wondered if my foot was caught and I was about to be dragged along beside the train car. But then the pressure on my shoe eased as my momentum carried me forward. I landed sprawling on the concrete of the station's floor at the same time as I heard the solid thud of rubber striking rubber, signaling that the door had seated.

Then the train pulled away.

I pushed myself onto my feet and moved toward the girl. She was squirming and flailing about with her arms and legs, trying to dislodge the bunny monster, but it held fast. And was steadily making its way up her back to her neck.

I glanced around, hoping another commuter or two would be able to help, but the station was empty. How was that possible, at this hour of the day? But it was, and all the wishing in the world was not going to change that. It was, again, all up to me.

A good solid kick had dislodged the thing from my back. I charged froward, hoping the same would work here.

But the bunny monster was waiting.

Maybe it expected my move. Or maybe attacking the girl was just a ruse meant to make me show myself, so it could exact some revenge. For whatever reason, it was ready. When I drew back to kick, it launched itself toward me. As it flew toward my face, I could clearly see its eyes, bright red to reflect its anger and blood lust, the pupils narrowed to tiny slits as it put all its attention on me.

I was moving forward with too much momentum. I could not

just stop, or hop backwards. In the split second before the bunny monster struck me, I considered doing both and just as quickly dismissed them. In the end, I did the only thing that seemed reasonable: I raised my forearms in front of my face and dropped to the ground, fully expecting to feel the bunny monster's claws digging into my arms, followed by its fangs on my throat.

But that did not happen.

Somehow, my dive made it miss.

Unbelieving, I rolled onto my back and sat up. Beside me, the girl had done the same, but unlike me she did not stop there, but was beginning to stagger to her feet.

The bunny monster lay at the base of a concrete pillar a few meters away. For a second, I thought perhaps it had sailed into the pillar and crushed its head. No such luck. It turned to face us - to face *me* - and stared for what felt like forever. Then it growled. No, roared.

"Oh my God," the girl breathed, scampering to her feet.

I was forced to agree. I wracked my brain, trying to think of something, anything I could do. But how do you kill a vampire?

"What?"

I had not realized I had spoken the thought out loud. I gestured toward the bunny monster. I had begun to advance, slowly for now as though savoring the moment of our fear. "How do you kill a vampire?"

I began backing away from the thing, toward the stairs leading up to the street level. The girl did the same, never taking her eyes off the bunny monster. "I don't know...holy water? Garlic?"

I was about to tell her that was not going to work, and we did not have those things anyway, but the bunny monster picked that moment to charge.

Predictably, it went for the girl first. Was it *trying* to piss me off, or did it really think I had so little thought in my head that it assumed I would act stupidly again just because she was in danger? More than likely the later. And, in its defense, I *did* do something stupid because she was in danger.

I leapt in front of her, shielding her with my own body.

If I had taken a minute to think about it, there is no way I would have put myself in the bunny monster's line of fire. A loud voice in the back of my head screamed, "What the hell are you doing?", but it was far too late to pay any heed to the voice of reason. The thing was coming right at me now, and I only had time to react by instinct. I barely had time to get my hands up before the bunny monster struck me.

But somehow, that was enough.

I stood there, stunned, and looked at the diminutive beast that I had somehow caught in midair before it would have landed on my throat. I held it beneath its front legs, and could feel the bones of its ribs quite plainly beneath my fingers.

For a second, we just looked at each other. I think it was as surprised at my miraculous catch as I was, if the widening of its eyes was any indication.

Then the second passed and it opened its mouth wide, barring its fangs. It began squirming around in my grip, trying to break free. It was all I could do to keep my hands locked around it, but I managed. Then it began scratching at me. Its forelegs clamped onto the muscles of my forearms, and the claws dug in. Deep. Far deeper than it had scratched at me before, even the first time when it was asserting its dominance. No, these blows were intended not to subdue but to punish, and punish severely.

And boy did they do the trick.

Searing pain, beyond anything I had ever felt, ran up my arms, and I saw red. I heard myself crying out - hell, screaming - but was not conscious of actively doing so. The world compressed until it consisted only of the pain and the image of the bunny monster's eyes, glowing as though lit by a red fire. That was all I could see.

Kneel.

The command crashed into my mind like a sledgehammer. I only *thought* the bunny monster had been forceful before. This... This was like nothing I had ever experienced or dreamt of. I was down on my knees in an instant; it was like the bunny monster had directly controlled my leg muscles to get me there.

The pain lessened slightly, enough that I could make out more than just the bunny monster's eyes: its entire face came into focus, now just inches away from mine. How I managed to not lose my grip on it completely, I had no idea, but somewhere beneath the pain and the pressure on my mind I felt the soft fur of its coat.

Release me.

This order was less like a sledgehammer and more like a soothing caress. It contained promises of an end to pain, of comfort even. It was like an offer of lemonade on a humid summer day while lying in a hammock with a gentle breeze blowing past you. I wanted to give in, and not because of the pain of my newest wounds, but because of that promised bliss.

I knew it was a lie, but all the same I felt my fingers beginning to relax. It wouldn't be so bad to just let go, let it all go.

No!

Somehow, I thought of all the people it had taken - had forced me to help it take. Of the vile babies growing in its belly. Of the havoc those babies would cause. And I became angry. Furious. That anger beat back against the pressure of its mental command, and I felt myself regaining control.

"No" I growled, and I began squeezing, as hard as I could.

The bunny monster's eyes grew wide, whether in surprise or anger I was not sure. But a moment later, as I felt its ribs beginning to give beneath the pressure of my hands, I knew the expression taking shape on its face was pain. And, I knew for certain, fear.

I felt more than a little satisfaction from that.

The beast began squirming madly. Its foreleg claws, already dug into my arm, began pulling downward toward my hands, and I saw deep ruts begin to open in my flesh. Its rear legs kicked up and I felt a new pain as those claws struck the undersides of my upper arms and held fast.

I was not going to win this contest. Either I would lose my grip from pain, or shock, or blood loss. But sooner or later I would let go, and then it would be all over.

Fortunately, I was not fighting alone.

From out of nowhere, or at least that was how it seemed to me, something crashed down onto the bunny monster's head. I heard the hollow clank of metal striking bone and, all at once, the bunny monster went limp.

It also dropped out of my grasp, unprepared as I was for the sudden additional force.

I stumbled backwards, reeling and for a second unable to comprehend what had happened. Then finally my vision cleared and I saw the girl crouching over the bunny monster, a fire extinguisher held in both of her hands.

She brought the base of the extinguisher down on the beast's head over and over again. There was a crack, then a squishing sound, and then its head broke open completely and grey matter splattered out all over the concrete floor. Only then did she stop. She pushed herself to her feet, dropping the extinguisher to the ground, and stumbled backwards until her back struck another pillar.

The only sound for a long several seconds was that of the extinguisher rolling away from where she had dropped it.

"Good Lord," I breathed. I wanted to say something - several somethings - more colorful. The burning in my arms alone seemed to call for it. But for some reason, just then I felt like swearing would have been wrong, sacrilegious almost.

The girl just stared at the bunny monster for a few seconds more. Then she looked back at me. Her eyes were haunted, but that quickly changed when she saw me. Or more in particular, when she saw the vast amounts of blood leaking from my forearms.

"Oh God," she cried, and hurried over to my side. "Are you alright? Put pressure on it."

Like I didn't know that. I somehow managed a half-smile. "I don't know. Hope so." I drew a deep breath and held it for a second, focusing only on that action. It seemed to help with the pain. A very little bit. "Thanks," I added.

She nodded, but only briefly. She took my hands and raised them so she could examine the wounds in my forearms more closely. "You're going to need stitches, quickly, or you're going to be in trouble." She turned her head side to side, scanning the station quickly. For what, I was not sure until she spoke again. "We need to put on a bandages. Can you get out of that coat?"

Despite the pain, I managed a resigned chuckle. My trench coat was totally destroyed. Between the scratches the bunny monster had put in the back and now the sleeves... The thing hung in tatters. All the same, it took some doing, and no small amount of assistance from her, to get it off.

She saw the t-shirt I was wearing and rolled her eyes, but said only, "That cotton will be a better dressing. Take that off, too."

That was quite a bit more difficult and painful to do, but I managed. Once the t-shirt was off, she began tearing it into strips using a small pocket knife she pulled from seemingly out of nowhere. It took me far too long to realize she kept it - duh! - in her pocket. I was losing a lot of blood.

Very quickly, she had what she needed, and she began dressing my wounds. She was very precise and neat in how she tied off the dressings, as though she had a lot of practice doing this sort of thing.

I cleared my throat. "Do this a lot?"

She blinked, pausing what she was doing, then flushed slightly. "I studied nursing for a while," she said. She went back to work. A few minutes later, my forearms looked like those of a mummy, but at least I was not dripping blood everywhere. "That should keep you until you can make it to a hospital."

"Thanks," I said, trying another smile. It was easier this time; the pain had reduced quite a lot, the way it tends to in the aftermath of wounds. A thought hit me. "You know, I never got your name."

The girl stared at me for a second. She looked surprised, then she just shook her head and laughed. "Sheila," she said, and we shook hands again. More gently this time.

"Barry."

"Nice to meet you, Barry."

"You too. I..."

I glanced past her shoulder toward where the bunny monster's body lay, and my words caught in my throat.

It was gone.

"Oh crap," Sheila breathed when she saw it. "Where the hell is it?"

I shook my head, unable to fully comprehend what I was seeing. How could it have gotten back up from that? It's brains were splattered all over the floor. Hell, some of them were still splattered all over the floor. So what the hell?

"Barry, what do we do?" She sounded well past freaked out. So was I, for that matter.

I drew in a deep breath and picked up what was left of my trench coat. My t-shirt was gone, so it was wear that or walk around topless, and it was getting a bit chilly for that. "We get the hell out of here," I said as I straightened.

Sheila nodded, her eyes darting back and forth in a fearful scan of the area.

She took my hand as we turned toward the stairs. Not from any romantic impulse, I was sure. But it still felt nice. I gave her hand a little squeeze and started up the stairs.

It was not until we reached the top that I realized how screwed we were.

"Are you freaking kidding me?" Sheila was well past scared and more than a little frustrated, and it showed in her strident tone as she shouted the words.

I could not blame her.

At the top of the stairs, the retractable steel bars that closed off the station after the T shut down for the night were closed and locked with a padlock that appeared nigh-on indestructible. I checked the time on my watch - somehow it still functioned. 2:30 pm. What the hell??

That explained why no one else was in the station. But why was it shut up? And why would the train stop at a station that was closed?

I shook the bars, knowing it to be futile even as I tried it. But that's what you do when you encounter a barrier in your way: at least try to see if there is an easy way to get past it.

"Oh crap, Barry. What are we going to do?"

That was the second time in as many minutes that Sheila asked that question, and this time I had no answer. The thought of going back down there, where the bunny monster waited, somewhere, was unacceptable. But waiting up here, where there was no where to go, was not much better.

I looked out, past the bars, at the street outside. The station was set ten or fifteen meters back, but I could see a number of pedestrians walking along the street. This area of town was much better than the one we had left not so long ago. If we could get one of those pedestrians to call for help, we might be able to...

Then it hit me how stupid I was being.

"You have a mobile? Mine's sitting on the coffee table at home."

Sheila blinked, then her eyes lit up. She fished in the inner pocket of the light jacket she wore, then pulled out her phone with a smile of triumph. She punched in 911 and held the device up to her ear. She bounced from foot to foot eagerly as she waited; she was practically dancing, the way she was going on.

A few seconds later, her eyes widened, and she said, "Yes. Hello? Look my friend and I need help."

She continued speaking with the operator, but I put the conversation out of my mind. Now that she was engaged, I went down a few steps and peered down into the station. The bunny monster was down there. It was certainly injured, and pissed off to no end as well - that was probably putting it mildly. And it would not be hard to figure out where we had gone. Fortunately, we ought to be able to see it coming from here.

Sheila hung up the phone and came down to stand beside me. "They'll be here in about fifteen minutes, with someone from the transportation department who can let us out." She did not sound particularly pleased. For that matter, neither was I.

"What did you tell them?"

She frowned, looking sidelong at me. "That we are locked in here and had been attacked by an animal."

I snorted softly. Attacked by an animal. While true, it was rich. "Well I guess we wait then."

Sheila nodded. She glanced down the stairs and I could see she was still more than nervous. She licked her lips. Her momentary elation at talking to the authorities was wearing off fast. I needed to get her mind off things, keep her calm.

I needed to do the same thing for myself.

"Why did you stop nursing school?"

Sheila gave a little start, then made a little sound that was half sob, half chuckle. "Ran out of money," she said, her eyes never leaving the landing, some thirty steps below us.

"There are scholarships..."

Sheila snorted. "Not for me. Just drop it, ok?"

I raised my hands defensively. "Ok. Sorry."

We sat in silence for a while. Or at least it felt like a while before Sheila spoke again.

"Do you think it's..."

"Dead?"

She nodded.

I shook my head. "Getting run over by a truck didn't kill it. I doubt a fire extinguisher will do the trick."

Frowning, Sheila looked back down the stairs toward the empty station below. I followed her gaze, not wanting to say what I knew to be true: that as soon as it got over the shock of being whacked on the head a few times, the bunny monster would be coming for us.

We didn't have fifteen minutes.

I crept back down the stairs slowly, easing each foot down onto the stair below before shifting my weight onto it to avoid making noise. It would have felt a bit comic - hell, I had to suppress the feeling that I looked a fool - but rising fear stamped down my self consciousness in favor of flight-or-fight.

I glanced over my shoulder to where Sheila sat, her back pressed up against the metal bars that sealed the entrance to the station. She managed a quick smile and thumbs up. Brave girl. She was clearly terrified, but was trying not to show it. I wondered how well I was doing in that regard.

Then I lowered myself down into the station proper, and I stopped, listening and looking.

The spot where the monster attacked me, and where Sheila knocked it for a loop, was easy to see from the smear on the floor. But aside from that, there was no visible indication of where it might have gone. The only noises were the soft hum of the fluorescent lights that illuminated the station and of ventilation fans whirring softly away in their ducts. Of course, the whole place smelled like crap.

It was not going to be easy to find this thing.

Listening to the fans, I considered briefly whether the bunny monster had crawled into the ventilation ducts and from there up to the surface, but quickly discarded the thought. It was not as nimble as it had been when we first "met", and the babies were clearly coming any time. Chasing Sheila and I, hitching a ride on the T, and surviving the truck and Sheila's attack must have drained a good portion of its energy. I let myself hope that it had crawled away into a corner to sleep, and maybe I could dispatch it while it was unconscious.

Fat chance.

I walked slowly across the wide open area past the entrance turnstiles, looking back and forth for any other sign of the monster, and saw nothing. Not a thing. There was not even a smear or streak leading away from where it had fallen. I continued on and found I had to force myself to breathe regularly. My heart pounded in my ears and it seemed like every step I took echoed loudly throughout the station, no matter how carefully I set my feet.

And so I was surprised to hear a rustling sound. Faint, almost inaudible, but it was there, off to my right, behind a closed-up concessions cart.

I thought for a second that it was just a rat, but I knew that was just wishful thinking. Part of me - a huge part - screamed to run, just get away from the thing. But the small little window of reason that I had been working so hard to maintain recognized that would be futile. The bunny monster had already proven more than willing and able to track me me down, and probably Sheila now as well, even on a moving train. Surely it would catch me on foot without any trouble at all.

And besides, where was I going to go? Down the train tracks into the darkness of the tunnels in between stations, where a train would likely run me down without noticing?

I froze in mid-step, not even realizing I had begun walking toward the concession cart, as the details of that idea struck me. Those tunnels all had maintenance accesses, walkways, things like that. Maybe we *could* get away through them, down to the next station. It could not be more than a quarter mile at most; that would just take a few minutes, and then we could get out.

Almost on cue, a low rumbling began to emanate from the

tunnel leading off to the south, where we had come from. It got slowly louder, and I felt my heart leap. Another train! Maybe I could flag it down, and we would not have to walk, even.

I turned and dashed back to the turnstiles at the bottom of the stairs and gestured frantically for Sheila to come back down. She blinked, looking confused, then unbelieving. She shook her head, lips turned downward in a deep, frightened frown.

The rumbling was even louder, and I could see the light from the approaching train's headlights begin to brighten the tunnel's curve where the track bent out of sight to the south. Damnit, we were going to miss our chance!

I gestured again, more forcefully, and pointed toward the track. She could not see it, not from where she stood. I silently prayed - it had been ages since I'd done that with any regularity - that she would get my gist and move it.

The rumbling of the train grew louder. Beneath it, the squeaks of wheels against the tracks as the train reached the turn began to sound. And finally Sheila seemed to understand. She moved down the stairs, tentatively at first and then with greater speed as she got lower and heard the approaching train. She reached the turnstile and vaulted over. I turned and ran back toward the track.

The headlights were brilliant in the tunnel; the train was about to round the turn.

I reached the edge of the platform and waved my hands, shouting at the top of my lungs, just as the train burst into sight and came barreling into the station. For a brief moment I saw the conductor - driver? What do they call those guys on subways anyway? - as he approached. He gave me a look that someone reserves for an idiot, and then he was gone, out of my sight as the train sped past. He never even applied the brakes.

The train sped off to the north, the red tail lights first bright but steadily dimming as it sped away, and I lowered my arms. I realized I was still shouting and stopped. It would alert the bunny monster. Not that it needed alerting, but still...

"Son of a bitch."

Sheila stood next to me, watching the train speed away with despair in her voice. I glanced toward her and saw it on her face as well.

"Come on," I said. "We're getting out of here."

I grabbed her hand - she did not try to pull away - and led her toward the northbound tunnel at the end of the platform. I swore under my breath when we reached it. There was not a service walkway, like I thought there would be. Would there even be one further down?

"You've got to be kidding." Sheila pulled back then, removing her hand from my grasp as she shook her head in denial. "You want to walk down the tracks."

"Better than waiting here for that thing to get its act together."

"We're waiting for the cops."

"Are you really sure they will get here first?"

Just then a loud thump echoed through the station. It came from the direction of that concessions cart. A cold spike of terror surged through me, and I could see from her expression that Sheila felt the same.

"No choice," I said, and held out my hand to her.

She looked back over her shoulder toward the turnstiles and the stairs leading up, then swallowed and took a deep breath. Then she nodded to herself and took my hand.

Together we hopped down from the platform onto the tracks and ran northward, into the darkness of the subway tunnel.

I've seen movies and shows where people creep down dark tunnels, whether subway lines or roads or just plain old walking tunnels. In those shows the light continues for a long time, and even after they round the corner from the light source they can still see, however dimly.

That is not at all how it is in real life.

Within ten paces I had a hard time making out details on

anything except for the subway rails themselves. Ten paces further on we came to a bend in the tunnel, and I could barely see anything. The thought of the bunny monster lurking behind us, or just as bad a train running up on us from behind, compelled me to keep running, though. So I did.

And within two steps, I tripped over a rail tie and fell headfirst to the ground.

My chin struck the edge of a tie as I landed and I felt a searing pain as my skin tore. I could not see it, but I knew I was bleeding. Badly.

I lay there for a long several seconds, clutching my bleeding, throbbing chin in my hand. Beside me, I heard Sheila panting heavily, sucking in great quantities of air as quickly as she could. I envisioned her bent over, hands on her knees as she tried to regain her breath, but in the darkness she was just one shadow on top of fifty more.

"Are you ok?" she asked between breaths.

Trying to ignore the metallic taste in my mouth - I may have bitten my tongue as well, though it was hard to tell, as ubiquitous as the pain was right that minute - I coughed and nodded.

"Great," was all I could manage, but it seemed to be enough. She took a deeper breath and I could almost hear her relief as she took my hand and helped me up to my feet.

I looked around and was surprised that I could just barely make out some details. A dim green glow came from ahead, around the corner. I had not noticed it before; my eyes must have been beginning to adjust to the gloom, but it was still hard to make out anything more than the curve of the rails and the outline of Sheila's body.

There was nothing for it but to continue on, so we did, more slowly this time. I tried not to reduce us to a crawl, but after that fall I found myself gingerly testing each foothold before shifting my weight ahead, to make sure my foot was on a good surface and not in a pit or on the edge of a tie. It made for slow going. Much slower than was wise in our circumstances, but I could not complain. Sheila did not either.

Eventually we rounded the corner and were rewarded with light that was bright enough to make out the tunnel in detail. It came from a small lamp that looked like one of the stoplights you can see at most street corners. A quick look at it revealed why: it *was* one of those stoplights. Except it only had red and green, not yellow. Right then, the green light was the only one lit.

I cast about quickly and found what I was looking for. Through a gap in the wall to the left, a gap which led to the south-bound track I was sure, I saw a small metal scaffold running along the wall. At last, there lay safety. Of a sort.

I felt my spirits buoy as I strode over to the gap and peeked through.

Looking right, all was blackness except for a dull glow a ways down the tunnel, although right there the glow was red. Probably to signal the proximity of the station and that the conductor needed to begin stopping the train. Although, with the station closed what would be the point?

Regardless, there was no train coming and the scaffold lay just past the southbound rails. The only problem was a lack of stairs or ladder leading up to it.

"That's you plan?" Sheila said.

I glanced aside at her and saw that she was nodding in approval, a hopeful gleam in her eyes. She no doubt thought as I did, that there had to be a maintenance access between stations. Some of them were miles apart, after all. And if that were the case, the access would almost certainly link up with the scaffold. At the very least, the scaffold would make for much better footing, and safer, than walking the rails. And best of all, the scaffold was lit by dim blue-white lights in fixtures that were set in the side of the tunnel at regular intervals. We would be able to see better as well.

I nodded. "We just need to find a ladder up."

Sheila sniffed and darted forward, hopping over the rails - missing the third rail by less than an inch - until she stood below the scaffold. Then she bent her legs double and jumped straight up. My jaw, pained as it was, fell open in astonishment. She must have pushed herself a good three or four feet off the ground, if not more. She grabbed the middle bar making up the guardrail at the scaffold's edge. There she hung for a second before she swung her legs up onto the walkway. She then shimmied the rest of the way on and rolled to her feet.

I just stood there, feeling like an idiot and no doubt looking far worse.

She just grinned back. "I was on the varsity gymnastics team."

All sorts of possibilities that were extremely inappropriate in that particular situation sprang to mind, unbidden. "Well," I said, clearing my throat and forcing those thoughts away, "give me a hand up?"

Sheila's grin became positively impish.

A few moments later, after much huffing and puffing and with a good deal of help from Sheila, I managed to haul myself up onto the scaffold.

That really sucked. But it sure beat walking the rails.

I got to my feet and we got moving, our pace a lot better now that we had sure footing. Things were looking up, and I began to think we might actually get out of this with our skins mostly intact.

So naturally, that was the precise moment when everything went right to hell.

The roar came immediately after the thud. And by thud, I mean more like an earth-shaking kaboom than the everyday thud of dropping a sack of potatoes. It was *loud*.

Problem is, the roar was even louder. And it was not some incoherent bellow. No, it was a single word - my name. My name, spoken with all the fury of a hundred, no make that a thousand, women scorned. It was enough to almost make me fall over dead from shock and terror.

How I managed not too was beyond me. Maybe it was Sheila's presence, her eyes widening in fear that I knew mirrored my own. Or maybe it was a determination that I did not even know I had. Regardless, after staggering for a moment before the onslaught of sheer volume, I looked back down the tunnel toward the station we had fled and, seeing something big moving in the shadows of the tunnel back there, I did what any red-blooded man in the prime of his youth would do in that situation.

I ran like hell.

I pushed Sheila ahead of me and just ran, thanking the good Lord that we had made it onto the steady footing of the scaffold before the bunny monster decided to get its act together.

Of course, from what I had seen when I looked back, bunny monster was probably the wrong term to use; the thing looked much larger than it had been, if the shadows were a good indicator of its size. But there was no time to dwell on that, not if we wanted to have a prayer of getting out of there.

So we ran, fast as we could.

Sheila impressed me right off. She needed no coaxing; she was off like a gazelle, running far faster than she had on the streets above. I can only assume the full understanding of what we were facing moved her to new levels of effort. Or she was not really giving it her all before. Either way, it was all I could do to keep up with her, and I'm no slouch in the running department. Or at least, I wasn't, back in the day. But as I panted and struggled to keep up, I found myself tallying up the number of years that had passed since I ran track in High School. It was a depressingly large number.

I did not have time to consider that number for very long.

Something struck me from behind in the center of my back, and I fell forward. I threw my hands out to lessen the impact of the fall, but all the same I once again struck my chin against the floor. This time, spots of light flashed across my vision and an intense ringing filled my ears. I literally lost track of everything that was going on around me, intense as the impact, and the pain, was.

Somewhere in the background, I heard Sheila scream.

A voice - a very loud voice - in my mind screamed at me to get up. Get up now, or I was a dead man, and likely Sheila would die as well. Normally a compelling argument, but I found I could not make my limbs move, at least not in a coherent manner.

Gradually the stars in my vision and the ringing in my ears began to recede and I became more aware of the environment around me.

I really wished I had not.

My back felt wet and sticky where whatever it was that struck me made contact, but there was nothing and no one else in the immediate vicinity besides Sheila.

However, somewhere not too far off, something large was moving down the scaffold toward me. The scaffold creaked and groaned with its every step, but still it kept coming. Sheila was crouched next to me, shouting at me to get up, to move. She held on to my right hand with both of hers and she was pulling frantically at me, trying to help me up.

I went with the force of Sheila's tug and rose to a sitting position. There I stopped as the monster strode into view. In fairness, it more hopped than walked. That much, at least, it kept of the bunny persona the beast had been wearing. Aside from that, though...

Its head was hideous, a twisting of the cute bunny face it had worn into something vile, hungry, vicious. Its snout was short, with an upturned nose, but its forehead rose quite a bit higher than the bunny's had. It bled slowly from a gash on its left temple; that must have been where the majority of Sheila's blows had landed, back in the station.

The rest of its body was...the best word that comes to mind is bloated. It was as though the bunny's body had expanded like a balloon until it reached the size of a german shepherd and then cracked in multiple locations as its skin stretched beyond the breaking point, leaving areas where it was covered by soft-looking white fur and other areas that were black, or maybe very dark green, and scaly. Ooze of some sort or other dripped from those scaly parts; where it fell to the metal walkway of the scaffold, a soft hissing issued and steam, or a mist of some sort of gas, wafted up. The analytical part of my brain put two and two together and realized that the ooze, whatever it was, was acidic.

The worst part, though, were the thing's eyes. They were different from when it wore the bunny mask. Still slitted, red, and piercing, but somehow now the red was that much redder and they almost seemed to glow with a burning light of their own. It gazed at us - at me - and I could see its rage, towering like the skyscrapers in the city above us.

All at once, the mental pressure that it had used on me all those times to force me to its will came crashing down. But it was stronger, so much stronger, than it ever had been before. My hands flew to my temples and I heard myself crying out as I fell backwards. Pain, far worse than any physical pain it had inflicted with its claws all those times, ran through every fiber of my being, down through to the depths of my soul.

Fool. To think you could beat me.

I thrashed around, mindful of nothing but the pain and the booming voice of the bunny monster in my mind.

I would have left you for last, as a reward for your service. Ended you quickly. But now...

The pressure redoubled and the world began to fade beneath a red haze that filled my vision. It was too much. I was going to pass out, and then it would finish me while I was unconscious. I know I screamed. I must have. But no sound reached my ears except the thumping of my heart and the gleeful mental cackle from my foe.

And then I blacked out.

Blacked out is not the right term.

I lost track of what was going on around me as the pain over-whelmed it all. By all rights, I should have fallen unconscious as my mind sought a last refuge from the bunny monster's onslaught, one last bit of peace before the end.

But that's not what happened.

Instead of the peace of oblivion, as my gaze filled with nothing but red and my mind registered nothing but pain, I blinked and found myself elsewhere. But not just elsewhere. Else*when*.

All at once, I found myself bathed in a soft, yet somehow sickly, white light and I realized I was standing upright. To my left and right stood walls that were painted a boring shade of pale grey. They stretched ahead, enclosing the corridor where I stood, for about twenty meters before bending sharply to the right. Looking behind me, I saw that the corridor did the same thing in that direction, except it bent to the left. Somewhere in my head, the analytical part of my mind took that in and decided that the corridor must double around itself to form a complete loop around a central core.

It all clicked together then. I was aboard Ketcham Station.

Of course, that made no sense. I had departed the station days ago, and it now lay adrift, uninhabitable, the victim of one of any of the thousands of stupendously unlikely, but deadly none-theless, mishaps that could befall a space station. There was no way I could be on the station. I knew for a fact that I really lay on a scaffold in the southbound tunnel of the red line of Boston's T network, just two stops from Downtown Crossing. This was just...well, I did not know what it was.

But damn if it didn't seem real.

Voices echoed down the corridor toward me, and a moment later two men and a women, all dressed in lab coats with security badges on their left breast pockets, strode into view. The men were nameless faces to me, but I recognized the woman immedi-ately as Dr. Liu, the researcher who had shooed me away earlier.

I didn't want to deal with her again, so I turned quickly back to the electrical panel I was working on. Then it hit me - I was working? I had not realized that at first, but then what else would I be doing? If this was not real, it must be a memory, and all I did on Ketcham was work. I presume.

The trio walked past me without slowing, though I thought I saw Dr. Liu cast a wary glance my way. They were discussing something in technicalese that was way over my head. I did not even bother to try listening, but then two words jumped out and grabbed me.

Quantum Tunneler.

Those two researchers in the cafeteria had used that phrase; one of the men flanking the Dr. Liu said it now. My interest piqued, I listened more closely.

"...the last test was very promising," the man, tall and lean with sandy-blond hair, was saying.

The other man, more dumpy and older, with a bad combover, snorted. "Promising? The damn rabbit came through in pieces."

"But it *did* come through. Horace and Shelby have high confidence that their adjustments are sound."

The balding man's responding snort contained entire levels of derision. "Really. And who checked their work? I would not trust those two to -"

"Enough!" Dr. Liu said in a stern tone, silencing both men. "We will proceed with the next test."

Baldy opened his mouth to protest, but she cut him off.

"As soon as you are satisfied with the adjustments, Leo."

They turned the corner then, and the rest of their conversation faded. Baldy's expression of chagrin as he vanished from sight spoke volumes, though. He had not planned on carrying that ball. Not one bit.

For the next several minutes, I finished up tightening the connections within the panel. It had gotten to the point that I could perform that particular job without paying much attention, so my thoughts began to wander. What was this tunneler thing?

They were sending rabbits through it, whatever it was, and it was doing bad things to them. To put it mildly. But what *was* it?

Some time later, I turned a corner, dull grey and bland just like every other corridor on Kethcam Station, and found myself outside the lab where I first met Dr. Liu. The memory of our earlier meeting, and of her dismissal, flashed through my head and I almost turned around before anyone saw me.

Curiosity stopped me. What were they doing in there?

Through the viewing window, I saw a large group of the researchers clustered together, Dr. Liu among them. Stretch and Baldy were there also, Baldy looking resigned yet also intrigued. The two junior researchers I recalled from the cafeteria were there as well. They stood in front of a whiteboard that was covered in greek letters and mathematical symbols that I found indecipherable, and were pointing excitedly to one part of the board in particular.

After a moment of discussion, Dr. Liu held up a hand and everyone stopped talking. Her lips moved and she looked to her left, where Baldy stood. He pursed his lips for several seconds while his eyes traced over the equations on the board. Then, finally, he nodded. I presumed whatever the cafeteria guys said, it had proven satisfactory.

Dr. Liu nodded and clapped her hands. The group dispersed quickly, each person going to a station around the room. They began throwing switches and making adjustments on equipment panels in the rapid, yet deliberate, way of people who were well practiced at their tasks.

A minute or so later, just as before, a man entered the room, but this time he only carried one cage. As before, when he grabbed the rabbit and lifted it out, the little creature struggled and kicked. But after a minute it settled down as the man set it down on a small black ramp that led toward the device in the back of the room that I could not see clearly last time.

This time I had no such difficulty.

The device took me by surprise. It was basically just a metal ring, about a meter in diameter, that rested atop a small table. It did not look like much of anything at all.

The ramp leading up to the ring began to move, and I could see that it was not a ramp after all; it was a conveyer belt. The bunny rode along placidly, chewing on some bit of food or other. I wondered if it was curious about the thing it was moving toward. Lord knows I was.

At that point, with the bunny about halfway to the ring, I noticed the other device. It sat about three meters away from the first ring and looked identical to it in every respect, except that the conveyer belt was moving away from its ring.

I began to have a notion of what was going on. But it was too incredible, like science fiction.

Of course, I thought this while standing in a research lab on an orbiting space station with artificial gravity, so who was I to judge?

The rabbit neared the end of the conveyer belt into the first ring, and Dr. Liu gave an order. One of the junior researchers threw a switch and lights turned on around the circumference of both rings. The lights began rotating, slowly at first then more quickly, until, as the rabbit passed the threshold of the first ring, I could no longer make out the individual lights but only a ring of light superimposed upon each metallic ring.

The rabbit crossed into the first ring and there was a flash of brilliant white light along with a small gust of wind - I could see the researchers' hair suddenly whip to and fro - as well as a barely audible popping sound. It must have been much louder within the lab, for me to hear it outside.

A heartbeat later there was a similar flash of white light from the center of the second ring.

And then there was a tremendous explosion and a deafening

roar. The researchers were knocked prone. Some lay still where they landed, others writhed in obvious pain. The plexiglass viewing window was cracked, the shockwave from the explosion was so strong.

I stood motionless, stunned. I knew I should have sounded an alarm, run for help, something. But the events inside the lab held me transfixed. Smoke and flame leapt from the table where the second ring stood. Electrical arcs shot forth, followed by another roar.

And then, from within the billowing smoke, I saw a pair of eyes. Glowing red eyes with vertical slits, like a cat's.

I jerked awake, or back to reality at least, sitting bolt upright as the shock of the vivid recollection hit home.

The bunny monster. It was the bunny monster's eyes I saw through the smoke on Ketcham Station. Dr. Liu and her associates *created* the bunny monster. Not intentionally, to be sure. But whatever they were doing with those rings - I had to assume it was some sort of teleportation device - changed that rabbit, made it into something...different. Something twisted.

And then Sheila pulled at me again and I remembered the situation I was actually in. The bunny monster, hugely grown now from what it had been at first, was approaching steadily, its eyes narrowed as it focused in completely on me.

"Get up!" Sheila shouted, and I wasted no time in obeying.

For a brief moment, I considered how to fight against the bunny monster. But then it roared again and I realized the futility of that thought. So instead, once again, we ran.

Fast.

It was only after I had put a couple dozen running steps behind me that I realized the crushing pressure that I had felt in mind my just moments ago - was it even that long? - was gone. I risked a glance over my shoulder. The bunny monster was still there, still coming. It's eyes still burned with fury, a fury that was directed at me with a fierce intensity.

And yet I suddenly felt nothing.

No, that wasn't right. I felt it, but its was somehow not as mind-crushing as it had been before. Because of what I had remembered?

I slowed, then stopped, and turned to face the monster.

"Barry, what are you doing? Run!"

Sheila's voice boomed in my ears, but at the same time it was like I was listening to her from within a glass bubble - the words came through but they were stepped down, slower and deeper than normal. Almost stretched out.

In the depths of my mind I heard another voice, also muffled and muted, raging at me and trying to force me to bend. To break. It was the bunny monster, that much was certain. But it was as though the beast had lost its power, or something was shielding me from it. Something strong.

Whatever mental strength or protection had manifested itself within me just then, it obviously did not offer physical protection as well. What trick of the mind ever did? But even knowing that, I found I could not turn away and run, no matter the urging of my mind. I stood tall and stared it in the eye as it advanced, and found, somehow, that I was smiling.

"You are an ugly bastard under all that fur," I said.

I did not say it particularly loudly. Hell, I did not even say it in my normal speaking volume. But the words cut through the air between us like a knife, the sound seeming almost deafening to me for a second.

The bunny monster reacted even more strongly. My words struck it and it recoiled, its eyes widening. In pain? Anger? Confusion? All of those? More?

Whatever the reason, it stopped its advance. In the brief respite I made a waving gesture with my hand toward Sheila. I silently willed her to take the hint and run, get away, while I ran interference here. And for a moment, I thought she did. Then a movement to the side drew my gaze and I saw her standing to my left, her jaw set determinedly despite the fact that she was visibly trembling. My heart sank even as my mind shouted her praises, both for staying to assist against the beast and for her composure in fighting back her fear.

The bunny monster growled and I looked back at it. It had drawn back on itself, crouching like a cat ready to spring at us. Which was a neat trick, since it still resembled a bunny, at least partially.

"Fools," it said softly. But again, soft as its words were, they reached my ears without difficulty. "I have seen a million of your worlds begin and end, watched the turning of ages unnumbered. *You* would stand against *me*?" A deep, rumbling chuckle, fill with mockery, issued from it.

"What are you?"

Sheila asked what I had been wondering for days. But I already knew the answer before the bunny monster replied. It came to me in a flash, an insight that blossomed seemingly from nowhere. I can only assume it grew out of my sudden recollection of the events on the station. I told myself that was all it was; the alternative, that it had come from...elsewhere...was too unnerving to think of.

The bunny monster was not just a warping of that poor rabbit by the teleportation process. No, in making their teleporter, Dr. Liu's team had torn a hole in reality, a hole with no distance, as we know it, between one side of it and the other, even though those sides in fact stood several meters apart. But creatures inhabit that world between the sides, between what we call space. The monster had taken the rabbit the way superstitious people used to believe a demon could take possession of a person. Now it was revealing itself. Maybe it really was what those people called a demon. And now it was prepared to give birth to its progeny, a progeny that would be at home in our world, not in the spaces between. And that would spell the end. For many people, certainly, and maybe for everyone and everything.

We could not let that happen, Sheila and I. Glancing at her again, I saw that she did not understand the way I did. But she could see it was an abomination, and for whatever reason if I was not going to flee it, neither was she. Her jaw, already set, firmed even more and her eyes narrowed in concentration.

The bunny monster spoke again, and its words were a call to battle if ever I had heard one. Not that I *had* ever heard one. But they seemed to fit, regardless.

"I am your death."

The bunny monster advanced, its maw opening wide to reveal an expanse of teeth. Big, sharp, pointy teeth by the dozen. It growled, and its breath was hot on my face even though it was still several meters away. Right then, my earlier question sprang to mind: how do you kill a vampire?

And I knew that was the wrong question. The same way I suddenly understood what the monster was and where it came from.

"It's not a vampire," I said to myself. "It's a *demon*. How do you kill a demon?"

"You don't," Sheila said, and I realized I had spoken more loudly than I thought. Reaching into her purse - it suddenly struck me how wonderfully feminine it was that, through all that had gone on since we bumped into each other on the streets above, she kept ahold of her purse - and pulled out a beaded chain that she wrapped around her right hand. "You banish it."

Sheila stepped forward to meet the bunny monster, her hand raised high, and I could see a small metal cross dangling from the end of that chain.

A rosary. She carried a *rosary*? Who carries a rosary anymore?

How many people even *know* what a rosary is anymore, dude, replied that annoying voice in my head that always told me when I was being a dummy.

"Be gone, beast," Sheila said in a firm voice of authority. Authority, and...faith.

She was a believer.

The bunny monster stopped for a moment. I could swear it was perplexed as it considered her and the small little cross dangling from her hand.

Then it began to chuckle. Slowly at first, then with greater gusto until its chuckle became a laugh and then a full-on guffaw. It was quite rude, actually. Sheila was not being funny at all. In fact, the more I thought on it, the more I realized she had the right of it.

I stepped up next to her and placed my left hand overtop her right. If she could believe, I could too. Hell, after everything that had happened and all that I had learned I could not *not* believe.

Scowling, I said in as firm and commanding a tone as I could muster, "Be gone!"

The monster just laughed harder. And it advanced. It was not moving quickly; it's bulk prevented very quick movements on the walkway, narrow as it was.

Wait. That did not make any sense. The thing had moved quite well just a moment or two ago, and the walkway was not any narrower than it had been. What the hell?

It was growing.

Son of a bitch, it was growing, expanding even further than it already had. Especially around its belly, where its babies were surely about ready to burst forth. The patches of fur were smaller now, more stretched. The oozing, scaly areas larger. Greater amounts of that ooze dripped off the bunny monster's bulk. One particular drop caught my eye as it pooled at the bend of its left foreleg for a couple seconds before dropping away.

My gaze followed the drop as it fell. I watched as it hit the metal of the walkway floor. And as it bubbled and hissed as wisps of gas rose from the spot where the drop landed.

Acid. The ooze was acid. I had noticed that before, but it had not clicked. I looked at the metal plating at the monster's feet. A few meters back, where it had paused last, several small holes were eaten through the walkway. The monster was moving now, though, and the drops did not have time to pool.

But it was also larger, and oozing more.

I squeezed Sheila's hand, a plan forming in my mind. She winced slightly and shot a glare my way. I nodded toward the floor and her eyes followed the motion of my head. They widened. She understood.

Together, we stepped forward, toward the monster which now crouched only three meters away.

"Be Gone!" I shouted, and I heard her shout it as well. Our words rang out in unison, amplifying each other as the sudden hope and resolve I felt seemed to give them strength.

Then, suddenly, the little cross dangling from our hands flashed. Just a little flash of light, but I saw it, plain as day.

The bunny monster stopped. Its eyes grew wide and its jaw dropped open, but not in a roar or in a show of intimidation. In amazement.

In fear.

"You know Him?" It said, its voice, so strong and mocking a few seconds earlier, now quivering and uncertain. "Impossible! You cannot -"

I moved forward again, and Sheila came with me. She needed no prompting; it was as though we both knew what we needed to do without discussing it with each other. Like our minds were one, just then.

"Be Gone," we shouted in unison, and the cross lit up again, brighter this time.

The bunny monster drew back, open fear on its face as it retreated. The ooze was dropping even faster now, almost a steady stream of the stuff.

The light from the cross remained; it even grew brighter. In fact the entire tunnel seemed as though it was becoming illuminated by it.

Then I heard the noise behind us and I realized it was not the cross that was glowing. It was reflecting the lights of the southbound train as it approached from further up the tunnel.

The beast noticed the train as well and its eyes narrowed once more. The fear lessened on its face, and it grinned for a second.

"Well played," it said, and it placed its foot down on the bit of walkway it had just abandoned in its retreat.

With a loud squeal of protest, the walkway, having reached the edge of its endurance between the beast's weight and the corrosion caused by its acidic ooze, gave way, its outer edge collapsing downward until it struck the floor of the tunnel, leaving a ramp where a minute before there was flat walking space.

The beast's eyes widened again as it tried to prevent itself from falling, and for the briefest of moments it appeared the bunny monster might succeed. But slowly, ponderously, it lost its balance and toppled down onto the floor of the tunnel.

The bunny monster rolled over as it fell, its momentum carrying it clear of the walkway wreckage. I heard the horn of the train sound as the conductor saw what happened - Lord knew what he thought of it. Then there was a flash of white-blue light as the bunny monster struck the third rail, the one that carried the electric current for the trains.

Brakes squealed, but even louder squealed the bunny monster.

And then the train barreled over it, its momentum too much to prevent a collision.

The front car lurched, bouncing off the tracks and slamming into the pillars dividing the southbound from the northbound rails. But the momentum of the cars behind it kept pushing the train along. Unable to leave the rails completely because of the narrowness of the tunnel, it ricocheted from one side to the other, rending the walkway to the south of us and the pillars on the other side, shattering train car windows, tearing open the metal of the cars' sides until finally it came to rest with the front car, battered and crushed, halfway out into the station to the south.

At some point during the crash, I threw myself atop Sheila and bore her down onto the walkway in a show of stupidity and chivalry. Chivalry because, hey she was a lady and men protect ladies. Stupidity because...duh I'm going to protect her from a train wreck with *my* skinny ass?

Regardless, it worked. As the dust settled and emergency lights kicked on - many of the nearby illuminations were either shorted out or flat-out crushed by the crash - I took stock of our situation and was gratified to find that neither she nor I were hurt. Or at least, no more hurt than we were already.

"Holy shit," Sheila breathed as I helped her to her feet.

"No kidding."

We looked down the tunnel at the wreck and I could not help but be impressed.

Then I heard groans and weeping from the passengers in the train and my moment of awe turned into sickness, guilt. People were hurt and we had caused it.

I had caused it.

"This is all my fault," I said, and I collapsed down onto my knees.

"Bullshit," Sheila said as she crouched down next to me. "It was that thing's fault."

She was right, of course, but that did not make it any easier to accept the fact. I think I might have shrugged. Or maybe I just shuddered. Regardless, I was unable to stand back up for a good minute or two. I just crouched there, looking at the destruction in the tunnel and feeling miserable.

Sheila lurched me back to reality. "Do you think it's dead?"

"What?"

She looked at me like I was an idiot. "It survived being run over by a truck and being brained."

I snorted and, finally, pushed myself back up to my feet. "It's a demon. You don't kill demons, you banish them, right?"

She flushed and looked away. "It just seemed right." She drew a breath, then added, hastily, "I don't really believe in that stuff."

She sounded like she was trying to convince herself as much as me.

I quirked an eyebrow at her and pointed at the rosary, which was still wrapped around her hand.

"Family heirloom," Sheila said. Then she cleared her throat. "Come on."

She walked over to the break in the walkway and, keeping three points of contact, lowered herself down the newly-made ramp until she reached the tunnel floor. Then she looked back up at me, expectantly.

"You coming?"

I actually had no intention of going down there. The smart thing to do would be to high-tail it north on the walkway to the next station, in case the bunny monster had survived. But then if it had died, or been banished or whatever, I would never know and I would spend the rest of my life looking over my shoulder for its return for no reason. On the other hand, if it was alive...

If it was alive, it was certainly injured at the least. This might be our best chance to finish it off.

I nodded and slid down, keeping contact with the ramp as Sheila had.

A moment later, we stood together between the rails and did not move. It was like we were rooted to the spot. Maybe it was because, up on the walkway, we were a bit more shielded from the real destruction of the crash. But down next to it, the debris thrown everywhere was all that much more real.

Or maybe we were both just re-thinking our decision.

None of that. I took Sheila's rosary-wrapped hand and smiled at her in a way that I hoped was reassuring. Then we stepped forward together to survey the scene and find the bunny monster.

It was like a scene from a nightmare.

The emergency lights only gave partial illumination, leaving most of the shattered train shrouded in shadow. Up ahead some-where, a fire burned; not large, but enough to provide a flickering yellow-orange glow to the scene that was positively eerie. An occasional electric arc, from the third rail or from some shorted system within the train or in one of the shattered lighting assem-blies in the tunnel, provided the final visual accent. The stench of ozone and dust filled the air, and above it a charred smell like rancid meat that had been left on a barbecue overnight.

And then there were the sounds of the passengers. Many more of them now that the initial shock had worn off. The groans and cries of the injured. The shouts and pleas for help from the panicked. And, in ones and twos, calmer voices from the few who had kept their wits about them and were trying to get the others organized, or at least to prevent them from panicking completely.

In all, Hollywood could not have done a better job if they were trying to make a scene to scare me out of my wits. Knowing that there really were injured people ahead, and maybe still the bunny monster itself, just made it worse.

I shivered, and not from cold; it was actually quite warm. Again I had the urge just to get back on the walkway and cruise north, away from the scene.

But I did not. Hand in hand with Sheila, I walked down the tunnel, hugging the gap between the southbound and north-bound rails, since most of the train wreckage had ended up nearer the wall with the walkway. And besides, the third rail ran through that central area, and that was where we would find the bunny monster.

Slowly, carefully we picked our way over broken-off pieces of cement and metal, shattered plexiglass from the train's windows, and the occasional sign or lamp fitting that littered the ground. At one point we had to clamber over an entire wheel assembly that had broken off of one of the train cars.

That was where we saw the first body. An older man, in his late 50s probably, he was pinned beneath the wheel assembly, his face locked into an expression of surprise.

Sheila gasped and turned her head away. I found myself doing the same as sudden guilt rushed through me again. That guy would be alive if it wasn't for me. I knew it was a lie - it was the bunny monster's fault, not mine. It had crossed over to our world to wreak havoc, of its own accord. I did not ask it to, and for a while there I was all but helpless to stop it.

"At least he didn't suffer, looks like." Sheila looked up at me and squeezed my hand as she spoke, and I could tell she was dealing with some shadow of the same guilt I felt.

I nodded and inhaled deeply, and instantly regretted it as the growing stench of the scene filled my nostrils. Reminding myself to breath through my mouth, I said, "Let's move." I tried to sound determined; don't think I did very well at it.

But Sheila made no comment. She simply turned fully away from the man and led the way further forward along the train.

About twenty meters further, we found it: a great mass of charred and twisted flesh. Or rather, two masses of charred flesh. It had been cleaved in two by the impact with the train and obviously cooked by its contact with the third rail.

"This has to be the beast," Sheila said. The she coughed and bent over, making little heaves and clutching at her stomach.

I did not blame her. Here, the stench was almost overpowering. Even breathing through my mouth, it was like I could taste it. And that was without trying to talk. I pulled the tatters of my trench coat up over my chin so it covered my mouth and nose, but that did not help much at all. It truly, *truly* stank.

"Let's go back," I said as quickly as I could to avoid getting more of the stench than I had to. But Sheila shook her head.

"We have to be sure."

She straightened, getting herself back under control, and managed a half-smile that I returned, for all the good it would do with my mouth beneath my shirt. So I just shrugged, which earned a snorted half-laugh from her. Then we both took deep breaths and turned back to the burnt corpse of the bunny monster.

It was big. No shock there.

What was shocking was the fact that it appeared to be charred straight through to its center. There was no blood, not even from the areas that were cut off by the train. That made no sense at all. The third rail carries high voltage, but not enough to completely fry a mass of flesh as big as the bunny monster. Not in that short amount of time.

I frowned and looked around for a tool I could use. I found it a short while later - a hand rail that had been ripped off its mounts during the crash. It was about four feet long, and jagged at both ends. It wold make a handy spear.

I took the spear and walked up to the bunny monster's remains. I hesitated only for a second, then thrust the spear as far into it as I could.

The spear went in like a hot knife through butter, and then a large chunk of the remains simply broken off and crumbled into a pile of ash at my feet.

I stabbed it again, in a different location. Same effect.

"Looks like it's good and truly dead."

It was hard to argue with Sheila's logic, but after being terrorized by that thing for so long, that was not enough. The anger that I had kept bottled up where it could not find it, even with its psychic bond with me, the shame at being kept powerless, the guilt at being unable to prevent its atrocities... That anger demanded more.

I heard myself howling as I brought the metal pole down upon the remains of the bunny monster. Again and again I rained blows down, and each time another chunk of its body fell apart and crumbled to dust. My arms and shoulders began to grow numb from the exertion, so different from what I normally asked them to do, but still I continued. Gradually, the anger gave way to a grim satisfaction.

That mother fucker was not getting back up from this.

Some time later - minutes, hours...seconds? - I reached a particularly bulky bit of char and brought my spear down. Like before, a big chunk of the bunny monster's remains broke off and crumbled. But this time something else fell out. A misshapen mass that at first was not anything I could recognize.

And then it moved.

It stuck an arm out and moved. It was certainly an arm because at the end of the limb as a hand, complete with an opposable thumb.

I stopped, dumbfounded, as the thing squirmed on the ground and the extended a second arm. And then first one leg, then another. Although I only recognized them as legs because of their location on the thing's body, down the torso from where the arms were. Aside from that, though... The arms and legs were the same length, as though the thing on the ground, whatever it was, was meant for walking on all fours.

I swallowed and looked at it more closely, where I presumed its head was. There was only an amorphous thing that might someday be a face of some sort on a stump that would probably contain a brain.

It was disgusting. Unnatural. Unlike any creature I had ever seen.

It was the bunny monster's child.

But it did not live long. Turns out, even though the bunny monster may have been a demon, its child was not. Or at least, not fully. I guess, having gestated here on earth, and having been nourished in the womb with human blood, it was bound by physical laws just like a human. Or maybe it was vulnerable because it had not been brought to term. Or it could not abide electricity.

For whatever reason, I found that a spear through the heart killed it just fine.

After that, Sheila found her own implement and joined me in breaking up the bunny monster's remains. It went without saying that we could not let any of its offspring survive. We found two more and dispatched them like the first.

It took a long time to get out of there.

Sooner than I expected, but longer than I had hoped, paramedics and other emergency crews showed up to take care of the train wreck. They came in through the station where Sheila and I had found ourselves trapped, and naturally they were not going to let anyone leave without giving them a clean bill of health.

Which was, frankly, ideal. And not just because I had several cuts on my arms and chest that required dressing, and perhaps a few stitches as well.

No, and I was ashamed to think this, the wreck made for ideal cover. Everyone was expected to be injured to some extent or another, and to have bedraggled clothing. No one asked Sheila and I if we were the people who had called asking for assistance in exiting the station earlier. The only focus was on treating the wounded.

And so I found myself sitting on a bench in the station, wincing as a paramedic applied alcohol to the smaller cuts on my legs and torso. My forearms, though, where the bunny monster had latched on so strongly...

"You're going to need stitches, buddy," the guy said as he pulled off the makeshift bandages Sheila had applied earlier. "A lot of them." He smiled apologetically then applied clean dressings to the wounds after applying antibiotic ointment.

"Where should I go?"

He shrugged and gestured toward the far side of the station, where a small gaggle of people with minor wounds sat or stood, waiting. "Just hang with those folks and we'll get you taken care of once we get the major trauma cases out of here."

That made sense, I suppose. Why tie up an ambulance with someone who was in no immediate danger when you could use it for a person who was going to die without help? And unfortunately there were a number of people from the train who met that description. For a moment, I was tempted to start beating myself up over that, but I forced my mind to other things.

Namely, Sheila. She waited on a bench by the gaggle of ambulatory patients, a few bandages recently applied where the bunny monster had dug into her. Thankfully not as many as I had. She smiled as I approached, and I pondered how quickly things changed. Not so long ago we were just faces on the street to each other. Me, a guy who might help her out with cash for the next meal. And her, a pretty but forgettable drifter, if only the bunny monster had not picked her out. But now, after the stress we had shared together, I felt close to her. Strange, considering I knew next to nothing about her.

Her smile said she felt the same.

I settled down next to her on the bench and let out a long sigh. "I honestly didn't think we were going to make it through that," I said.

Sheila glanced sidelong at me and pursed her lips, but was silent for a while. When she finally spoke, it was in a subdued tone. "I never in a million years would have imagined something like that was possible." She shuddered slightly. "You could have just run away and let it take me." Her smile returned, and I could see the gratitude in her eyes. "Thank you."

Part of me felt good about that. Another part was insulted. Like I would just abandon someone to that thing's ministrations. But then, I reminded myself that I had pretty much done essentially that many times before encountering Sheila. So why was she different? Just because she was young, with a pretty face? I wanted to think there was something deeper to my decision-making process, but looking back on it, I was not sure.

But did it really matter?

Yes, said that inner voice that tended to annoy me so. Yes, it really does.

That was something that would take a long time to figure out. Fortunately, I had all the time in the world. So instead of waxing philosophical, I simply said, "You're welcome," and shook her hand.

I quickly wished I had not. Now that the adrenalin and stress of the incident had worn off, my arms really did hurt. I winced and let out a little groan as she squeezed my hand, and Sheila's eyes widened.

"Oh geez. I'm so sorry."

"No worries," I said through clenched teeth. "Dude said I need a bunch of stitches." I indicated the paramedic, who had moved on to a man who appeared to have a broken leg.

"You know," Sheila said, a mischievous twinkle in her eye, "there's a free clinic a few blocks from here. I'm on good terms with the manager, if you don't want to wait around for the ambulance crews to get back."

That was a great idea.

An hour later, I had fresh sutures in both arms, a new shirt and jacket on my back, a full antibiotic series and painkillers in hand, and a contented smile on my face. Sheila's medical friend had come through with flying colors. Even better, if anyone even noticed us leaving the T station they did not care. We were just another couple of people who were unlucky enough to get caught up in the wreckage, but also lucky enough to escape relatively uninjured.

Which was great, because having to answer questions about what we had been doing there would have been...awkward.

I stepped out of the clinic and waited on the sidewalk while Sheila thanked her friend again before following me out. During those few moments alone, I took in the street around the clinic. It was neither run down nor swanky, just sort of middling, with storefronts of all varieties and the usual cross-section of humanity walking, running, driving, or riding along in the late afternoon. The sun was low enough in the sky that it had sunk below the tops of the surrounding buildings, leaving the street in shadow. The sounds of hustle and bustle, the scent of cooking food, the perfume from a woman who brushed past me, the exhaust from the passing vehicles, and the chill of the breeze on my cheeks felt so much better than I ever recalled before. It was like it was all new, and I was noticing it for the first time.

I understood why: just a couple hours ago I thought sure I was going to die, and maybe many more people with me. Instead, I was alive. And it felt great.

Sheila pulled the clinic door closed and slid up next to me, linking her arm with mine. "Well, we've got a new lease on life. What do you want to do first?" The euphoria of having survived was hitting her as well, it seemed.

I shrugged. "I don't know. I shouldn't stay out too late, though. I've got work..."

I stopped, and not because of the incredulous look that appeared on Sheila's face. Something struck me then. She had mentioned it back on the train after I told her the story of what was going on. She thought everyone on Ketcham Station was dead. Hell, everyone on Ketcham Station *was* dead. Which meant...

I was dead.

I burst out laughing, and I felt all the worries and concerns that had been haunting me for weeks, hell months, maybe years, fly away with the sounds of my merriment.

"Hot damn," I said. "I'm dead."

Sheila looked askance at me. "Huh?"

"Everyone probably thinks I'm dead, killed up on Ketcham Station. Hell, I'm amazed they still haven't come and taken all my shit out of my apartment." Delighted, I looked at Sheila with a big grin. "I'm dead. I don't have to do a damn thing." Another thought struck me then. It was beautiful. Perfect, even. "Sheila, you said you were on the road?"

She nodded, still looking a bit confused by my sudden antics.

"Were you going anyplace in particular?"

Sheila shrugged. "Not really. Just seeing where the road takes me, experiencing the world."

My grin felt like it was going to split my face, as wide as it became. "Would you like a traveling companion?"

Sheila blinked, surprised. She was silent for several seconds, just looking at me and obviously thinking it through. Finally, she said, "Sure why not? Sounds like fun." Then she smiled again, and that smile contained the promise of freedom and happiness. Maybe not forever, but for a while. And that was good enough.

MAILING LIST

If you enjoyed this book and would like word on new releases and special deals from Michael Kingswood, sign up for his newsletter on his website. Guaranteed to be spam-free, you can opt out at any time. And you can rest assured he will not share your information with anyone, for any reason, without a court order.

https://michaelkingswood.com/newsletter-signup/

ABOUT THE AUTHOR

Michael Kingswood has published more than 80 short stories, novellas, and novels. He has appeared in anthologies from WMG Publishing, Stark Press, and Knotted Road Press. A twenty year veteran of the US Navy's submarine force, he has four children and currently resides in San Diego.

Fans can contact him through his website, on Twitter, or on Gab.

Michael has a weekly podcast, Story Time With Michael Kingswood, where he reads his work and discusses writing, philosophy, and history. Subscribers are always welcome!

Listen on: YouTube Rumble Bitchute Odysee Podcast

MORE BOOKS BY MICHAEL KINGSWOOD

GLIMMER VALE CHRONICLES

Glimmer Vale

Out-Dweller

Tollard's Peak

Robbed Blind

The Falconer's Stairs

Campaign Season

Glimmer Vale Chronicles Books 1-3

STORIES FROM GLIMMER VALE

Legacy

Hidden Magic

Captive Hearts

Wedding Gifts

Lost Credit

THE PERICLES CONSPIRACY

Passing In The Night

The Pericles Conspiracy

SHORT FICTION

Michael has also published a number of shorter works, which can be found at michaelkingswood.com/store.

www.ingramcontent.com/pod-product-compliance
Lightning Source LLC
Chambersburg PA
CBHW021522240626
47154CB00002B/744